The Liberation of Bella McCaa

Catherine Aitken

Handbag Press

Copyright © 2023 by Catherine Aitken. The right of Catherine Aitken to be identified as the Author of the Work has been asserted in accordance with the Copyright, Designs and Patent Act 1988.

All rights reserved.

ISBN 978-1-7394756-1-1

All characters in this publication are fictitious and any resemblance to real persons, living or dead, is purely coincidental.

No part of this publication may be reproduced, stored in a retrieval system, or transmitted, in any form or by any means, without the prior permission in writing by the author.

Handbag Press 2023

ABOUT THE AUTHOR

Catherine Aitken always wanted to be a writer and couldn't believe her luck when her first job was as office junior for Jackie Magazine. But wanderlust took her travelling until she segued into a career in the film and TV industry, eventually working in script development and producing drama. To supplement the lean years in film development, Catherine created an accessories brand that she ran in tandem with feature film pursuits. Now she is concentrating on her own stories and The Liberation of Bella McCaa is her first novel. Catherine hails from Dundee but lives in Leith, Edinburgh and is currently writing her second book.

Find out more at www.catherineaitken.com

ACKNOWLEDGEMENTS

Many people helped me get to this stage and I have appreciated all the wonderful support. But there are those who need a special mention – my sisters, Maggie Aitken and Janet Begg have read every draft and happily given feedback - and allowed me to speak about Bella ad nauseum – thank you for everything. My good friend, author Alison Craig, has played a big part of getting to this stage, with all kinds of help and advice, including drinking Margaritas in the sun when necessary. Crime writing author duo CC Gilmartin have been generous with their practical tips and passing on their own experience of publishing. Insightful editing skills and assessments came from editor Sam Boyce and Ellie Hawkes of Elspells Writing Feedback. The beautiful book cover design is by Raspberry Creative Type. And last but not least – to all the friends and colleagues who commented on and critiqued early drafts and covers – a huge thank you.

Dedicated to all those who believe in second chances.

PROLOGUE

Thirty years ago

The Student Union bar was awash with beer and cider and condensation dripped down the walls, adding to the sauna-like atmosphere. Undeterred, the audience slithered and shimmied their unique moves to The Danfans as the band belted out their recent number one triumph from the stage and the sweaty crowd yelled along at high pitch. Bella and Jem were tight in the middle of the throng as they screamed the lyrics to each other, brandishing their glasses for emphasis, their pints of Snakebites splashing into the air as they lost themselves in the palpable energy in the room. Bella slipped on the soaking floor and she felt Jem's strong arms save her from falling. Not letting each other go, they swayed more slowly to the music, their bodies pinned together. As the song ended and the jubilant fans called for an encore, Bella stood on her tiptoes and kissed Jem, slowly and passionately, oblivious to her surroundings, lost in her love for him, knowing they would be together forever and she would never let him go.

CHAPTER 1

The dress was stuck. Desperate for something to wear, Bella had forced it over her ballooning breasts, and could barely breathe, the tight trap forcing her arms out at right angles. She didn't have to see her reflection to know she looked ridiculous – this little black dress was miniscule.

'How are we getting on in there? Do we need any help?' the assistant called from the other side of the heavy curtain.

'No, thanks. All fine.' Bella gritted her teeth as stiletto heels clip-clopped away.

Blasts of hot air wafted in from a heater she could hear whirring away in the corridor. She wriggled her shoulders to see if the movement would create more give in the fabric. Nope. Stuck. With a resigned sigh and great difficulty, Bella angled her body to root around in her backpack, pulling out a set of keys. Attached was a trusty old penknife. She opened it and, with a painful contortion, managed to nick the tiny stitches open. But it was a laborious process in the stifling space and she leaned her head against the wall, panting. Ditching the knife, she wangled a finger in the hole she'd made and gave it an almighty yank. Her left breast, encased in a heavy-duty bra, was released, creating room to manoeuvre the dress over her shoulders and off. Relief. The dress was returned to the hanger but there was no way it could go back on the rail. Damn. It was the ninth dress she'd tried on that morning in as many shops, and here she was in *Janine's* – the last chance saloon for 'formal attire'. Bella regarded the other option, which had been handed to her by the assistant with, 'This might flatter your shape better.'

It resembled a giant bin liner hanging up, and once on, a glance in the mirror confirmed the resemblance. At least it fitted and was baggy enough to hide her bloated belly. It covered all areas – high neck, long sleeves, scraped her knees. A pair of opaque tights and black heels, and she would be sorted.

Bella hauled on her jeans and flannel shirt and escaped the changing room, coming face to face with the offending convector blasting the baking air. As if she wasn't already broiling, her own internal radiator erupted. She battered the digital button of the thermostat to below freezing. *Ha!* Beads of perspiration popped out of her forehead as she went out to the sales desk.

'I've decided to take both, thank you – and I don't need a bag.' As Bella squashed the dresses into her backpack, the assistant grabbed hold of them too and a silent tug of war ensued over the counter, with both women determined to win.

'I need to scan the tickets!' Janine, for it was indeed the eponymous owner, shrieked in exasperation and Bella surrendered, forcing her adversary into an awkward stagger. Recovering her composure, the woman held the first dress up and pointed with an imperious pink nail.

'This dress is torn!'

'I had a little accident. It's fine. I'm paying for it.'

The woman had a smirk on her face that Bella could have cheerfully slapped off but she waited, arms crossed, while the dresses were folded in rustling tissue, placed in a presentation box, then packed into a stiff white carrier emblazoned with a massive *Janine's Boutique. Dressing Dundee since 1972.*

'£650.98, please.'

What? Bella hadn't even looked at the price tags, she'd been so focused on finding a dress to wear. She fumbled out a card and shoved it in the machine, stabbing in the pin when prompted. A bead of sweat ran down her cheek and dripped onto the counter. It gave her a sliver of joy to see the distaste on Janine's face, pleased she would have to clean it off.

'Enjoy your party!'

Bella glowered and turned. 'It's not a party, it's a funeral, actually, and you should size your dresses properly!' She banged the door shut behind her.

Relieved to have found a dress at last, despite the excruciating cost, Bella threw the carrier in the boot of her Mini. She pulled her parka on, shivering as the hot flush abated. Firing up the engine, she drove off into the afternoon traffic, through Dundee city centre and out onto Riverside Drive towards home. She could see the Tay flowing on her left and the sight, with Fife in the distance and the impressive rail bridge winding across the water, relaxed her. Bella loved this view along the river, even under unwelcoming March skies. She sang along to Chumbawamba's Tubthumping as it played, like a sign from providence, on the radio. That was her – she got knocked down but she'd get up again and no hot flushes or expensive dresses were going to ruin her mood – she was free and would be in London as soon as the house was sold. She trilled out the lyrics as she bounced along Riverside then, screeching a sharp right towards the Perth Road, gave a deft turn of the wheel and whipped the car into a parking spot.

She eyed the local florists from the driver's seat. Every week her mother ordered a bouquet and Bella collected it; autopilot had brought her to their door. The house was full of sympathy flowers; people had been so thoughtful, but she wanted a less formal selection. Inside she splurged on daffodils, tulips and sunflowers then added her mother's favourite hyacinth for the hell of it. Pleased with her freedom of floral choice, she jumped in the car and shot off, earning a loud beep from an irate driver.

'You stupid… *wanker!*' Bella yelled.

She planted a heavy hand on the horn for a satisfying long and loud blare and glared at the offending driver in the rearview mirror. Two more extended blasts evaporated the anger that was constantly simmering under the surface these days. The Mini pootled towards home, leaving the shops behind, and into a residential area with glimpses of imposing Victorian villas half hidden behind high walls and tall trees. Not much further and she turned into a wide driveway and parked in front of the family home, a period detached house set in generous grounds, with sweeping views across the river.

Bella gathered her packages and opened the front door. She stood in the hallway, with its cold mosaic floor, wood-paneled walls and stained-glass windows, listening to the silence. The lack of her mother's presence was deafening, the house no longer overshadowed by Dorothea's commanding personality. Looking up the curving staircase, she expected to hear her mother call her name. *Annabella*. Never Bella, or Anna, or any other diminutive pet name. Always Annabella. After the stroke, her mother had ruled from her bedroom the same as she'd done from her office, and without Dorothea to attend to, Bella stood, unsure what to do, listening to the tick of the grandfather clock.

The loud chime on the hour broke her reverie and she entered the kitchen. No more prevarication; she had to get on with preparations for tomorrow. She would be guessing as to how many people would come for the funeral tea – aiming for at least thirty seemed sensible. Bella totted a mental list up – brother Roddy and his much younger wife, Lorna, their teenage children, Heather and Gordon, and Aunt Nettie. What would she have done without Aunt Nettie over the years? Every Thursday she would come for lunch and spend the afternoon with Dorothea. It was always a pleasure to see her; her aunt insisted her time with Dorothea be respite for Bella, who would meet up with friends if they were free or go for a solitary cinema date, shutting out the world for two blessed hours. Aunt Nettie was her father's sister and after his death became close to Dorothea. Bella loved the old woman, who was still tootling around in a social whirl at eighty-four.

She kept counting – friends and their partners, staff from McCaa Properties, her mother's friends. Dorothea's stroke had severely limited her mobility, and at eighty-two, many of her contemporaries had fallen away over the years. Never a happy woman, Bella's mother had excelled herself with a constant critique of her daughter's care and housekeeping efforts, but seldom had a bad word to say about Roddy, who did nothing to help. To cope with the habitual disapproval, Bella thought of the anger and the loneliness behind it, and mostly forgave her mother's ill temper. Even so, there were nights over the years when Bella had wept at her own frustrations and loneliness – the aftermath of the stroke had trapped them both in a symbiotic dance neither could break free from.

Bella put the radio on and ramped up the volume till it bounced against the walls. She danced while dusting, hoovering, setting out the ancient Royal Albert, shining up the silver and putting guest linens in the downstairs loo. She was off to London and nothing was going to stop her getting her life back. With Duran Duran pumping away, she got her tools out and fixed the dripping tap, re-screwed one of the loose hinges on a shutter and put a new plug on the coffee machine. Living in such an old house had made Bella a dab hand at DIY. And, of course, she wanted it to be in the best condition for potential buyers. In time to the beat, she plumped up the cushions in the living room and pummeled the seat of the armchair to remove the well-earned bum impression.

'Annabella!'

She fell onto the chair and turned to see her brother standing in the doorway.

'What are you doing?'

'I'm cleaning.' Bella clicked off the radio. 'I didn't hear you coming in.'

'I'm not surprised.' How very droll.

'How've you been? Do you want a coffee?'

'Busy, busy. A coffee would be grand. Thought I'd pop in for a chat.' Roddy never had time, always with the *busy, busy*. A chat? Really?

He led the way to the kitchen and Bella placed the kettle on the Aga.

'Everything all set?' He stared out of the feature window to the garden and the view beyond.

'Flowers, crematorium, catering...' Bella counted off her fingers. 'Cars are booked. I'll pick up Aunt Nettie. Will you go for a viewing beforehand? If so, you need to call them today.' She spooned out instant and poured the bubbling water.

'No! I mean ... the crematorium is fine.' Her brother rarely sounded so unsure of himself and was fidgeting with the figurine ornaments on the window ledge.

Topping the mug up with milk, Bella handed it over remembering a time, even with the eight-year difference, when they'd been close. How she'd idolised the big brother who spoiled and teased her. When their father died, with Bella at fourteen and Roddy newly graduated, the siblings grew apart and, once she'd moved to London, were only in touch when she came home. Along with Dorothea, Roddy had taken over the day-to-day running of their father's property business and many nights Roddy and their mother would be closeted in the study while they discussed the ins and outs of it all. He opened his mouth to speak and firmly closed it again.

'You alright?' Bella asked. He did seem distracted.

'A lot going on. It's all a bit of a blinder, isn't it?'

'Yes. Yes, it is.'

'I mean, she'd been ill the last while, but wasn't she getting better?' he said.

'She was getting better, but the doctor did say there was a chance of another stroke.'

'You didn't tell me.'

'Yes, I did. You didn't listen.'

Bella couldn't think of anything more to say and they sat at the kitchen table, lost in their memories of recent events, while Roddy drank his coffee.

It had been a shock, especially for Bella, who went to attend to her mother as usual and discovered she had died in her sleep. Dorothea had been chipper the day before, spending time on the phone with an old friend, giving Bella her orders for the shopping and taking a couple of slow turns around the garden with Bella's support. Thankfully Andrea, the carer, had arrived and taken over. She was the one who called the doctor while Bella phoned her brother and aunt. The day had been a blur, and a week later, it was still difficult to process. She swung between happiness that she could move on with her life and guilt in wanting to do so.

'Annabella?'

'Yes?' Bella looked at her brother.

'Erm.' Roddy removed a piece of fluff from his suit then abruptly stood up. 'OK, I'd better be off. Thanks for the coffee.'

Bella followed him to the front door, where he placed an uneasy hand on her shoulder. 'Thanks. I mean thanks for... I know it's not been easy.' He gave her shoulder a firm shake. Was it an encompassing thanks for all the care she'd given her mother, for what she'd given up? Bella was surprised and touched – recognition from Roddy in their adult years was rare.

'We'll speak tomorrow, OK? Once it's over, get stuff sorted.' Another shake of the shoulder and he was off. 'I'll see you at the crematorium,' he called with a backward wave.

Bella stood at the door and watched as her brother got into his shiny black Merc and purred up the gravel drive. So much for the chat.

CHAPTER 2

Bella measured the ingredients for a tray bake. Tonight, she was going out. Wracking her brain, she couldn't recall the last social occasion she'd had – was it afternoon tea with friends at Christmas? Now it was March. When her mother had the first stroke ten years ago and Bella had returned from London to care for her, she'd often gone out and met with the old school friends she'd stayed connected with. Initially the nursing was twenty-four hour care and Bella had time for herself, but as Dorothea's condition improved and plateaued, and she was as well and capable as the doctors advised she'd ever be, the nursing had reduced to one carer from the agency for half an hour each morning, leaving Bella to manage alone the rest of the time. Her mother, used to getting her own way, hated being left without Bella's service at night and although she accepted a carer getting her up and dressed for the day, she only wanted her daughter's help to get ready for bed. Bella had tried to resist, to keep a small part of a social life – she'd organised her mother's friends to come in the evening and paid agency nurses to be on hand to help her to bed. But her mother's belligerence and self-centredness were harder to deal with on a one-to-one basis and the friends' visits had tailed off to the occasional afternoon. The desire to do their duty and secure generous donations for their charities became less important than having their ears blasted for an hour about how much better things would be if Dorothea ruled the world. Bella would close the door behind their pitying looks and embarrassed farewells and extended the hours of the intermittent evening nurses out of her dwindling savings as Dorothea refused to pay.

'What is a daughter for but to look after her poor mother? Think of all the things I've done for you.'

The aftermath of an infrequent night out became unbearable as it unleashed the worst of her mother's complaints and criticism until, worn down and depressed, with no support from her brother, Bella had given in and given up on a social life.

No more. Bella shook her head to rid her mind of the past. Time for pastures new. She continued weighing the ingredients as her mobile pinged.

Could you pick up Pam and Jean – you won't be drinking, will you? X

Keren – her oldest friend and in whose house the gathering would take place, a monthly ritual Bella had rarely been able to attend. She'd been intending to walk, as her friend's house wasn't far, and have a drink – only a glass or two – to mark the occasion of how her life was changing. But she feared once she started she might not stop and she didn't want a hangover for the funeral. Taking the car was best – for her head and her friends' feet.

Hours later, armed with a tin of rocky road and with Pam and Jean in tow, Bella rang Keren's bell.

'Windy!' Keren beamed as she swung the door open. Bella plastered a plastic smile on her face. Jeez Louise, would she never get away from such an inane nickname – she hated it. Inspired by her middle name, Winifred, a smart aleck at school had abbreviated it to Windy. Ha bloody ha. It had stuck, stalking her through school and university, and she only escaped by moving to London. But Keren had persevered and asking her to stop had been futile. It still rankled. Every. Single. Time.

'Sorry about Dorothea, Windy, but you've got no excuses anymore for staying in!' Bella was crushed by Keren, and Jean and Pam joined in with a group hug. Her friend accepted the tray bake. 'Thanks, Windy. I knew you'd have time on your hands.'

Soon they were sitting round a table laden with bottles of fizz and bowls of crisps, nuts and the rocky road. Bella nursed a glass while the others downed theirs with remarkable speed. The lack of alcohol didn't diminish her enjoyment of a convivial atmosphere and catching up on what was going on in their lives. Keren was having a conservatory built. Jean's husband, Will, an architect, had drawn up the plans and Jean, with a successful interior design business, presented a portfolio of how it should be. They all cooed at the sleek furniture and style suggestions laid before them.

'Has to be wipe clean! Those little fingers get everywhere.' The incredibly house-proud Keren was butter in her granddaughter's hands and she regaled them with tales of the child's smallest achievements.

The conversation moved on to Pam's latest conquest. Ultra-feminine, impeccably dressed and perfectly manicured, Pam attracted men like the proverbial honey drew in bees. She broke their hearts and messed them around, doing it with such sweet style and lack of malice that they all stayed friends. Bella couldn't remember the last time she'd even been in the company of a single man, but Pam always found them.

Jean brandished her mobile phone. 'You should try it too, Bella.'

'What?' She'd been in a dream and had lost track of the conversation.

'A dating app.'

'Maybe when—' Bella's response was obliterated as Keren's arm reached out and squished her face into her friend's neck, cutting her off mid-sentence.

'You don't want to wind up with another Sam!' Keren said. 'He was a right tosser. You're much better off on your own, past all that nonsense.' Bella couldn't get a word out; her mouth was trapped in Keren's hold.

Pam shouted, 'You need to get a Brazilian! Or a Hollywood!' She'd downed several scoops by this time while Bella was still contemplating why she would be 'past all that nonsense'.

'What? Why? I've had a Brazilian before but what's a Hollywood?'

'Gerrit all wheeched off. Men expect it these days. No wild bushes anymore. They even wheech it off their own bits.' Pam unzipped her trousers.

'Noooooo!' Bella raised a hand to cover her eyes. 'Don't show me!' She laughed.

'You won't catch me whipping it all off. Too many plooks when it grows in again. I use Will's beard trimmer,' Jean triumphantly declared.

Keren raised a hand. 'Speaking of men, Pam. Dal's colleagues will be up from London – let loose on their own for the weekend – and you'll be the only single woman at the party!' Bella's head was jerked into another stranglehold, her nose in an armpit this time. 'You'll be there too, of course, but you know what I mean; it's not your thing.'

'What party?' Bella managed to pull away from Keren's grip as her attention was taken by the traybake.

'My birthday, of course. Last one to fifty-two. You'd better be there – we're all coming tomorrow to support you. Where's the do after?' Keren shoved a huge piece of rocky road into her mouth and slurped it down with Prosecco.

'Roddy wanted it at the house. Less formal, and—'

'You're not doing the catering, are you? Don't let that brother of yours bully you.' Keren slopped her drink over Bella as she wagged her finger. Inebriated, the hostess didn't notice.

'Fisher and Donaldsons are delivering a buffet and I've got all the drinks. Sherry. Whisky. Prosecco.'

'Goody.' Pam and Jean raised their glasses in salute.

Bella stood up. 'I'd better go – I've got to finish sorting the house for tomorrow.'

'Aww. *Stay*. Have a proper drink. Leave the car. It's not far. Get a taxi?' Keren's eyelids were drooping under her sleek, black-fringed bob: her signature style since forever.

'No, I can't. It's been lovely, though, to see you all—'

'Dorothea's house'll sell in a minute,' Pam gushed.

Bella laughed as she put on her coat. 'I'm counting on it!'

'Then you'll be off to London. To another top-nosh City job?' Jean was at the slurry stage. 'What could London *poshibly* have that Dundee hasn't got?'

They all sniggered.

'Yup. Once the house is sold, I'm on my way. Shirley – remember my old London pal – she's already found me a great flat; should work out timewise.'

'But we won't see you. We never get the chance to see you,' Keren wailed. A twenty-minute walk away and stuck in the house virtually twenty-four-seven, it crossed Bella's mind that Keren could have seen her if she'd tried harder. And then she remembered the occasions they did come over, Dorothea petulant about her daughter's attention being taken away to the point that having her friends over became hopeless, with Keren, Pam and Jean drinking and chatting in the lounge while Bella attended to her mother's imaginary needs. Over the years these rare evenings had fizzled away too, locking Bella into a cheerless, lonely life. She left her friends downing the Prosecco, another popping cork ringing in her ears.

Bella was in the hallway when Dali, Keren's husband, came out of his study and pecked her cheek. 'Bella. I'm so sorry. If I can help, with the house or whatever, you will let me know, won't you? Roddy will have it all under control, I'm sure. But if you need advice about anything, I'm always here.' He gave her a hug.

'Thanks Dal.'

'You still here? S'everything all right?' Keren had poked her head round the door. Dali released Bella.

'Just saying goodnight.' Bella waved at them both. 'Thanks. See you tomorrow.'

She drove home, wondering if Keren was right and she was 'past all that nonsense'. Bella didn't want to believe her romantic years were over. Caring for her mother had dictated her life. Ten years she'd been at home. Ten years. Where had the time gone? The years, months and weeks had drifted by frighteningly fast, and achingly slow at the same time.

Bella kicked off her Docs, leaving them where they landed halfway up the stairs, and unzipped her jeans. In the kitchen she selected a diet Irn-Bru from the fridge and rummaged in the biscuit tin, plucking out a couple of Caramel Logs. On her return to Dundee, she'd regressed to her childhood sweet treats, an immature rebellion against her mother's disapproval. Padding through the house in her stockinged feet, Bella switched on the TV and, pulling the drapes, shut out the twinkling lights from across the river. Lamps turned off, Bella settled on 'her' armchair, ready as anything to create another bottom indentation and happy with the light from the flickering screen. Pulling the pouffe into position she hit the remote, thumbing through the stations to see what was on. Ah: *Working Girl*. Marvelous. She'd only seen it a hundred times but it made her think of returning to her career in London. And a possibility of romance – she wasn't past it – there was life in the old girl yet. Popping the can and munching into the biscuit, Bella put her feet up and got lost in the film.

CHAPTER 3

Before she'd even opened her eyes, Bella had heaved herself upright. The sound of the buzzer on the bedside table had woken her. Her hair was clamped to her head, her scorching face slick with moisture, the supposed-to-be-over-sized-but-not-quite-over-sized-enough Duran Duran T-shirt clinging soggily to her curves.

'I'm coming. Don't worry,' she mumbled, pushing herself off the bed and stumbling into the hallway. She was halfway towards her mother's bedroom when she came to. *What the hell?* She must have been dreaming. The sound of the buzzer – she could swear she'd heard it. She stood, bare feet clammy in the deep pile carpet. Ugh. Her head was pounding and she supported her tender breasts as she padded downstairs to the kitchen. The stone-flagged floor was refreshingly cold on her sweaty soles and, opening the fridge, she stuck her head in, trying to defuse the heat coming off her body in waves. She peeled off layers of kitchen roll and mopped her soaking face and neck. Jeez Louise – would this ever end?

Bella's temperature dropped at last and, as the chills took the heat's place, she lifted an ancient suede car coat from behind the garden door and slipped it on, instantly warmed and comforted. Wrapping the coat around her and shoving her feet into wellingtons, she unlocked the door and stepped outside into a rare, cloudless sky. The house was built on a slope with a panoramic view of the water, and the moon shone brightly, sparkling on the Tay as she hugged the coat closer in the cold spring air. The coat had been her father's, the one he'd put on when he went outside to bring in coal – and have a sneaky cigarette. She'd join him in the cold, contemplating the constellations, and enjoying the father-daughter time. He would puff away with an arm around her shoulder. She would inhale the smoke and coal aroma from the coat, her troubles melting away. Both her father and the coal fires were long gone and the coat hung there as an illustrious memorial, a reassuring presence used for all forays out into the garden, whether hanging the washing on a blustery day, going out with the rubbish or wrapping up tight when you were at the freezing end of a blooming hot flush.

In the bedroom, Bella removed the coat and peeled off the ancient T-shirt, the only garment she could bear against her skin at night. Years of wash and wear had made it so sheer you could see through the blurred faces of the band. She shrugged on an ancient pink candlewick dressing gown. Not keen on getting into a damp bed, she settled into the winged armchair with a tartan blanket. The moonlight shone into the bedroom and her flowers, in a vase and placed on the dresser, cast shadows against the wall. Was it the strong scent of the hyacinths permeating the night that had made her dream so vivid? It didn't matter. She may well be a fifty-two-year-old frump with raging hormones, but her life was about to change. Smiling to herself, she snuggled into the dressing gown and, pulling the blanket up, was soon asleep.

Standing in front of the mirror with dress and shoes on, Bella concluded the outfit passed muster, only her feet were a tad nippy. Thank God she wouldn't be going far. She'd made an effort with makeup, alien on her face after such a long time. Wearing a dress was unfamiliar, too. In London she'd worn smart trouser suits to work, with the very shoes she had on today, getting through an eighteen-hour day without any problems at all. These days her uniform consisted of jeans and an array of checked shirts – and her Docs – so wearing the dress was discomfiting and rather airy. She needed protection against the March weather, so Bella staggered to her mother's bedroom. Dorothea had outfits for all occasions; there would be something she could wear – the parka would not do today. Picking out a black wool stole and wrapping it around her, she was enveloped in her mother's perfume. Bella breathed it in.

They'd had a tortuous relationship, but today Bella was unperturbed by the evocative scent. She spotted a black clutch sitting on a pile of shoe boxes and commandeered it; this wasn't a day for a shabby backpack either.

Keeping a firm grip on the banister, she tottered down the stairs just as the doorbell chimed. Opening the door, Bella was met by a huge spray of flowers, the little card poking through the cellophane: *Thinking of you today, babes. Lots of love, Shirl girl xxx*. Behind the flowers the funeral car pulled up and, opening the window, the driver raised a palm towards her.

'No worries, dear. I'm early. You've got plenty of time.'

The patronising 'dear' set Bella's teeth on edge but she stumbled inside, placing the flowers in the sink, and had a last-minute look round – all seemed in order. Bella opened one of the buffet boxes and inspected the contents: a mixture of tiny cream cakes and mini savouries. She licked her lips as her stomach growled; pinching a dinky roll and shoving it in her mouth, it was time to go. With the stole, clutch and house keys, Bella walked with as much dignity as she could muster toward the limousine.

Aunt Nettie didn't live far and it wasn't long until Bella and the driver were helping her into the huge car – a difficult operation when you had tiny legs. They sat holding hands, drawing comfort from each other. Bella barely had time to relax when an intense heat broke out from her core. She threw off the wrap and attacked the window button, craving cool air.

'Do you mind?' The bitter east coast wind flew into the car.

'No, don't be daft. We've all been there.'

They leaned back, hair whipped by the wind as the driver discreetly slid the partition glass across. Bella tucked the wrap around her aunt's knees and before long the car crawled to a stop outside the funeral home and, with well-timed efficiency, a hearse pulled out in front and led the way to the crematorium.

Bella could see the coffin in the hearse up front, and imagining her mother inside filled her with a deep sadness. Despite their constant conflict, there'd always been the hope of a mother-daughter reconciliation where Dorothea would become a loving mother and she would be a beloved daughter her mother was proud of. This could never happen now. Bella felt her aunt slipping her hand into hers again. 'Nothing's ever black and white. Your mother was hard on you and we don't understand why.' Aunt Nettie tucked Bella's hair behind her ear. 'I'm not sure Dorothea was cut out for motherhood but it's alright to grieve for what might have been.'

A tear snaked down Bella's face as the memory of her first day at school came to mind – Dorothea reaching over her to open the car door. 'Remember, you're a big girl at school. No more "Mummy" – it's Dorothea. Off you go.' Bella had slid out at the towering school gates, bewildered and alone, watching the car drive into the distance. Roddy, who liked to walk to school with his friends, had appeared and taken her hand, walking her to the classroom with the other children and their parents.

Bella's aunt reached up and wiped the tear away. 'You just need to get through today and then you can live any life you choose, away from Dorothea's influence.'

Bella hugged her aunt to her as they arrived at the crematorium.

The traditional service passed in a blur and she soon found herself at the exit beside Roddy, ready for the line of people to pay their respects.

Pam came up first and said to Bella, 'Quick. Give me your keys. Jean and I are going to take Aunt Nettie. She's a bit shaky on her pins and we'll get the tea and coffee on. You might be ages here.' She indicated the queue of people waiting and Bella gratefully handed them over.

'I knew Dorothea from the Women's Guild. Helped raise so much money for charity.' This from an old woman who smiled benevolently while holding Bella's arms in a vice-like grip. The queue of mourners continued; old friends who had tales to tell about how they knew her mother, business associates of Roddy's who remembered their father, too. Keren and Dali, with Will, shuffled along the line, hugging and offering condolences, and then her hands were encased in a strong clasp and in front of her was a face she hadn't seen for thirty years.

'Annabella, sweetheart. I'm so sorry for your loss, hen.' A man in his eighties, who had once been very tall, kissed her cheek.

'Mr Adam! It's so...' A surge of emotion charged through Bella, and she clenched her fists to keep control as he drew her into his arms.

'It's OK, Annabella. Dinnae worry.'

Bella found herself blubbing against his coat, sniffing inelegantly. Mr Adam handed over a laundered hanky.

'I'm sorry.' Bella gave her nose a good blow. 'How are you? God, it's been years. It's so good to see you.'

'I'm fine, lass. Cawin' awa as they say. Cawin' awa. Jem's coming home.'

'Coming home? When?'

'Not long.' Mr Adam glanced behind him; a small huddle had formed as the last of the black-clad attendees waited. 'I'd better move on. It's good to see you, lassie. I'm not coming for the tea and sausage roll if you don't mind, but I wanted to come and pay my respects. I remember Dorothea well from all these years ago.' His smile was rueful. 'I hope ye'll no be a stranger.' He pecked her cheek and went off at a slow pace.

The last mourners came up to express their sorrow and before long she was sitting in the limo for the solitary journey home. As they exited the gates she could see Mr Adam in the distance, walking away.

CHAPTER 4

When Bella entered the kitchen, she could see Pam and Jean had been as good as their word. People were picking up cups of tea – or more often a stronger tipple – to carry to the lounge, and Bella followed. Aunt Nettie and two older ladies she vaguely recognised were perched on the sofa. Bella moved among the guests, monitoring the supply of refreshments, and gradually people bade their farewells, leaving Roddy and Bella alone. She gratefully kicked off her shoes, sinking down on her chair, glad the worst was over. Roddy was picking up and replacing ornaments, peering closely at pictures he'd seen ten thousand times before.

Bella was irritated at his constant movement. 'Why don't you sit down? Do you want another drink?'

'A whisky, if there's any left? I noticed Will getting stuck in.'

'Your friend Clarkson was giving it good welly, too.'

Bella fetched Roddy's drink and the last of the buffet, helping herself to a couple of bridge rolls.

'Ice?' Roddy waved his glass.

What did your last servant die of? She strode off to the kitchen, got the ice bucket, and served cubes into Roddy's glass. She demolished the buffet rolls as she regarded the skies through the window. They were darkening; threatening clouds loomed and the river was dark and choppy.

'I'll miss this view. Even on a day like today.' She enjoyed the bustle of London, but the sight of wide-open skies was rare.

'You're definitely off south then?'

'Shirley says I'll be able to get a job, if I can catch up on what's been happening the last decade. And she's lined up a great flat rental; it should time well with the house sale.'

Roddy had taken a seat but was immediately up again, pacing with his drink.

'I suppose we put it on the market with an agent, or should we go private? What would work best? It's your area of expertise. By the time it's sold, I'll be ready to move.'

'Annabella...'

'What?'

'The house...' Roddy took a good draught of the whisky.

'What about the house?'

'The house is mortgaged.' He deposited his empty glass on a table.

'Mortgaged?'

'If it's sold, there'll be no capital.'

'What are you talking about? The mortgage was paid off when Father died. She always said we'd have the house.'

'Listen. This development we're invested in, we needed more capital and re-mortgaging the house was part of the plan. We needed the investment, Annabella; it was Dorothea's suggestion.'

Bella was astonished. She had no inkling there was any mortgage on the house, or that the building development she knew so little about was precarious. She sank onto the sofa. 'When did this happen?'

'About six months ago, after the building work was underway. It won't be long before we're out of the woods, then we can sell the flats and repay the investment. It's just a bit ... tight.'

'Tight? Dorothea never said a word.' Many times her mother had explained that the house would be left to her, and that she and Roddy would be 'taken care of and more'. Recently, as her mother's health had deteriorated, Bella couldn't help but dream of a future. Hope would be followed by worry that she was wishing her mother dead. Bella was angry at not being party to what was happening. When Dorothea last spoke of the house, she would have known that any sale would have yielded nothing. She was hurt her mother had lied to her and hurt to be deemed unworthy of the truth about the family's affairs.

'There didn't seem any need to tell you. Mother's stroke. It was ... bad timing.'

'Bad timing?'

'I didn't mean it like that. We knew she was unwell, but it was ... unexpected.' Roddy fumbled around with his top pocket handkerchief. 'It won't make any difference to your plans for London. You can still go.'

'How? I don't have any money.'

'You can't have spent it all? All the money from the house in Hampstead? What have you done with it?'

'The US partners in our last deal went bust and we lost our investment, we never quite pulled ourselves back from it.'

Roddy joined her on the sofa. 'Why didn't you say?'

'I didn't want to give you both the satisfaction. You always seemed so successful with the business.' She wished she'd poured herself a tumbler of whisky and could down it in one. 'I also paid out for a lot of the care in the beginning and the allowance wasn't exactly generous. I've hardly anything left.' She felt sick, the buffet threatening to make a return. 'How long is all this going to take?'

'Well, if Lorna and I move in here—'

'Move here? Why?'

'Wait, wait. Let me explain. If we move in here, we can sell our place, giving us the extra capital we need. It will all go as planned and we should have flats to sell in twelve months.'

'You must have money in the bank; there was a hefty sum sitting there when I helped you out with the book-keeping last year. You could lend me money to go to London. In fact, you could give me it; think how much I've saved in carer's fees over the years.'

'For God's sake, Annabella, don't you get it? I'm up shit creek without a paddle. The kids – I can't take the kids out of school, and every spare penny goes to the financiers. It'll be worth it in the end, for all of us. I'll make sure you get a share of the profits.'

Whoop de doo. 'What kind of deal did you make?'

'It's a perfectly good deal. We had a couple of setbacks. It's none of your business, anyway.'

It kind of is, Bella said to herself, but she let it go. She had learned over the years that her input and experience were never going to be welcome.

'What am I supposed to do in the meantime?'

'You can stay here, too. I mean, there's plenty of room. There's four bedrooms.'

'No. No, no, no. It's not possible. What about the portfolio – isn't there any property you can sell?'

Roddy prattled on about how they'd got rid of the smaller flats to invest in building and they had no assets left. The company was seriously in the red and the financiers' accountants were watching every penny. This was the only way out. If Mother had lived a bit longer, Annabella would have been none the wiser. Building your own properties was the way forward; small fry to have individual places and rent them out these days. *Blah. Blah. Blah.*

'Mother and Father, they would've wanted this. Us coming together to save the business.'

'Us coming together? Don't make me laugh.' She didn't want to hear anymore.

'It's for the best. I can't let McCaa Properties go down the tubes, for God's sake.'

Bella could imagine sharing the house with Roddy and family, being at their beck and call, with only her bedroom offering sanctuary.

'I don't want to live here with you and Lorna and the kids. I'm not going to be a sad old aunt relegated to a corner of the house.'

'You won't be. The place is huge. The kids would love it.'

'No, they wouldn't, and I doubt Lorna would be happy.'

'Listen—'

But Bella wasn't in the mood for listening anymore. 'Roddy, it's been a long day, you should go.'

'Annabella, hear me out. If you don't want to live here, there is a place. It's been empty a few months and needs a bit of work. You could have it till you go, if you don't want to stay here.'

'What flat? Where?'

'Broughty Ferry. It's near the—'

'Broughty Ferry's miles away! It's full of old ladies and charity shops. People go there when they're ready to die.' Bella shook her head. 'None of my friends live there.'

'Come on, it's not bad at all.'

She clutched her hair in frustration and pressed her head against the window. 'I've had enough for today.' She stormed past Roddy and he trotted to keep up as she reached the front door and opened it wide.

'I'll come over tomorrow and see what you think. If you want me to, I'll take you to see the property. Annabella – it'll all be worth it in the end.'

Bella saw her sister-in-law waiting in her spanking new BMW; the value of a small flat in Dundee. Lorna gave her a wave as Roddy got in the passenger side but Bella slammed the front door shut without acknowledging it.

In the living room, she closed the curtains as rain spattered the panes. Was she wrong to have expectations? She'd always tried to shut out desperate hopes for the future, as the only way she could have one is if her mother didn't, and she didn't wish her mother dead. There was no way her mother would ever have moved into a home and Bella knew her position had no all-round happy ending. After a couple of years had gone by, Bella realised she was in it for the long haul. In her worst moments, she'd imagined her mother hanging on until she was a hundred years old, leaving enough for a little retirement place Bella could shuffle around in during her twilight years on earth. But over the last while and especially the last week, these long-held but submerged hopes had allowed her to imagine a different future, having her life back; being able to return to London and pick up her career, a chance she could only allow herself to occasionally fantasise about while caring for Dorothea.

She switched on the TV, flicking through stations and absentmindedly eating the remains of the buffet. As night fell, a coldness descended, and Bella wrapped the stole around her. She quickly flung it off as she caught hint of the scent. Her mother had lied to her. Dorothea may well have had plans for her to be 'taken care of' but Bella had been kept ignorant of the reality. She sat for a long time staring vacantly at the screen.

In the bedroom, she unplugged the buzzer connected to her mother's room and threw it in the wastebasket. Her life had been ruled by that sound for far too long. In the morning the others would be removed. They were set at strategic points throughout the house so that Bella could be called any time. Of course, she had to be aware of her mother's needs, but they were used incessantly – buzzing into her brain at various times during the day and night – for a vase to be moved; a table to be dusted; to bring iced water. There would be no more buzzers. Bella placed the flowers on a table in the hallway – she didn't want the nightmare again.

Rolling fully-clothed under the duvet, she snapped off the light. What was she going to do? Exhausted by the events of the day, and knowing she would not rest easy while anxiety jittered through her system, she started her breathing exercise. Inhale for four and hold for four, exhale slowly. And repeat. Inhale for four, hold for four, exhale slowly. Gradually, she relaxed, fear subsided, and amongst the turmoil of the funeral, worries about her uncertain situation and the darkness of her mood, it was Jem who drifted into her mind as she fell into an unsettled sleep.

CHAPTER 5

'Annabella!'

Bella withdrew inside the bedroom and softly eased the door closed.

'Annabella! I know you're there.' Roddy's brogues thumped upstairs and stopped abruptly on the landing. Bella held her breath. She had no desire to face her brother this morning. The grandfather clock tick-tocked in the distance as the siblings waged a voiceless battle.

'Please yourself. I'll leave the keys in the kitchen,' he called out. A further minute of stillness ensued – then Bella exhaled as she heard him clomping downstairs, and eventually the front door banged behind him. She waited as the car crunched up the drive before descending to the kitchen and picking up the keys left on the counter. A large tag heralded *McCaa Properties @ 173a Long Lane*.

Roddy had left a note: *Utilities on. Needs cleaning.*

Big woop. Bella threw it all in the cutlery drawer. No way was she being banished from her home; she had as much right to be there as anybody else. She'd woken in the early hours and decided the best plan would be to stay in the house with Roddy and family. Her outgoings would be minimal as the bills were covered by McCaa Properties. She would get a job, keep expenditure at rock bottom and it wouldn't take long to save enough money for London. And if she managed to have a job to go down to, she wouldn't need much behind her. But it would still be thousands more than the £397.26 her bank account had revealed this morning. Those damn dresses.

She sat at the kitchen table and lay her head on her arms. She'd already lost ten years; how much more of her life would it take to save enough money? She was wretched with despair, the hope and excitement of a return to London replaced with bitterness and anger. Her chest exploded with heat and she hurriedly stripped off her clothing as perspiration popped out all over. Down to her bra, she opened the garden door and was frantically opening the windows when she spied her mother's Royal Doulton figurine collection on the ledge. Picking one up, Bella launched it at the wall, where it gloriously shattered, covering the kitchen floor in tiny fragments. She weighed another in her hand and smashed again, then another and another and another, lost in a frenzy until they were all gone and she stood breathless and sated and no longer hot.

Putting her clothes on and adding her father's coat for extra warmth, she opened her notebook and wrote, in large figures, '£397.26'. Wow. Not a lot to show for a successful career in the City for twenty years. The company Bella and her husband, Sam, had created had initially thrived, until they decided to invest everything, including the house, into an international property deal with a US company – a perilous decision it turned out as a mini crash in the US stock market wiped out their partners and sent their own company into administration too. Bella had used her savings and personal investments to make sure the staff could cope after the sudden loss of income. She and Sam had disagreed about paying them, with Sam insisting they would quickly pick up new jobs, but Bella felt responsible, especially since most of the staff had been with them since the beginning.

The disintegration of the business carried over into their marriage. It had been happy during the good times, but the bad times exposed dissimilar approaches to life Bella could no longer ignore. She secured a job as a financial analyst and was trying to rent a flat when Roddy had rung with news of Dorothea's stroke. Within twenty-four hours, she'd packed up her car and headed north. What had been left in the bank had dwindled over the years to today's measly amount.

Bella opened a can of diet Irn-Bru as she contemplated her options. To go to London, she would need at least four thousand pounds. The rental deposit for the flat Shirley had organised was two thousand and she would need money to live on while she found a job and got settled. So, she needed two jobs – one in Dundee to save money to go to London and one in London for when she moved. Time to bring her friend up to date. Bella video-called Shirley and, although it was a Saturday, her friend was at work surrounded by piles of paperwork and files heaving on her desk.

'You mean you can't even sell the house?'

'No, so there's not going to be any money at least for a year. Roddy's tied it all up in this block of flats he's building.'

'Can he do that? Legally, I mean?'

'I suppose so; I've never been part of McCaa Properties. Once Father died, Roddy and Dorothea were left the business, and they never wanted me to be part of it. And I never wanted to be part of it either.'

The two women had met when Bella had moved to London and were twenty-two-year-old interns working towards the end of their degrees. They'd been friends ever since and their careers had mirrored each other's, moving from personal mortgages on to corporate finance, where they worked as analysts. They would assess corporations – their shares and assets – and their worth in the market. If necessary, they would organise refinancing and loan schedules. Five hundred miles apart, Shirley was the friend Bella confided in when life was difficult. In all the time she'd been in Dundee, Shirley hadn't deserted her. She'd made short trips to the city even though Bella couldn't reciprocate by going to London. In turn, she listened to Shirley through her ups and downs, and heard about the men who came and went, as Shirl got bored easily. They celebrated her deals, remotely of course, but the discussion of the ins and outs faltered as Bella became distanced from what was happening in the financial world they had shared.

'It means I'll have to get a job here first and save up. At least it's rent-free and expenditure will be minimal. I'm hoping by the end of the summer?'

'I don't think the owner of the flat would wait; he was only holding on as a favour to me. I'm sorry, luvvy, but there'll be other places.'

'Yeah, I suppose so... I thought I'd be able to borrow money from Roddy until the sale was concluded, but he hasn't got any, so he says.' Bella swigged at the can to swallow the threatening tears. 'On the positive side, it gives me time to catch up on what's happening in the market – and all the big deals over the last ten years.' They laughed.

'Sounds like a plan. Give yourself a bit of time. There'll be loads of jobs in a place the size of Dundee and anywhere would be lucky to have you. I'll keep my ear to the ground here, too. Don't worry; all will be well.' Shirley's attention was taken by a voice off-screen. 'Sorry, I'd better get going.'

'Jem's coming home.'

'What? Jem Adam? What do you mean?'

'His father came to the funeral and told me Jem was coming home – soon, I think. I mean, I won't see him. I don't want to see him.'

'I always forget you went out with *the* Jem Adam.'

'He was plain Jem Adam when I knew him. Before he went to New York.'

'But I don't forget how heartbroken you were when we first met. Little shit.'

Bella waved the mention of Jem away. 'It's irrelevant. I've got plenty of other things to be thinking about and I'll be in London in no time.'

'You will, babes. With a cracking job – here in the swing of the metropolis and all it has to offer. Right, I'd better get moving. We're going to be burning the midnight oil on this one. Don't you miss it? *Ciao.*' Shirl switched off.

Bella did miss it – missed the teamwork and the adrenaline when a deal was finalised, and the celebrations after. Telling Shirl about Jem came from nowhere; she hadn't been thinking about him. Not much, anyway. Only a bit of googling, but the information hadn't changed much from when she'd occasionally looked him up over the years. *The Courier* had published articles on the 'local man made good' theme – about Jeremy Menzies Adam (they stated his full name for some reason) inventing a successful video game and how it sent fans crazy worldwide each time there was a new edition. She'd googled 'Jem Adam wife' and 'Jem Adam partner'; nothing came up except interviews in trade magazines with the 'notoriously private games designer' talking about the next big thing his company would produce – nothing about his personal life, not even in his Wikipedia entry.

There was one picture taken about twenty years ago at an awards show: Jem in a tux with a beautiful woman by his side, shimmering in an elegant evening gown. Other photos online were slight variations on the standard shots from the company website. Bella would peer at them to see if anything of the man she once knew was still there.

She clicked on the job pages. Jem was a door not to be re-opened. She had moved on before and she was moving on again.

CHAPTER 6

The next couple of weeks were spent browsing, phoning, being interviewed at the job centre and registering at agencies with zero results. She'd dusted off her CV and what had once been impressive was dated and jaded. No one was interested in her career as a financial analyst in the City.

'Have you worked as a secretary?'
'No.'
'What programs can you use?'
'Umm... Word. Excel.'
'Any graphics? Adobe Suite?'
'No.'
'Have you done any retail work?'
'No.'
'Worked in a restaurant? In a bar?'
'No.'

And on and on. Most frightening was when she tried to bring herself up to date by reading the financial news, researching who headed up what institution, who the main brokers were and what had been happening over the time she'd been away. Her brain had turned to mush and she couldn't seem to hold information in her head; it was like ploughing through a fog. If it wasn't the fog, she would fall asleep; yesterday she'd woken in the afternoon with her face in her laptop, having sent an email with a zillion 'f's. Night sweats and fear for the future woke her in the small hours. One minute she was incredibly excited about the opportunities to come, the next she was in an impotent, murderous rage when employment agency staff barked questions at her. There was the gaping hole of ten years caring for Dorothea – impossible to hide. Even though she'd served for a short while as Roddy's bookkeeper, she didn't have any bookkeeping or accountancy qualifications – she had a worthless thirty-year-old business degree.

Besides the constant job search, Roddy and Lorna appeared at any given time during the day, invading her space and poking around the house, deciding what would go or stay, ignoring any input from Bella. She'd retire to her room, seething into her pillow as family heirloom furniture vanished daily. She tasked herself with sorting her mother's belongings because they were in such a hurry and the process speeded up the emotional rollercoaster even more. It was unpleasant doing a clear out so soon after her mother's death. Yes, there were times when Bella hated her mother – her easy unkindness, the put downs, the constant criticism – but you couldn't care for someone when they were at their lowest without compassion. The way her mother had fought against the results of the stroke, would not be beaten, would not be bedridden – in fact, she wouldn't even move her bedroom downstairs – had stoked grudging admiration in Bella and made it easier for her to act as carer. And housekeeper. And head cook and bottle-washer. Day in, day out, for a long ten years.

All these abilities were worthless for the kind of job she wanted and Bella knew she didn't have it in her to work in a care home; she was prone to bursting into tears or exploding with anger, and the residents would be miserable.

Keren's party was tomorrow. Dali's legal practice seemed to be constantly growing, with their two daughters joining as partners. Would he have a vacancy? She could file, type, make coffee – she didn't mind – anything to get work. She'd ask him tomorrow. Excited by having a plan and looking forward to the party, she moved on to studying the Financial Times. Bella was still doing research when Lorna's face appeared at the kitchen door.

'And how's Annabella?' Lorna tilted her head to one side, patronising and pitying. Bella's delicately balanced temper teetered on the edge as Lorna joined her at the table. 'I've got a huge favour to ask. You love your niece so much and I'm sure you won't mind.'

Bella boggled at what might be coming. Lorna was nice enough, she supposed, but only engaged with poor, divorced and therefore insignificant Bella when she had to – usually to ask her to make tea for them all when they visited. She bristled, waiting to hear what was coming.

'Heather is a bit of a late starter, but she's becoming a woman, sprouting everywhere, and dreadfully embarrassed all the time...'

This was news to Bella, who had seen a less embarrassed Heather on occasion hanging outside the school gates with a motley crew of boys, seemingly proud of her growing assets.

'Would you let Heather have the bedroom with the en-suite? Saves her padding about the hallway when she needs to attend to ... women's things.'

'You mean give up my bedroom?'

'Yes. There's the other one – at the end of the hallway – and it means Heather has room for the desk she needs for her studies. You don't need much space, do you? What do you say? I guess we all must make do under the circumstances. We'll take Dorothea's room, of course. Don't worry, I wouldn't have you moving in there.'

'But—'

'You remember how mortifying it was in your teens and how privacy was so important? You don't mind, do you? I knew you wouldn't. I said to Roddy, Annabella is generous, of course, she won't mind.'

The shriek inside Bella's head was so intense she feared it had come out of her mouth, but Lorna was still sitting there with her simpering smile. What about the embarrassment of the menopausal woman? The middle-of-the-night bladder calls awash with sweat? Bella bashed out gibberish on the keyboard to distract her from grabbing a plate and ramming it into Lorna's face.

'Thank you so much. We'll all be moved in by the afternoon; we brought bits and pieces ourselves to start.'

'You're moving today?'

'Yes, did Roddy not tell you? He's so busy. It won't take long to move rooms, will it? Can I help you with it? No time like the present.'

'No, thanks. Off out. Just need to grab my coat. I'll sort it later.'

'I knew you'd agree and I sort of made a little start ... hope you don't mind...'

Bella didn't trust herself to speak as her blood pressure ratcheted up several notches and, banging the laptop shut, she grabbed backpack and keys and fled the kitchen. Opening her bedroom door she saw what Lorna meant – the top dresser drawer had been emptied onto the bed – her most private possessions lying out for anyone to see. Bella's insides twisted with rage and mortification and she ran into the hallway, determined to do damage to whatever or whoever was at hand – only to be met by her niece, who visibly cowered from the ferocious spectacle Bella presented.

'Erm, Mum asked me to see if you needed help... but it doesn't matter.' Heather bolted.

Bella, remorseful at frightening her niece, soon followed and ran outside, giving the front door a good thunk as she went. Why was she the one who always had to compromise, to move over? She spied Lorna's roadster parked up beside her old Mini. If they needed money so desperately, why hadn't the car been sold? In a flash her penknife was out – and she stabbed the blade into the rear tyre. She stabbed repeatedly until her fury died away. She dived into the Mini, the door swinging open wide enough to hit Lorna's shiny red passenger door. Buoyed up by the satisfaction of her vandalism, she wheeled round and out the driveway onto the Perth Road.

'Aaaaaaaaaagh,' she screamed like a wailing bat out of hell. 'Aaaaaaaaaaaagh. I'm so sick of this.'

CHAPTER 7

Bella sped into town and avoided disaster by centimetres when she screeched to a halt at a red light, almost rear ending the car in front.

For God's sake Bella – pull yourself together. But the tap had opened and tears gushed freely, salty on her face. Heading in no particular direction eventually she found herself chugging up the steep brae of the Hilltown and didn't stop until she climbed higher and higher and round and round on the narrow road leading to the top of The Law – an imposing hill in the centre of Dundee. Miraculously empty except for an old man and his dog, Bella pulled up and got out of the car, buffeted by the wind.

'Smile, dear, it may never happen.' The old man dared to show his membership to the patriarchy.

'Oh, bugger off!' Bella yelled and the man beetled away, rightly scared. The dog scampered behind and they were out of sight in no time. Bella sobbed openly. Why couldn't she shout at Roddy or Lorna – or even her mother? When had she become such a wimp?

The wind whirled through her hair, making it even more unruly. She didn't mind; being out in the elements reflected her wild mood. Of course, Heather should have the en-suite – puberty is hellish and privacy is important. Her own teenage years were long before the house was modernised and she would have appreciated a private bathroom. Bella regretted her petty actions. Imagine slashing the tyre – Jeez Louise, she'd lost the plot. Not to mention the dent in the car door. She'd examined her own and there wasn't a scratch.

Wandering over to the war memorial Bella sat down, taking in the panoramic view of the river and Fife beyond. It wouldn't take long to pull the money together, enough to have as a cushion while she found a job and place to stay in London. Surely, Shirley would put her up on the sofa if it came to it. Her friend had gone for location rather than size and had an impressive apartment with a wraparound balcony and panoramic view of London, but no spare room – a deterrent against too many relatives coming to stay.

She could ask Roddy again for money but he'd pleaded poverty the day of the funeral and every time she'd seen him since. Aunt Nettie would be delighted to help her, but it seemed wrong to ask an eighty-four-year-old for a loan. It had crossed her mind when, on seeing her aunt recently, she'd asked how the London plans were going. Bella's toes had curled in her boots and the words could not pass her lips. No doubt any of her friends would oblige, but even the suggestion of borrowing from them filled her with shame and a sense of failure. She could ask Dali? A loan against the house sale in the future was more like a business arrangement. But she knew she would never approach him, either. Her insides soured at the thought of people finding out how broke she was. She would stick to the plan of asking him for a job; he would understand she needed to reacquaint herself with the world of employment, be part of a workforce before she headed to London. Meantime she couldn't face going home and having to deal with the damage she'd done to the car. What would she say to Lorna?

By late afternoon Bella's Mini was on the road again; she'd had her fill of coffee and cake in two separate cafés and couldn't put off the confrontation any longer. Lorna's car was there, facing the opposite direction and with an obvious flat tyre. Bella couldn't deny a surge of happiness at her success. The front door was open and she could hear raised voices. Lorna was shouting and, at the sight of her sister-in-law, said, 'You won't believe it, Annabella. Your nephew Gordon did wheelies in the driveway in my car – flattened one of the tyres!'

'I'm sorry! But you do want me to learn to drive.' Gordon stuck out a defiant chin.

'But not doing wheelies – and you're only sixteen. You can't drive like a maniac.'

'Aunt Annabella does. I saw her hurtling down the road. Must have been doing seventy. She nearly rear-ended an Audi.'

Thank you, Gordon. Bella had been struggling to get the words out to say the tyre was her fault but the little clype made her keep shtum. He was in trouble for the wheelies; why not busting the tyre, too? And perhaps the dent hadn't been noticed yet. Bella crept upstairs, leaving them to it.

'Don't bring Aunt Annabella into this...'

Ignoring the fracas, she found a pile of boxes stacked either side of her bedroom door, all marked in bold coloured pens: *Heather! Hands Off! Keep Out!* She'd forgotten about the move.

An hour later, she'd squashed her belongings into the small space and plonked herself on the bed. How had it come to this? The single bed saddened her the most. There was an immaturity about a single bed. A double bed was the size of hoping a lover might share it, although God forbid; she'd never bring anyone home. Bella knew she should have refused – it was unfair of Lorna to ask. This pile of boxes, the clothes hanging in the wardrobe, her toiletries in a carrier bag represented all she owned. Not much to show for a life.

She realised she could sell pieces of her mother's jewellery. She entered Dorothea's bedroom, soon to be Roddy and Lorna's. The room had been stripped, except for the imposing, handmade bed and antique dresser. Bella searched but all the drawers were empty. No jewellery box. It was uncomfortable to be in the room bereft of evidence of her mother's life, as if she'd never existed. On cue, the distinct sound of her mother's buzzer shattered the peace. Bella covered her ears – was she imagining it? *Buzz, buzz, buzz.* She was sure it wasn't in her head and dashed into the hallway. The speaker was re-attached to the wall and buzzing away like crazy.

'What the hell...?' Bella ran downstairs into the kitchen – Lorna was standing beside the sink, pressing up and down on the mechanism. 'What's going on?'

'It's working? Great. It's the best way to get the children down, save me shouting all the way up the stairs. This house is too big for calling out.'

'Lorna, it's right outside my door. And will the kids even hear it when they have their headphones on? Which is most of the time!'

Roddy came in. 'It's working. Great! I hate shouting through the house.'

'Can't you text them?'

'This way we get them both together. Saves Lorna's voice.' Roddy was well pleased with the plan and attacked the buzzer himself. This time it did bring Heather and Gordon.

'What's going on?' Heather glared at the adults while they all ignored the question.

'Where has Dorothea's jewellery box gone, Roddy? I left it in the bedroom so we could go through it.'

'I put it in the office safe.' Lorna was smug.

'What?' Bella was put out. 'You ... you shouldn't have done that. Roddy?'

Roddy at least appeared uncomfortable. 'I suppose it's better in a safe place. You can come to the office tomorrow and we can go through it all. No problem.'

'I'll come too.' Lorna interjected. 'Heather must have keepsakes to remember her grandmother by. Those emerald earrings are magnificent.'

Bella scowled and left. On the landing she wrenched the buzzer off the wall and ground it to a pulp under the heel of her Docs. No way was it going to be salvaged out of a wastebasket a second time. She carried the pieces downstairs to an empty kitchen. The family had made themselves scarce but could be heard, banging and thumping as furniture and boxes were moved to make the house their own. Placing all parts of the system into a bag, Bella battered them with a rolling pin and tossed the shattered residue in the bin outside. There would be no more buzzing in this house.

The fire pit was smouldering in the corner of the garden, and Bella wandered over to investigate. Horrified, she extracted a remnant of cloth and inspected it. A sleeve. A single brown suede sleeve. The rest of her father's car coat underneath was reduced to burnt rags. Even her mother had never suggested the coat should be taken away, and it had hung on the garden door all these years. Bella bent double, hugging the pain until she replaced the sleeve on the pyre and watched its smoky cremation complete before retreating to her new quarters. The door clicked firmly shut behind her as she sank to the floor.

Night had fallen as Bella stood up and extricated a large suitcase from the wardrobe. She shoved her clothes, with the hangers, into the case. The toiletries were next. She folded the single duvet and heaved it along to her old bedroom. Flinging it on a chair she reclaimed her double one, along with the pillows.

'These are mine,' she averred to no one, and stomped along the hallway. She gathered as much as she could in her arms and carted it downstairs, out through the front door, opened the Mini's doors and shoved it in. To and fro she went, undisturbed. She could hear arguing from the lounge – with a definite reference to the scratched door. Ha! She no longer cared. Back and forth she struggled with the boxes, ramming them in as best she could.

She gave the bedroom a final inspection. It was empty of all her own possessions, but she snatched up the table lamp and mirror too. With her free hand, she unhooked a painting from the staircase on the way down. It wasn't her favourite landscape but it was leaving with her. Bella continued to the Mini and jammed it all in. She retrieved the keys from the kitchen drawer. One last deed: she thumped along the hallway, past the lounge, ignoring the arguing inhabitants, and on to the living room. She then lurched outside with the huge TV, managing to slide it over the top of all her worldly goods.

Bella slammed the front door with as loud a bang as she could make. It reverberated through the house and a wail from Gordon rose through the night:

'She's taken the TV!'

Bella spun her car round, zoomed up the drive and out onto the Perth Road, straight through the city centre and out the other side, on the way to 173a Long Lane.

CHAPTER 8

Driving towards Broughty Ferry, Bella considered the fact there was nothing wrong with the 'suburb by the sea', as tourist blurb called the area. In fact, she'd rather liked the place as a teenager, when she and Jem first met and he had a summer job in a harbour café. There was a long beach with fabulous sand dunes and, despite the Scottish weather, they'd picnicked happily. The only real negative, she supposed, was it not being the West End. Her friends lived near home, as did Aunt Nettie. She loved the little shops, tea rooms and galleries up and down the Perth Road.

She turned into Long Lane and could see how well it lived up to its name, running parallel to the sea front and the high street – an irregular mix of tenements, villas and small cottages. She winced as the Mini edged along, dodging badly parked cars, over uneven cobbles and road-calming ramps. Crossroad after crossroad went by. After a bumpy age, and squinting into the darkness to see the numbers, she parked at the shabby front door of a cottage that was squashed in between two tenements. A seagull cawed into the night and chose the occasion to expunge its guano on the car window before screeching loudly off into the air.

Welcome to the seaside.

The main door stuttered as she pushed it open and stepped into an open plan living and dining area. A foetid stench made her gag and cover her nose as she felt along the wall for a light switch. The dim glow revealed the room was dotted with a bizarre collection of furniture long past its best. A bluebottle buzzed round her head and Bella waved it away, horrified.

Bracing herself and moving forward, she came to a small scullery and utility space. An adjacent door appeared to lead out to a garden and she grappled with the handle, but it wouldn't open and none of her keys fitted the lock. She peered against the window just as a neighbour's security light came on and momentarily flashed up the sad vision of a dilapidated wooden shed, rusted tools and a wheelbarrow lying around in the weeds.

A spiral staircase led to the upper floor and a small oval window halfway would offer another view in daylight. Unable to see a light switch, Bella used the torch on her phone. To the left of the stairs was a bathroom with a small tub ingrained with a black rim of dirt. To the right was a bedroom, only large enough to hold the double bed and chest of drawers. One side had a coombed ceiling with the windows set in the roof. The bedroom door was off its hinges and standing in the narrow corridor.

The shaft of light skimmed over the messy leftovers of a stranger's existence. Bella poked some tissue up each nostril and used her free hand as a guide as she crept about.

What was that odious aroma? Was it just filth, coupled with unopened windows and locked doors? The atmosphere was dark and depressing.

Downstairs Bella poked around in the scullery, with its manky free-standing gas cooker and overhead grill. She opened the oven door and quickly recoiled after catching a glimpse of a mouldy roast. Yuck.

Surveying the dilapidated quarters, Bella wondered whether she'd made the right decision. This was dismal and dank; years of ingrained dirt had penetrated the chocolate brown walls and floors and it wasn't only musty – the smell was rank. But she would stick it out, no way was she crawling home.

Bella woke to a cacophony of squawking seagulls. After the first look round the night before, all she'd done was decant her belongings from the car and pitch them into the living space. Managing to identify her duvet in the various heaps, she'd covered the sofa with bin bags, flung on the duvet and launched herself on top. She was sticky and sweaty, and regarding the surrounding mess of possessions with a bleary eye, Bella gingerly plucked the tissue from her nostrils. The ghastly smell had woken her during the night, and she'd stuffed her nose again to obliterate it. Bella peeled damp clothes away from her skin. Yuck. Her head was splitting, and she was dying for *coffee*. But first, she needed to wash and find clothes – clean knickers, at least.

Pulling a towel and the carrier bag of toiletries out of the case, she made her way up the rickety stairs, peering out the small window halfway up. With a corner of the towel, she wiped away filth and saw a young woman in the garden of the tenement next door, preening and posing while taking selfies against a coloured backdrop. Jeez Louise. What a state to be so up your own bum you spent time cavorting about and taking photos of yourself. The neighbour expertly flicked her long and admittedly luscious locks into a faultless style and modelled a jacket while adopting what appeared to Bella to be absurd poses, pouting all the while. Bella shook her head and continued upstairs.

She perched unsteadily over the loo, determined her posterior should not meet any part of the porcelain. The tap burped out brown spurts of water before running clean. There was a soft boom and with joy she knew a combi boiler had come on; lo and behold the water ran warm. Her fortunes were changing.

In clean clothes and with purse in hand, Bella exited the front door and, once out in the street, she banged into the preening, posing neighbour.

'Hello. Have you moved in? I saw you unloading last night. I'm Amina from next door.' There were big, friendly smiles while she indicated the ground floor tenement flat adjacent to the cottage. 'Do you need a hand with anything?' Amina tried to peer over Bella's shoulder into the cottage. 'It's been empty for a while, but it'll be great to have a neighbour again.'

Bella shut the front door. 'It won't be for long, just a short stay. And I think I'm fine, thanks.' She eked out a minimal smile.

Amina appeared unfazed by Bella's rudeness. 'If you're sure. But shout if you change your mind. See you later.' She whirled away down the lane, all jangling earrings and maxi skirt with those luscious long black locks billowing out behind her.

Bella trundled off hopefully in the opposite direction, finding not just coffee, but a shop selling bacon rolls and an assortment of cleaning materials. Breakfast consumed and donning fetching neon rubber gloves, she got stuck in.

Hours later a neat line of black bags was ready for the bin, together with a heap of rubbish that Bella would take to the city dump and an odd selection of furniture she would make do with until she went to London. The floors had been swept and washed, all surfaces decontaminated, and the chocolate brown walls had been wiped down. She'd prised open the windows with her penknife and the breeze alleviated the choicer odours dominating the space. A loud knock at the door broke into the assessment of her travails. It had better not be Roddy – she wasn't ready to face him yet. Yanking it open, she found her neighbour, who whooshed confidently past her.

'Ah, you're cleaning! Old Peter was not the most hygienic of individuals, so I brought vittles to sustain you.' Amina placed a tray of millionaire's shortbread on top of a box and offered Bella a choice of canned drinks.

Bella, caught between the unwelcome invasion of her space and the realisation of how hungry and thirsty she was, found she couldn't resist the offering of her favourite tipple and the temptation of the scrumptious-looking shortbread. 'Thanks, it's kind of you. The Irn-Bru, please. Can I give you cash for it?'

'No, it's a welcome to your new home present.' Amina delicately handed her a slice of the shortbread on a paper napkin.

Bella wolfed it down, relishing the heavenly sweet flavours, and accepted the next proffered piece.

'Oh, God. Mmm.' Bella chomped while speaking. 'Did you make it yourself? I was never good at millionaires.' She was won over despite herself. 'I'm Bella, by the way.' She was ogling a third slice and being nice and polite was the way to get it.

'What are you going to do with all this stuff?'

'Take it to the bin or the dump.'

'Are you taking these to the bin?' Amina gingerly poked a stylish boot at a pile of throws on the floor, ready for exit.

'Yes, they're disgusting.'

'But they're such a gorge vintage pattern underneath all the crud – you could give them a boil wash and they'd come up like super new. I'm always picking up stuff in charity shops and you'd be amazed how a little bit of TLC can transform.'

Bella looked doubtful. She'd had her fill of the shortbread and didn't want anyone questioning her decisions. 'I'll think about it. I—'

Amina looked at her watch. 'Shit. I need to go. I'm supposed to be bagging a table at the pub and it's always so busy on a Saturday.'

'Saturday!' Bella jumped up, crumbs scattering. The day of the week had been lost on her. Tonight was Keren's party. 'Shit. I'd better get a move on too.'

She ushered Amina out the door – but at least had the decency to thank her for bringing the much-needed sustenance.

'Hand in the tray when you're finished. Nice to meet you properly.'

CHAPTER 9

Bella had been tempted to slip another slice down, but seeing it was 6.45 pm she put temptation aside. The party kicked off at seven o'clock. Bella rummaged and found the white shirt and smart black trousers she'd spent part of her remaining cash on, justifying it as an interview outfit. They were crumpled and, with no iron, she laid them out hopefully across the sofa. She had a quick bird bath at the sink and washed her hair using an ancient, cracked jug she'd found in a cupboard. She couldn't find a comb, brush or hairdryer so she would have to go for 90s bed-head style. Thankfully, she found her makeup bag and whacked on as much as she could without looking like a clown.

Dressed and ready to go, she dared a look in the long mirror she'd found in the bedroom and instantly wished she hadn't. The trousers didn't look too bad, but the shirt was crumpled, and not in an expensive-linen kind of way. And the Docs – they looked wrong with the smart trousers. Her hair was dry, but not the sexy, tumbled-out-of-bed look she was aiming for. It was shapeless and the wiry texture it had of late at the roots made it all sit slightly up from her scalp, highlighting the grey showing through the mousy brown. Why hadn't she gone to the hairdresser? Her diary had hardly been full recently.

Bella sat down on the bed. She didn't have to go to the party; no one would notice if she didn't appear. So many events of this kind had been missed over the years while she looked after Dorothea. But she wanted to go; it was a chance to speak to Dali in case there was a vacancy in the offing, and there may be other possibilities if she got chatting to the right people. And it might be fun, and fun had been missing from her life for such a long time; she had to go.

In a last-ditch effort, she added armour in the way of red lipstick, hoping people might be so distracted by the vibrant colour they wouldn't notice the rest of her. Bella threw an uneasy smile at her reflection and, frightened by the result, turned away. Picking up her coat and backpack, she set off in the car – all the way to the other end of Dundee. If she fancied a drink, she could leave the car and pick it up tomorrow; she was going out tonight to have a good time.

CHAPTER 10

'Windy! Thank God you're here.' Keren dragged her inside. 'Please help me. Only one of the caterers has arrived and I must get the drinks and canapes handed out.' Bella was led into the kitchen and Keren started fixing an apron round her friend's waist.

'Do you think Dali might have any vacancies at the practice, for secretaries or a clerk, an admin kind of thing?' asked Bella.

Keren rotated Bella around to face her. 'Why? Aren't you going to London?'

'I am, but there's going to be a delay in the house getting sold and I need to get into work, remind myself what it's like – and I want to earn my own money again.'

'Dali won't have any vacancies; his staff stay forever.' Keren gave Bella's outfit a critical once-over. 'Thank God you're wearing black and white, it looks the part, but, Heavens, Windy, have you not heard of an iron?' She thrust a tray of champagne into Bella's hands and, turning her to face the door, pushed her out of the kitchen.

Bella found herself in the doorway of a large lounge crammed with people. She saw Pam and Jean through the throng – *why hadn't they been commandeered to help?* She gravitated towards her friends while people picked up champagne and dumped their empties on the tray. She manoeuvred her way between the guests, uncomfortably hot and breaking into an uncontrollable sweat.

'Oh, excuse me, waitress?' An old man leered at her. 'Take this red wine would you? I think it's corked. I'll have champers. Much more fun, eh, what?' As he banged the glass down, most of the contents sploshed over the front of her pristine top and Bella looked down in dismay. The glass had a force of its own and teetered dangerously on the edge. Mesmerised, Bella tried to balance it, but a big drip of perspiration caught in her eyelash and when she shook her head to remove it, the glass went off on a journey of its own and landed on the carpet. An artistic splash of red splayed onto the inevitably cream fibres, and Bella got down on hands and knees to save the glass before it was crushed by oblivious party feet. She put the tray down beside her and, using her apron, tried to wipe the wine off. This was not how she had envisaged her first Saturday night out in forever.

'Belle! Bella?'

She heard the voice and her heart jolted so wildly she nearly fainted. Thirty years may have passed, but she recognised it instantly and he was the only person who ever called her Belle. It was Jem. Bella wanted a big hole to open and swallow her, and she contemplated burrowing under the sofa. Instead of escaping, she found herself being hoisted upright; Jem was also picking up the tray from the floor.

He looked so handsome – nothing like the gangly youth she first knew nor the gawky young man of twenty-two she'd last seen. His brown hair had taken on a golden tinge, with only the slightest grey at the edges. He'd filled out – he was no longer skinny but still lean and broad-shouldered. Bella was aware of her splodged, un-ironed attire as she casually drew a sticky hand through her wiry hair.

'Jem. Hi. Imagine seeing you here. How are you?'

He looked confused. 'Are you working here?'

'No, I'm helping Keren out. I—'

Keren barged her way between them.

'Let me take those, Jem. Oh my God, look at the carpet. What happened, Windy?' Keren took the tray from Jem and returned it to Bella.

'I'm sorry, one of your guests put a nearly-full glass on the tray and it fell.'

'I'll take the tray,' Jem headed out of the room with it, and Bella followed behind, regarding the front door like an emergency exit on the way.

In the kitchen, he deposited the tray and she dabbed the dishcloth at her front. His eyes burned into her until she had to look up.

'It's been a long time,' he said.

Bella gave up the fruitless attempt to reduce the stain. 'Yes. Yes, it has.' Her heart thumped in her chest.

'Bella...' Jem appeared as nonplussed as she was and there was a long, awkward pause as they studied each other. 'I'm sorry about Dorothea. Dad told me. How are you coping?'

Keren came into the kitchen and linked onto Jem's arm. 'Jem, I've got people you have to meet and they're not staying long. Windy, could you look at the canapes. *Please*?' Keren gave her a pleading look as she ushered Jem out of the kitchen. He looked at Bella from the door and gave a faint wave.

If there was a way to meet an ex, this was not it. She went over to the sink and tried soaking her blouse with water, but the splatter was there to stay, and was now surrounded by a dark wet mass. God. He looked so good. She'd forgotten how tall he was. And his shoulders... His eyes the dark, denim blue she remembered.

Keren came in. 'Oh, please can you give me a hand? You can see how busy it is.'

'You didn't say Jem was coming?'

'I only found out yesterday. Dali invited him and didn't tell me. He's home for a while, seeing his father.'

Bella watched Keren check her hair was still in its precise style in the mirror.

'Jem said he would never have recognised you. You're so changed. He's changed too – for the better!' Keren laughed.

'Keren.' Dali joined them in the kitchen. 'Let's put the trays of food on the table. I've taken the samosas and stuff already – put the rest out and people can help themselves. Same with the drinks.'

'But I want to serve the guests and Windy doesn't mind—'

'Come on, we don't have enough waiters and it'll be so much easier. No one will care.' He handed a tray to Keren and she huffed off with it.

'Sorry about your blouse, Bella. Is there a top of Keren's you can borrow?'

'No, don't worry. Let's get this stuff out there.' Gathering up more trays, she and Dali went out with the rest of the food and drinks and placed them on the table.

Looking around, Bella could see Jem in close conversation with an attractive woman who put her hand out and touched his arm while making a point. She caught sight of herself in the mirror over the mantelpiece and stared. So changed, he wouldn't have recognised her. Cheeks burning with embarrassment and head bowed to avoid guests, Bella retreated into the hall and picking up her bag and coat she headed for the door.

'You're not going, are you? So soon?' Dali had come out from the lounge.

'Oh, Dali. I don't think I'm ready for society yet.' She tried to make light of it but she couldn't raise the slightest smile.

'I get it. It's all such momentous changes. Roddy told me about the house and needing work. Why don't you give me a call on Monday? We're always looking for office staff.'

'Daljit!' Keren's voice rang out from the lounge.

'Oops. I'm being summoned. Take care, Bella.' Dali followed his wife's call and Bella crept out into the night.

In Broughty Ferry she parked and wandered down to the beach. It was dark and the pools of light from the streetlamps occasionally highlighted people out enjoying the night air. The constant swish of the sea as it slowly ebbed and flowed was comforting, reminding her of her breathing exercises. A drizzle of rain came on, but she didn't mind; it was light and refreshing on her face. She noticed she still wore the apron and, ripping it off, stuffed it in the nearest bin before taking a seat looking out over the water.

Jem was back.

She was surprised at the intensity of her feelings when she saw him. Thirty years may have gone by but she could still feel the hurt. And he thought her so changed. It didn't surprise her, she barely recognised herself these days. The worst was over. They'd met, were civil, end of. She could stop thinking about it. Bella hoped Jem's trip home to see his father would be a short one. Besides, she was off to London and a fresh start.

CHAPTER 11

The following days were spent cleaning and scrubbing, going to the recycling centre, washing, and more cleaning. The mystery of the foetid stench was solved when the grate was emptied of its rubbish and she found not one but two seagull carcasses. Holding them at arm's length, Bella retched her way to the outdoor waste bin. Despite all efforts the garden door remained resolutely shut but with the windows open and the sickly stench dealt with, the air was much improved.

She spent an hour wrangling the mattress out of the bedroom and down the spiral staircase – and the delivery men spent ten minutes expertly bringing the replacement in and throwing it on the bedframe. At least she would be off the sofa; she stripped the covers to add them to the laundry pile. She contemplated a raid at home to release necessities like toolbox, iron and ironing board. But she couldn't face seeing anyone. Keren, Pam, Jean, Roddy and Shirley had all left messages, but she didn't want to speak to anyone, either. Why hadn't Keren told her Jem was coming? They had gone out for eight years, for goodness' sake – wasn't it worth a heads up? Jem being home unsettled her. The fact he didn't recognise her hurt – she would have had no trouble spotting him in a crowd.

Bella let the house cleaning act as therapy; it kept her mind off Jem, jobs and money, and had satisfying results. The nights were different, filled with worry and sleeplessness.

One night after tossing and turning for hours, she gave up on sleep and flicked through old photographs. They had looked so happy together, from when they first met at fourteen through to drunken parties as students. From polaroids to photobooths to grainy prints; smiling at the camera or each other, kissing, pulling faces, looking so young and innocent. She trawled through all the mementoes: ticket stubs from concerts; silly gifts he'd bought her; necklaces and earrings he'd saved to buy and that she'd kept all these years; birthday and Valentine cards; mixed music tapes. Jem thinking she was working as a waitress at Keren's made her cringe. Why did she let herself get railroaded?

It was a pattern set when they were at school – Keren was great fun, boisterous, always the centre of attention with her confident air, precise bobbed hair and immaculate school uniform. Bella was grateful this self-assured individual wanted to be her friend and spend time with her. It was Keren who would decide what to do and Bella would happily follow. Meeting Jem was the first thing she'd done on her own. He had brought out the best in her – she flourished in his company, and she knew Jem did in hers. The end of their relationship had been swift and heart-rending, and they'd gone their separate ways. He'd become a multi-millionaire games designer and she had a failed career with an ever-decreasing bank balance.

She opened her banking app: £212. Lordy, why couldn't she get a job? She no longer planned to ask Dali; Keren had said he never had vacancies and she didn't want to be a charity case, although it was good of him to suggest she get in touch. Besides, he was too close to Jem and Bella wanted everything she was doing to be private. She would keep her desperation to herself. The only person she'd contacted was Aunt Nettie, phoning regularly, making sure she had everything she needed. Bella spent another fruitless day online looking for work and, totally disheartened by her lack of success, went off to the supermarket to gather up the staples: diet fizzy drinks, Caramel Logs and coffee. A selection of ready meals were added to the basket. Reaching the checkout, she spied a remarkable offer on cans of cocktails. Not much of a drinker generally, she wanted alcohol tonight and this would hit the spot. A bargain box of twelve Passion Fruit Martinis went into the trolley.

Outside the cottage, the meticulously groomed Amina appeared and helped her unload the car.

'I can see what you're up to tonight.' Amina indicated the cans. 'A favourite cocktail?'

'I fancied a drink, to toast the new place.'

'Got friends coming round, then?'

'No, not tonight anyway.' Crikey, she'd shown herself up as a complete Nora No-mates. Bella wished Amina would leave but instead found herself saying, 'Do you want one?'

'Mmm. It's a bit early for me.' Amina checked her watch. 'Oh, go on, why not?'

'Straight from the can or in a mug? Your choice.'

They went inside and dumped the shopping. Amina popped open her can. Bella did the same and they touched tins. 'Here's to your new place. Lang may yer lum reek and all such silly sayings.' They swigged. 'Hmmm, not bad for a tinnie. But you're not staying long, are you?' Amina sat down on the sofa.

'Off to London soon, get my career back on track.' Bella glugged at the cocktail. 'What is it you do for a living?'

'I'm an influencer.'

'An influencer? How does that work, then?'

'Mostly on social media. I post images and engage with my followers, answer questions about my life. I write articles for magazines and newspapers, get sent stuff to review and promote.'

'But it's not a real job though, is it?' Only one can and Bella was losing any tact she may have had.

'I think it's important and yes, it is a real job, actually. I make a good income from it. You should check it out. I'm @*aminarecycled* on Insta.'

Bella offered another can, but Amina turned it down. 'I have to get going, got stuff to do.' Bella was ashamed she'd hurt her. What was she thinking, being so rude? 'I'm sorry; I'm a bit ignorant about how it all works these days – out of touch.'

Amina left and Bella popped another can. She had no job and here she was dissing Amina's. 'Jeez Louise, these Martinis are tasty,' she announced to the cottage as she extricated the crisps from the shopping, digging in while opening another cocktail. She upended one of her packing boxes and seized a well-worn Walkman and cassette tape. The mixtape. Did people create them anymore? She jammed in a tape and a tinny selection of 80s tracks filled the room.

She got up to dance, swigging at the drink while she got her groove going. *Reflections of Us*. So corny. It was a tape Jem had made for her, and she'd kept it all these years along with the Walkman so she could play it. The tinny sounds squealed out – Madonna, Deacon Blue, Bananarama – and a few dodgy ballads. Bella was lost in the music, giving it laldy at the top of her voice, drunk and dancing like no one was watching. She tripped over her feet giving too much oomph to striking a pose for Vogue and went headlong into the table; the ancient Walkman hit the deck and speeded up, chewing the tape. Bella whacked the stop button, but it was too late, the tape was completely entangled by the mechanism.

Bella sat on the floor and sobbed. *Why was she so useless? Why couldn't she find a job?* She sat in a stupor for a while before pulling herself up and went into the scullery to make another attempt at the garden door – twisting the handle as far as it would go, but she could get no purchase at all. She rattled the handle furiously; why wouldn't it open? Determined she would not be thwarted and armed with the poker from the fireplace, she rammed it in the space between door and wall and pressed with all her might – zilch. She rammed it in further and used all her weight to lever it open. No movement. She bashed the door with it. One of the small windowpanes broke and it was a catalyst for Bella losing all control, whacking at the door and handle, breaking another pane and denting the wood, and with a final massive overhead swipe there was a loud clang and a key, previously hidden along the top of the door, hit the floor. It was huge and rusty. Bella swayed down to pick it up and ram it in the keyhole. With one easy turn, the chambers engaged and the battered door sprang open onto the garden – a reasonable half-concreted space with long grass and overgrown weeds.

The old wooden shed was in the corner, padlocked. Bella was on a roll and, attacking it with her trusty weapon, the door burst open and a bunch of old chairs rained down, sending her flying. From her prone position, she could see there were more inside, all piled on top of each other. Fat lot of use they would be, considering the size of the cottage. She opened another can to celebrate access to the garden and stood outside, drinking into the night.

CHAPTER 12

Bella peered gingerly over the duvet. With a clanging head and dry mouth, she admonished herself. Enough of the adolescent behaviour; it was time to stop wallowing in self-pity and get on with her plans to move to London. Washed and dressed, she headed for the beach. It was only 6.30 but joggers and dog walkers dotted the promenade and she found a seat looking out over the sandy beach. The sky was clear, heralding a promising day. Squeals and shouts caught her attention and further along the beach she saw a bunch of women running into the waves. Idiots. What a state, to be caterwauling like fools in public. The group splashed and jumped around to acclimatise. Bella got up and distanced herself from the foolishness, stopping at the next bench along.

There had to be a job somewhere in Dundee for her – an office would be fine. She could work a PC and answer a phone, couldn't she? It was time to stop making excuses about getting the cottage habitable and focus on real work. Get fit, eat healthily; no more biscuits and fizzy drinks, no more Passion Fruit Martinis, either. Bella got up from the seat with determination and surprised herself by breaking into a run. She was free, life was good and the future was hers. Picking up speed, Bella flew along the walkway but it all went terribly wrong as the momentum forced her into a running fall. She whirled her arms to pull herself out of it. An oncoming runner was mesmerised by her actions and just as Bella managed to right herself, she noticed the runner was about to step off the promenade. Bella swung to the right and saving the woman from the edge, they fell to the pavement in an ungainly splat.

'You were about to fall off!' said Bella.

'You looked like you were going to go headlong.' The woman peered over. 'God, I would've been on the stones. Thank you.' They helped each other up.

'Did you hurt yourself?'

Bella was inspecting her skinned knees and hands and looked up to see the grey-haired woman was running on the spot.

'I'm fine, thanks. I just had a notion to run.' She waved her hands to cool the stinging.

'You start with small spurts, walking in between, and it all gets joined up. No one can run a long distance from the off, but I can run 10k.'

Bully for you. The woman launched into overhead arm stretches.

'I'm out every day at this time if you want to join me. I can show you the ropes. You'll need better shoes, mind.' The woman pointed at the Docs. 'Those are no good.'

'It was a mad impulse. Don't intend to run.' Bella blew on her injuries.

'It's recommended. Great for your mental health – for women of a certain age, if you don't mind me saying. The effect it had on how I coped with the unmentionable was the main reason I kept going with it. I'm Celeste, by the way.'

'Bella.'

'OK. See you around.' She was off, jogging along the front, grey ponytail swinging behind her.

Bella ambled to the cottage, her sore breasts more painful after the spurt of exercise. The hangover was kicking in. Grabbing the duvet from her bed, she rolled herself into a ball on the sofa and went to sleep.

CHAPTER 13

She woke for the second time that day in much better condition. The priority was to find a job, but the need for coffee and a bacon roll was strong, so she multi-tasked by wolfing them down as she ambled up and down the High Street, glancing in shop windows for sales vacancies. Despondent there was nothing on offer, Bella crossed the road to the ironmongers; repairing the garden door glass couldn't wait. She loved an ironmonger shop, full of practicality and interesting gadgets you were unaware you needed in your life until you saw them – all with a most enticing smell. Entering the shop, Bella was happy to see that this was an old-fashioned one, crammed so full that customers could hardly move down the narrow aisles. Bella measured the panes of glass available and added two to the basket, along with a Stanley knife and putty. *Kerching*, more money left her bank account as the ancient man behind the counter totted up the goods.

'Would you like a bag, young lady?'

'Yes, please.' As the assistant slowly bent down behind the counter, a sign appeared on the wall behind him. *Help Wanted.*

'Oh, do you need help?'

'No, thank you, young lady, I can manage; only it takes me a while to get up again.'

'No, I mean the sign on the wall – *Help Wanted* – are you looking for staff?'

'I might be. Are you thinking of applying?'

'I need a job and I'm honest and hardworking—'

'Have you worked in a shop before?'

'No, but I've worked in a bank so I can count, deal with cash. I can be pleasant to people, and helpful. And I'm punctual.'

'Hmm, I suppose I was thinking of a younger person ... a school leaver, teenager.'

'But why, when you can have a more experienced person for the same money?'

'But you told me you were not experienced, young lady.'

'And you keep saying "young lady", so I must be young enough?' They laughed.

'Tell you what, give me your name and phone number and I'll think about it.'

'It's Annabella – Bella – McCaa. My number is...'

'McCaa? Such an unusual name. Are you related to George McCaa of McCaa Properties?'

'He was my father. Did you know him?'

'He sold me this building. He wasn't planning to, but I rented the shop and we rented the rooms above and I told him I wanted security for my family, so he sold it to me for a very reasonable price. Oh yes, I remember your father very well. He was a good man. Taken too early from this earth.'

'Yes, he was. What a coincidence he owned this building.' Bella reached out and touched the wall as if she might be able to channel her father in some unfathomable way. 'Please think about it and call me. I live close by and I'm dependable. Here's my number—'

'Maybe it's time for me to return your father's favour. You can have the job on trial from Monday. What do you say? I pay the real living wage – I'm a very fair employer and you get one hour for lunch, and holidays, too. Let's shake on it.' He held out his hand. 'I'm Mr Mirza.'

'Mr Mirza – thank you so much. You won't regret it. I'll be here on Monday bright and early. Thank you, thank you!' Bella packed the shopping into her backpack and exited the shop. She couldn't believe it. A job! OK, it was in an ironmonger, but she did love an ironmonger – and he had been a tenant of her father. Better times were coming. Working in an ironmonger. Bella laughed to herself. Her mother would have a fit.

Bella did a quick tally in her head; she was rent-and-overheads free, and with a tight budget she could be on her way by the middle of summer. She'd save a couple of hundred by cutting the sweetie budget alone and her heart would thank her for it.

A job. She had a job. Things were looking up.

To celebrate her good luck, Bella went into Visocchi's and ordered her old favourite – a double-scoop 99 with a sugar cone – and walked to the front. A bunch of screaming children were running wild on the Castle Green play area and Bella was turning away to find a more peaceful path when she heard her name called. It was Mr Adam and she joined him, watching the children.

'Jem's in there.'

Bella looked again and saw that Jem was running around the green, being chased by a small gang of children. He was jogging in action-man, slow-motion style and they managed to grab his legs and bring him down, laughing hysterically at their success. For a while he played dead and the children jumped all over him to wake him up. Then he was up and off running as they chased and brought their man down again onto the grass.

'He set this charity up years ago, for youngsters who haven't had the best start in life. They do day trips, respite holidays and picnics like this one. Jem always joins in when he's home.' Jem hoisted a red-haired boy about five years old onto his shoulders. The little boy had his arms raised aloft in triumph, a huge grin on his face that she saw reflected on Jem's.

'Does he come home often?'

'Long weekends every so often. I mostly go over there. I see you've been to Visocchi's?'

'It's hard to resist.' As her tongue protruded to take a big lick, a seagull dive-bombed from the skies, grabbed the cone in its beak and flew off with it. The ice cream detached itself and landed on her front, dragging a slow descent down her clothes to the ground. The flake flew off into the grass, where it was immediately swooped upon by the perpetrator's compatriots.

'Oh, Bella,' Mr Adam laughed, as did all the kids who had witnessed the attack. Jem came running over as she was wiping the ice cream from her front, an action reminiscent of the party night. What a slob.

'Hi.' But his attention was immediately drawn away by the children who were dragging him back to play. 'Give me a minute,' he laughed, obviously delighted at the attention.

'We're off to Visocchi's,' Mr Adam called after him. 'C'mon, Bella, let's get you a replacement.'

'How long has Jem been running the charity, Mr Adam?'

'It has to be Fergus after all these years,' he linked into her arm.

Bella laughed. 'Old habits die hard, Fergus.'

'Since the first game was launched, I think – twenty years?'

'It's a wonderful thing to do.'

'Yeah. He gets all his rich pals to chip in as well. Not bad for a bin man's son, is it? Or a Waste Operative, in today's parlance. Sometimes I can't believe it's my boy who's been so successful. You should see his place in New York.' Fergus smiled, plainly proud of his only son.

'Stop it, Dad.' Jem had caught them up. 'He's always bragging to his mates.'

'I won't stop, either,' Fergus said as they arrived at Visocchi's.

'Double-vanilla 99 with a sugar cone?' asked Jem.

'Well remembered.'

Bella and Jem tentatively smiled at each other, and he joined the queue inside the café.

Fergus put an arm around her and squeezed. 'It's good to see you, Bella.'

'And you. Are you living in the Ferry these days?'

'Jem bought me a house along the front. I always fancied a house at the beach.'

Jem came out and shared the ice creams. He'd gone for what had been his favourite – a squasher: a slider with a snowball inside. They carried on towards the front, absorbed in their ice creams as Bella kept lookout for flying thieves. It was a stunning day for April with a blue sky and soft white puffs of cloud chasing each other. The wind chill factor was bearable.

'Are you living in the Ferry, too?' Fergus licked his cone.

'I moved when Dorothea died. Long Lane – a little cottage squashed in between two tenements. I fancied a change.'

Fergus moved off to a bench to 'take the weight off his legs', leaving Bella and Jem to carry on to the shore.

'You left Keren's early. I looked round and you'd gone.'

'I couldn't face it, so many people – and all that spilt wine.' Bella snorted. 'I'm not much of a waitress. Are you here on holiday?' They were standing close together, quietly appraising each other. Bella resisted the temptation to reach out and remove a small drop of ice cream trickling down his battered leather jacket.

'I've moved back for a while. Dad isn't very well and needs looking after. I'm hoping I can persuade him to return to the States with me. Better treatment, I think, and better weather.'

'Have you and Dali always kept in touch?' Bella asked.

Jem raked his fingers through his hair, an action so disarmingly familiar she had to look away. 'I asked Dali to deal with the purchase of Dad's house, years ago, and we email occasionally.' He bent to examine the stones, picking up and discarding them before he weighed a flat one in his hand. 'You stayed in London all these years?'

'Not the last ten, but before, yes. And you've been in New York. I saw … in the paper once. The games business worked well for you?'

'I was lucky, got in at the right time. You remember how much I loved it.'

An invisible cold wall appeared between them. Yes, she did remember. It had been a cause of disagreement all these years ago when Jem dropped out of full-time education to become a runner in a games company in Dundee. Bella thought it unwise to throw away everything he was studying for. Her mother was horrified. 'A tea boy! I always knew he wouldn't come to anything. A wasted scholarship on a stupid young man. You could do so much better.'

But Jem had come to something. He'd gone to New York soon after they'd split, had created the game *Shrifters*, became a partner in the studio he joined and had been leading the New York office when the company went public and the share price stratospheric. She'd gleaned as much from the papers over the years. It was ironic, she supposed – Bella had been less than supportive of his career choice and he'd become a huge success while she'd lost everything. She had no desire to tell him about the job with Mr Mirza.

Jem skimmed his stone across the water.

'Two. Out of practice.'

Bella scrabbled around to find her own stone and expertly fired it.

'Four!'

'Shit!' They both rooted around for stones and started firing them, giggling like the teenagers they once were, competing for the best ones. Occasionally their hands touched and a spark of excitement would run through Bella. She could see Fergus smiling as he watched from the promenade.

'Three!'

'Four!'

'Two... You haven't lost your talent for skimming stones, Annabella McCaa.'

'One leg!' Bella called, harking back to how they used to play at school as she balanced unsteadily on one Doc. She fired the stone but the effort made her fall and Jem, laughing, caught her in his arms and they rocked unsteadily together.

'That was a long time ago.' She could feel his breath on her neck. Jem held her until Bella stepped away, unsettled by the surge of happiness running through her.

'It was.'

'It was weird seeing everyone at the party.' Jem fired another stone across the water – unsuccessfully. 'Maybe we could—'

'Jem?' Fergus was calling from his seat, sounding out of puff. 'We need to hit the road. Sorry, love. I need my tea.' They clambered up the steps to reach him.

'Thanks again for coming to the funeral.' Bella hugged Fergus and said to Jem, 'Thanks for the ice cream.' They did an uncomfortable head dance as Jem bent to kiss her cheek and their brows clunked.

'Ow!' They rubbed their respective heads in amusement.

'You need to come over for tea, Bella.' Fergus called as he moved off, slightly unsteady. Jem extended an arm to balance him and Bella watched them walk away.

At the cottage, Bella looked at herself in the mirror. Crikey, she looked a fright – her hair was like an explosion in a mattress factory. When was the last time she'd got it cut? There was an ice cream path down the front of her jacket and a hole in the knee of her jeans where she'd fallen saving Celeste. She needed to smarten up – for the new job and for going to London. And Jem – it would be nice to bang into him when she had decent clothes on, with no slobbery down her front and her hair in a bit of a style. She had to admit it was good seeing him. It scared her to think of the feelings lurking, but she was no longer a young woman wearing rose-tinted spectacles. She wondered if seeing her had stirred up any memories in him.

CHAPTER 14

Bella trachled up the stairs in Aunt Nettie's tenement laden with shopping and was soon in the kitchen packing it away.

'Do you want a cup of tea before we go?' Her aunt filled the kettle.

'Why don't you have a cup and let me zoom around with a duster while I'm here? Save you doing it later?' Bella had noticed the kitchen and living room needed a bit of TLC.

'No, you will not. I'm absolutely capable of doing it myself. I've been busy; I do have a social life.' Aunt Nettie chuckled. 'Why don't we get on the road, I'm looking forward to seeing your new place.'

As they drove along Long Lane her aunt expressed surprise that the property was still owned by McCaa's. 'Dorothea never mentioned it. Mind you, she never took an interest in your Father's business until after he died. It was his first property.'

'I didn't know that. It's only the house they re-mortgaged for the development. It's going well and it's such a fantastic project. Roddy's brilliant with the property business.' Bella didn't want to worry her aunt with the true state of affairs and luckily the subject was dropped as they arrived at the cottage.

Aunt Nettie loved the transformation. Bella had sent mobile pics when she first moved so her aunt could see the difference. Amina had been right – a good wash had not only brought the best out of the throws and their dazzling 70s prints, but the sofa covers were usable and once on, it was as if a new piece of furniture had arrived.

After lunch they went for a 'constitutional', as her aunt called it. 'This is where I'm going.' Aunt Nettie pointed in the direction of a residential building on the front – the Tides Retirement Home for Ladies. 'I'm on the list and it'll soon be time. I've got good friends in there.'

'Not yet, though.' Bella hurried her aunt along the road. They stopped off at Mirza's and later Aunt Nettie congratulated her on getting the job.

'An excellent re-introduction to work – it'll help build your confidence for moving to London.'

Bella hugged her. Driving back, she told her aunt about meeting Jem, at Keren's and at the beach.

'Jem? There's a blast from the past. What was it like? Didn't he move to the States and become stinking rich?'

Bella smiled. 'Yes, he did. He's here to look after his father who's not so well.'

'I remember Fergus, such a nice man. You and Jem were inseparable for years, then it was all over and you moved to London. Dorothea told me you'd come to your senses, but I didn't get the full story. I liked Jem.'

'Jem ... it was just ... well ... he went off with another girl, slept with her. We'd been having a rocky patch. Even so...' Bella struggled to speak, surprised the historical pain was still there. 'What is wrong with me? It was thirty years ago!'

Her aunt patted her arm. 'These hurts never go away. They linger inside and become part of us – make us who we are.' She sounded like she knew what she was talking about. 'And you're very vulnerable.' She handed her a tissue.

'Vulnerable? I don't think I'm vulnerable. I'm getting my life back.'

'You need to look after yourself. It's not long since Dorothea died and whatever your relationship was, it's a huge thing, losing your mother. There's the stuff with the house and you've had to move. Joining the workforce again – it's all incredibly stressful. And here's this old boyfriend popping up who broke your heart. Be careful, is all I'm saying. You're always so hard on yourself. Be as kind to yourself as you always are to me.'

She leaned over and kissed her aunt's cheek, squinting to keep her eyes on the road at the same time.

'Stop it. You'll get us both killed and then what'll we do?'

Bella laughed.

Later, Bella went into her garden, such as it was, and set to clearing out the shed. The array of chairs – some in pairs, other individuals – seemed a random collection but the design and craftsmanship were easy to admire and she wondered why they'd all been stuffed away. She ran her hands over the wood, enjoying its beauty through the ugly stains and paint splatters. The fabric of the seat cushions was threadbare and mouldy in parts. Bella investigated the shed more closely and hidden in a corner under a blanket of cobwebs, was an ancient treadle sewing machine. With oil and TLC, Bella coaxed it to sew. She got to work on the cleaned throws, creating simple cushion covers and little curtains, her mind never far away from the reactions the conversation with her aunt had thrown up. Bella remembered everything so vividly – she was devastated when Keren had told her what Jem had done. The first weekend they'd spent apart in years and he slept with someone else. Keren had been such a support; if it hadn't been for her she'd have missed the internship, and within days she had been working in a private bank in London and had met Shirley. Bella nursed the pain; keeping it close would stop any stupid romantic notions she might have been flirting with.

CHAPTER 15

On Sunday night, Bella set alarms on both her clock and phone. Worry about her capabilities for returning to work plagued her dreams. Would she be able to use the payment machine? Her knowledge of tools and DIY was hardly encyclopaedic – would it be enough? Could she be nice to people for an extended period without losing her temper? Would it be cool in the shop? Would she get through the first day? Bella arrived at Mr Mirza's, not exactly perky as a teenager, but at least on time.

'Good morning, good morning, young Annabella. I'll teach you the ropes today, the system we have, and you can do it all to my liking.' With patient customers, she learned how her new boss liked to do things. It was a busy little shop and it amazed her how, with the hundreds of items there must have been in store, Mr Mirza knew exactly where each product was.

'It's taken me years!' he exclaimed. 'Years and years I've worked here, and if you do well, you too can work here for a very long time.' Bella hid her face by shuffling paint tins on a shelf. No point in stating her plans yet, was there?

'I don't expect you to learn the trade immediately. It will come, it will come.' Despite her misgivings that it was 'only working in an ironmonger shop', Bella enjoyed it; the day went fast, and so did the next day and the next. Mr Mirza would go out and leave her for short periods on her own as she gained confidence. In the evenings, she would cook a meal and where once she might have lazed in front of the TV, she worked on the chairs. She enjoyed sanding down the wood, seeing the grain gradually appear. Occasionally she saw Amina outside doing her pouting and preening routine in the garden. Bella was sceptical that being an influencer could be a proper job but she'd started to admire Amina's confidence and belief in what she was doing. She'd looked at her Instagram page and understood better what she was all about, feeling worse for being so dismissive.

Her first wages twanged into the bank. Insignificant in comparison to what she'd commanded ten years ago, Bella was delighted to be earning her own money again and was looking at her bank balance and making projections for the umpteenth time when there was a loud knock on the door. Half hoping it might be Amina with another tray bake she opened the door to find Roddy and reluctantly invited him in.

'What a difference. Did you do all this yourself?'

'Yes, I did.' Bella had used her staff discount to buy paint and the downstairs area was transformed by stark white. Roddy scanned the cottage and she could see pound signs coming out his ears. 'Upstairs is still a mess though.'

'We were along seeing Aunt Nettie. She's in good form. Brought us up to date with what you'd done to the cottage and the job... I never hear from you.'

'And vice versa.'

'But you're still making plans for London?' Roddy continued nosing around.

'A couple of months and I'll be gone. Why don't you have a seat?'

Roddy sat down on the sofa and Bella perched on the other end. 'I hear you're working for Mirza's,' he said. 'Nothing better on offer these days?'

'I need money to go to London, remember? You may not have noticed but I gave up ten years to look after *our* mother, and that has consequences.'

'I didn't mean to dismiss it, I genuinely meant...' Roddy petered out. 'Anyway... Look.' He held up his hands in a sign of surrender. 'I came round to see how you were doing here, to tell you Aunt Nettie was fine. I'm going to look after her so you don't need to worry about getting over there while you've got your job.'

'I'll manage.' Bella was suspicious.

'I... umm... things have got a bit easier and... umm... I can lend you money for London. I know it's been a real disappointment for you.'

'You said there was nothing?'

'I managed to move accounts around. Annabella, I want to help.'

Bella got up and filled a glass of water from the tap and sipped, looking out into the garden as she weighed up this new option.

'You could give up Mirza's and be off to London next week, footloose and fancy free. Repay me when you get a job – I won't even charge interest. You don't need to worry about the house, or what's happening up here.'

It was tempting, but she was even more dubious – where did the generosity come from? Was he embarrassed that his sister was working in an ironmonger's shop? On the other hand, she would be able to go to London, get on with her life. But what if he suddenly demanded she repay the loan? The past year he'd been so greedy, even quizzing her about the housekeeping costs at one point until her mother had stepped in. Being beholden to him sickened her; it was bad enough with the cottage.

'Thanks, I appreciate it but it's better I go under my own steam, you having been so strapped for cash and everything. You might need it.'

He stood up and examined the painting on the wall. 'I saw this was missing. It's one of a pair; shouldn't be sold separately if it's what you're planning.'

'No, Roddy. I wasn't planning a sale because it belongs to both of us, doesn't it?'

He wandered over to the staircase and peered upstairs. 'I was talking to Jem Adam at Keren's party – you should have stuck in there.' He laughed.

'I seem to remember you and mother were in agreement when we broke up – happy and relieved.'

'OK, OK. Are you sure about the money?'

'Yes. This gives me time to look at my work options for London and do my homework for a job there.'

Roddy appeared disappointed. 'Please yourself. But come over to dinner one night; the kids would love to see you.'

'I doubt it. I imagine Gordon misses the TV.'

'Oh, we got a home cinema unit, much better for us.'

Bella headed towards the door and Roddy followed.

'What about the jewellery, Roddy? When can I come in and sort through it?'

'Oh, erm, Lorna sent it all off to be valued. It's the proper thing to do. Should be back soon.'

Bella scrutinised her brother, wondering if he was telling the truth.

He squirmed under her attention, changing the subject. 'You're making this place an attractive proposition. I need to think about putting it on the market.'

'You could at least wait until I'm gone.'

'This is the best time to sell. Timing is what this business is all about.'

She opened the door and he stepped into the lane, appraising the exterior in more detail. 'You've even painted the windows outside. Looks good.'

'Goodnight, Roddy.'

I bet he does put it on the market, Bella thought, as she flung the door shut. Her brother had become such a shark. Easy to see why he wanted rid of her to London. His superior attitude got up her nose – and one minute so broke, the next buying a home cinema? Waiting until she heard his car move off along the lane, she shrugged into her coat and went out. She'd console herself with chocolate.

CHAPTER 16

Arriving at the shops, Bella spotted Roddy's Merc parked at the off-licence, and there he was inside perusing the shelves. No doubt buying expensive wine with the money he hadn't had until it miraculously appeared in a random account. *Wouldn't charge interest.* Bloomin' cheek. She'd better keep a check on the property pages as he'd sell the cottage from under her. She didn't trust him at all these days, and imagined the jewellery would be kept away from her, or already sold. *This'll teach him*, she thought, and quick as a flash, her penknife was out and she scored the blade along the side of the car, making a deep and gratifying mark.

'Windy!' A male voice called from behind. Bella's heart leapt into her mouth. *Cripes, it's the police.* A tall, uniformed man was coming towards her. What did you get for wanton vandalism these days?

'Windy? It's me...'

'Chinner?' Bella recognised an old school chum – had he seen her in action? She didn't want to hang about in case Roddy saw the damage. She jogged towards Chinner, stopping him in his tracks, heading him off from the scene of the crime. He was laughing.

'It's Iain these days.'

'And I'm Bella.'

'Of course, Bella! I'm sorry. It was such a surprise to see you, I didn't think. How are you doing, anyway? Don't you live out the West End?'

'I moved not long ago. How are you, *Iain*?'

'It could be hell at school, couldn't it? We both hated our nicknames. Anyway, those days are long gone. It's good to see you. What are you doing with yourself? This is not fancy dress by the way – I did indeed join the police.'

To prove a point, Iain's radio sparked into life and a voice chittered unintelligibly.

'Right, I've got to go. Think the seagulls have stolen a local's fish and chips. Hey, you don't fancy going for a drink one night, do you? Catch up on old times?' Determined to get rid of him before Roddy exited the wine shop, Bella agreed it would be nice thing to do. 'What's your number?' Iain whipped his phone out and as she reeled the numbers off, he tapped them in. 'Ok, I'll give you a call. Better go.' He was off.

Jeez Louise, imagine if he'd caught her. She was worried about her capacity for vandalism but more terrified about getting caught. On the other hand – it had been extremely therapeutic. Should she do the other side? Deciding not to chance her luck, she retreated to Long Lane.

Chinner. Bella hadn't seen him since school – *he* obviously didn't think she was so unrecognisable. Didn't find her 'so changed'. He was a policeman – surprising, as he'd been shy at school, or his awful nickname made him so. Yes, he'd been imaginatively called Chinner because he had a long and pointy chin. She supposed it wasn't terribly pointy, but kids could be cruel. Now it was covered with an attractive greying goatee.

At the cottage, the chocolate was forgotten and her fingers itched to get to work. The night wasn't cold so she went out to the garden to sand the chair. She got lost in the rhythmic motion of the simple task, looking forward to restoring it to its former glory.

'Mid-century Scandinavian.'

'What?'

It was Amina – she was out in the garden too and peering over the wall. 'The chair – it looks mid-century style. You should look them up. They may even be antiques; if you do them up you could sell them.'

'Sell them?'

'Yes. I did a whole feature on it earlier this year and it's totally super vogue. Look.' Amina scrolled through screeds of images on her phone. Bella peered in. 'See. These were done by a woman in the Borders – she sold them all.'

'She got 2043 likes? They must be popular.'

'I reach about 1500 for my posts on average but this series had super traction.' Amina flicked on – past the chairs were shots of her, in various poses.

'But what's the point?' She stopped Amina's hand at an image. 'Over three thousand likes? Heavens.' Bella was impressed. 'And you've got over 100,000 followers. I don't get it. How can you make a living out of this?'

'My speciality is zero waste. I advise people how to live a greener lifestyle. I hunt around second-hand shops for clothes and other accessories, tart them up, model them and sell them online. I also feature designers and makers, like the chair woman, and tell people where they can buy second-hand or upcycled and how to choose. I'm often invited to write about it all, too. And I've got a revenue stream from my YouTube channel.'

'YouTube?' She'd misjudged Amina, thinking her an airhead. How ignorant she was. 'I'm sorry, it's a new world to me.'

'And in my world it's a fact – if you do up those chairs, they will sell.'

'Wow.'

'Yes, wow.'

'Thanks, Amina. You've inspired me. I'm going to crack on.'

'Goodnight, Bella.'

Bella started working on the chair with gusto. Who needed Roddy's money? She'd be in London off her own back in no time.

CHAPTER 17

Bella was at work, her head buzzing. If she wasn't thinking about refurbishing chairs or London, her mind was full of Iain and when they were going out. He had phoned a couple of nights ago and they'd had a laugh on the phone, talking about school days and who was doing and had done what. They'd made a date for Saturday night. But was it a *date* date? Had there been a flirtatiousness about their call? She was so out of practice. Whatever, it excited her to be going out on a social occasion and with a person of the masculine variety.

Ruminating on the male species made her think about sex. It had been such a long time and forever since she'd been aroused by anything more than a bag of sweeties. Was it like riding a bike and you never forgot? Would certain parts be in working order? Was she getting ahead of herself? It was a drink with a friend for a bit of company. But whatever it was, she needed a replacement for the outfit she wore to Keren's party, which was still in a heap in the laundry basket. She didn't want to be mistaken for a waitress a second time. Bella also couldn't believe her meagre wardrobe had been supplemented over the years with items of her mother's. There was even a skirt with an elasticated waist she'd worn on desperate occasions.

She was jolted back to reality by a customer – Mr Mirza had moved on to trusting Bella to look after the shop alone during the day, so she had to get to it. There was stock to put out and dusting to do. She needed to sell – but a customer bought a penknife and it reminded her of Jem. Meeting him had thrown up a whirlwind of memories and reminded her of the love and despair she'd experienced with him during their relationship. She'd enjoyed seeing him but was confused by it, and shy and a bit ashamed. Ashamed he must think she'd let herself go, if he hadn't recognised her – and ashamed because she knew she had. What an abysmal failure; nothing to show for all the study and hard work. In the last ten years she hadn't altered an iota of her life. Nada. Zero. Zilch. Looking after her mother, the constant care, the lack of company – she'd become a hermit. But what else could she have done? Dorothea was so demanding. The prospect of a night out with Iain helped steer her mind away from Jem and any stupid impulses she might have. She hadn't heard from him – and why should she? He didn't have her number. But he came into her mind uninvited every time she heard the ping of a message coming in.

The door opened and she looked up to see Keren.

'So, it *is* true, Windy!'

Bella's knuckles were white as she tightened her grip on the pricing gun. They'd been friends forever but often she wanted to slap Keren. 'Dali was speaking to Roddy who told him you'd moved to the Ferry and got a job in the ironmonger's. What's going on? And why did you dash off from the party so early?'

'It was busy, and I'm not ready for company yet. Not to mention your guest had sloshed wine down my front. Did you have a good birthday?'

'It was great. Shouldn't have had it in the house though; too much to worry about. Of course, everyone came.'

The door opened and a customer arrived, a frail-looking old man in need of an extension lead two and half feet long. Bella told him the one marked one metre would do the trick and with room to spare. After a bit of convincing he went off happily. Keren hung around.

'But why are you working *here*? It's so not you.'

'Roddy and I are putting off selling the house for a while. There's a bit of work to be done that he's going to oversee before it goes on the market, and I'd prefer to move to London in August, towards the end of the summer. This job is ideal – and you know I wanted to earn my own money again. Gives me cash while I study the financial markets and bring myself up to date. I'm enjoying it.'

Keren didn't look persuaded by Bella's babbling. 'I couldn't move out of the West End.'

'I fancied new horizons and Roddy had a nice little cottage here, so all good.' Bella tried to look busy by shuffling papers around, hoping Keren would go.

'It's London I've come to talk to you about. Are you sure you want to wait so long before you go?'

'It fits in with my plans and being ready for a good job.'

'Because if it's money, I could lend you some? You can be in a position to "take your life back", as you always say.'

'No!' Bella was horrified. 'I'm sorry. I mean – no, thank you. I don't need to borrow money. I appreciate the offer but I don't need money, I'm just doing this for pocket money and to get into work mode.'

'You're sure?'

'Of course. But thanks.'

'There's another thing. Dali and I have that place in London – he uses it for business and we rent it out, not very often though. You could stay there, for free?'

'A place to stay?' The cogs of Bella's mind were whirring. Staying in Keren and Dali's house for free was not the same as borrowing money. 'But wouldn't you lose a lot of rent?'

'A bit, but you would also be doing us a favour as it needs work done and it would save one of us going down if you were there. It could be soon?'

Bella's brain whirred; even with a place to stay she would still need a decent amount of cash to tide her over until she got a decent job. But this offer was fantastic.

'Can I think about the date? Thanks so much, Keren. It's so generous of you and will make a huge difference to my plans. I can't believe it. I'd only be there long enough to get myself sorted.'

'Good. You could be in London in a couple of weeks. By the way, we're all going out on Saturday night – do you want to come? Me and Dal, Jean, Will, Pam and her man du jour. Food and drinks. Nothing crazy.'

'I can't, I'm going out.'

'Where are you off to? Hot date?' Keren laughed at the notion but Bella felt uncomfortable under this scrutiny of her private life.

She reddened. 'No, a drink with a neighbour.'

'You've gone all pink – who's this neighbour? C'mon, out with it.'

'It's a hot flush.' She fanned herself with her pad, disconcerted the blush was indeed turning into a deeper heat.

'HRT is all I'm saying.'

'But doesn't it just put it off?'

'No. It stops everything till you're over the worst. What's the point of putting yourself through all these stupid symptoms? No thanks.'

Bella continued to fan herself. 'I'll think about it.'

'Keep in touch,' said Keren. 'We need to find out about this neighbour who brings on the heat.'

'He doesn't. It's—'

'Oh, it is a *he*. Is it a Jem *he*? He's staying in Broughty Ferry with his father.'

'I met them, we went for ice cream.'

'Get you. Hobnobbing with the rich and famous.'

'Hardly.'

'And is it?'

'What?'

'Jem that you're meeting?'

There was a welcome ting of the door and a family piled into the shop, filling up any spare space.

'Hello,' said Bella. 'Feel free to browse and if you have any questions, I'm here to help.'

'I'd better go. Leave you to your "customers". Give me a date for London.'

Bella watched Keren leave. A place to stay in London. She couldn't believe it, such a generous offer.

'Do you sell plungers?'

Bella shook London from her mind and got on the case. Like an old hand, she guided the customers down one of the aisles and pointed. 'We have a fabulous selection here. We have the common sink, or cap, plunger. We also have a flange plunger – for the toilet.' Bella brandished one proudly. 'And we mustn't forget the accordion plunger – this is also for the toilet but despite its attractive shape and name, it's not as good as the flange. I'll leave you to take a closer look.' She walked to the counter, pleased with her recently acquired plunger knowledge. Her mind drifted to Keren's generosity. She was also thinking, ungenerously, that Keren must be very keen to have work done to want her down there so soon. She didn't care – she would take the offer. It would make such a difference to her plans.

The family approached the desk. 'We'll take the flange, thanks.'

'Excellent choice!'

CHAPTER 18

The week rolled on. Shirley was swamped but had time to send a string of emoji champagne bottles and exploding fireworks at the news Bella had a place to stay. She had to settle on a leaving date but her excitement for the future was dulled by the disappointment she would have to inflict on Mr Mirza by handing in her notice.

The other fret was what to wear for her date with Iain, but Amina came to the rescue by offering to initiate Bella to the joys of the second-hand shop. They had previewed Bella's measly wardrobe but other than the Armani business suits – currently too tight but hope for the future – they agreed additions had to be made and items taken away to charity.

Bella surprised herself by being loath to get rid of the ancient elasticated skirt and her mother's wrap. She found comfort in them hanging in the wardrobe. Her fashion guru understood, even if Bella couldn't put it into words. Bella had a wobble when her flannel shirts were given their marching orders but added in the heels she'd worn to the funeral and their never-to-be-worn-again colleagues. She didn't want to totter ever again, even in

London. The funeral dress was staying – it was a consummate catch-all sack, useful for emergencies. The other black dress she'd repair and give to Amina to sell. Close inspection revealed many of her T-shirts had holes and couldn't go to the charity shops. Amina suggested cutting them up for kitchen cloths. She also recommended the method for old pants – Bella's were certainly big enough, but perhaps that was a recycle too far.

The shop bell tinged and Mr Mirza appeared, breaking into her wardrobe daydreams. 'I'm happy with you, Annabella, and I'm going to give you more responsibility. Please could you open and close the shop on the days you're here? I'll come and let you go for lunch, but this would save me at either end of the day. For this I'll give you an extra £1.25 an hour. What do you think?'

'I think thank you very much, Mr Mirza.' Bella was delighted and proud her boss was happy with her work. Then she remembered she'd be leaving and skulked away, pretending to dust the shelves.

Amina arrived and off they went, for all the world like they were hitting Bond Street, and Bella had so much fun. Amina knew the staff in the charity shops and was treated like a star, allowed into the inner sanctums to see the latest donated pieces. Bella's influencer friend wanted her out of her wardrobe rut and every time Bella laid a hand on anything baggy, she would stop her.

'No. You have a figure. Look!' In front of a mirror, she got behind Bella and tightened her current baggy shirt from behind. 'See? You have boobs and hips, but your waist goes in. You have a classic shape and if you dress to your shape you'll look much better.'

Amina searched out soft, feminine tops that emphasised Bella's curves instead of hiding them. Bella loved the sheer fabrics and pretty florals, surprised she liked how she looked in them. The prices also helped her get over her initial reticence about wearing people's cast offs. By the time the mission was accomplished, ten tops, jeans (Gap – brand new with tags), black jeggings, a pair of Chelsea-type boots, trainers (unworn; she hoped she would be more worthy than their previous owner) and a pair of leggings from an 'activewear' section were in her shopping bag. Amina also lucked out – she loved vintage and was delighted when Bella spotted a gorgeous Chanel jacket – and she herself picked two geometric print skirts, a 60s shift and a pair of thigh boots, setting her up for the coming week on Instagram.

In the evening, the darling Amina, fast becoming Bella's most favourite person in the world, coloured her hair using a natural highlighting pack and conditioner. The fringe was straightened off – Bella's DIY had unsuccessfully extended to her hair – and the rest trimmed. Bella was delighted with it; gone was the mousy brown and even the wiry texture had improved, the grey blending in under the highlights. Not too blonde, but a bit blonde. She was unsure how she might repay Amina until the fashionista mentioned what a mess her accounts were in, and she was unsure exactly what kind of company she should be. At last, Bella's experience could help her young friend and she took away an impressive (and slightly daunting) bin bag of *AminaRecycled* receipts and other paperwork.

Armed with her new hair and almost-new clothes, Bella was ready for her date with Iain.

CHAPTER 19

All she had to do was keep the butterflies about meeting Iain under control. She knew it was natural to be nervous, and there were also the physical changes her body was going through. She'd been researching natural aids for menopausal symptoms – eating yams with virtually every meal, drinking Black Cohosh tea – she had even ordered pine-bark extract from the internet but hadn't yet had the courage to boil and drink it. Other research made Bella give thanks she lived in the twenty-first century; Victorian remedies included a dangerous belladonna plaster placed at the pit of the stomach and vaginal injections with an acetate of lead solution. Her personal favourites in the fight against brain fog were less extreme; a more gentle and palatable diet of coffee, energy drinks and chocolate cleared her mind but brought with them an accelerated heart rate, thumping head and fitful sleep.

She centred herself with deep breathing exercises – it wasn't a date; she was meeting an old friend.

On Saturday night Bella put the finishing touches to her make-up. The Gap jeans were a good fit and the freshly laundered floral blouse comfortable in a casual-dressy kind of way. If she held her stomach in when she sat down, all would be well. Having followed Amina's advice for the boots – using perfumed wipes inside, adding insoles and leaving them stuffed for a night with newspaper – she couldn't tell they were pre-worn.

She looked in the mirror; the change in clothing style and highlighted hair gave her confidence and she was excited about a night out. Bang on eight o'clock she arrived at the Ship Inn and saw Iain leaning on the bar, pint in hand.

'Hey, Bella, what you having?'

She wasn't sure what her drinking preference was these days, but a woman next to her ordered an Aperol Spritz and Bella followed suit; its resemblance to Irn-Bru was comforting.

'Let's get a seat over there,' Iain suggested as he led the way with drinks in hand. 'So, what've you been doing the last thirty years?

They laughed at how unbelievably fast the years had passed since they'd met as school children and it broke the ice a little.

'Business degree at Edinburgh, moved to London to complete it. Worked in corporate finance for years in the City. Gave it up ten years ago to come home and look after my mother when she had a stroke. She died two months ago and I'm having a bit of a break before I return to London.'

'Thirty years in a flash. Sorry about your Mum. Both my parents have gone, too – I remember your dad died while we were at school.' Iain took a draught of his pint. 'Didn't you go out with Jem Adam for years? What happened there? You were so solid together. Of course, he went sky-high with *Shrifters*.'

Bella twiddled with her glass. 'We grew apart; you remember how it is with first love. But what about you – you joined the police?' She didn't want to dwell on Jem; it was weird discussing him with Iain, who remembered them as a couple.

'It was all I ever wanted to do. A bobby on the beat then worked my way up. Was a detective for a while but decided it wasn't for me.'

'Married? Children?'

'Two girls. Both in the police – one in the Met and one in Edinburgh.' He showed her photos of two smart looking young women who thankfully hadn't inherited the MacBain chin. He was understandably the proud father, detailing their progress and awards.

'They'll do much better than me. I'm taking early retirement soon. Got a jippy hip and I don't want to wait until I need a stick to get around. Another three years should be enough.'

Iain didn't mention a wife, so Bella didn't press it. They raked through other classmates and he was full of gossip, who had done what to whom, when and where. She had less to pass on.

'I see Keren. Pamela and Jean, too. And Dali, of course. But I haven't kept up with anyone else. I suppose you see people around town?'

'I think when you stay home you're always banging into old classmates.'

Iain ordered another round and wouldn't let Bella get her purse out. They relaxed into general chat. He was easy to talk to, interested and interesting, with stories to tell from the police. He'd had a stint in financial crime, so they had more common ground besides reminiscing. The drinks kept coming and by the time it got to the fourth round she insisted it was her turn to pay. She negotiated her way to the bar and returned balancing drinks and sustenance – prawn cocktail crisps and dry roasted nuts – which they devoured instantly. They'd got to the giggly stage and by the time the bar called last orders at midnight, they were at the low (or high) point of singing the school song.

They pitched outside. The bar was on the front, and it was such a fabulous view in the night, the sound of the water drifting in and out of the darkness.

'I'll see you home; where are you?'

'Not far. Long Lane.' They set off. It was good to be in the company of a man after such a long time alone and she threaded her arm through his, enjoying his strength and masculinity.

'I always liked you, Bella. Had a wee crush on you at one point.'

She laughed. 'No, you didn't. You were always mad for Alice Elder – I remember.'

Iain chortled away. 'Oh yes, I did go out with her once. Then she stood me up! I was devastated. Left me standing at Burtons for ages. It was called Duffer's Corner for good reason. I had to scuttle away with my head down but it makes me laugh. She became a Mormon. I know, I know – what's that got to do with the price of mince?' They both found this hilarious in a drunken, uncontrollable kind of way, as they couldn't work out why it was a saying. They stumbled towards the cottage and were soon at the door.

'Don't think I've ever noticed this building before; it's kind of squashed in between the tenements. Which came first?'

'Exactly what I said! Thanks, Iain. I had a good time tonight; I hope I don't regret all those Aperol Spritz in the morning.'

'You'll be fine. I had a fun time, too; good to have a laugh. Life is too serious.'

Iain stepped closer and leaned in. Before you could say 'tongues' they were into a full-blown, hearty snogathon, only pulled apart when Bella tripped slightly in her new boots and they both giggled.

'I'd better get in. Thanks for seeing me home.' It didn't feel right to invite Iain inside, even though she'd enjoyed the snog.

'I'll give you a call, OK? See if you fancy going out for dinner. Or a film?'

'That would be lovely.'

Iain swung in for another shorter snog that Bella happily reciprocated, then she watched him swagger down the lane.

Bella unlocked the door and headed to the scullery. She needed to soak up the alcohol and, in slow deliberate movements, managed to make toast and take a pint of water up to bed. Placing them on the bedside table, she bent down to pull off her boots, lay down and conked out.

CHAPTER 20

'Ugh,' Bella groaned. She was lying naked, face-down, having woken during the night, bursting for the loo and desperate to remove her clothes. She peeled her tongue from the roof of her mouth and could taste the dry roasted nuts from the night before. Yuck. Grabbing the water from the bedside table she glugged it down and got up for more – and paracetamol. Oh, her head was rough. Worse than the night of the martinis. Thank God she hadn't invited Iain in; she might have got carried away.

She sat on the sofa and put her head between her knees. There was a lot to do today: finish the chairs she'd been working on, do Amina's accounts and drive over to Aunt Nettie. It was early but a windy blast on the beach would get rid of the cobwebs. She had a quick wash, dressed and wore her new trainers to give them a test run – or rather a test walk. There would be no running today.

On the esplanade she was blasted by the bracing wind and it helped her clanging head. She missed much about being in the West End – the comforts of home, the garden, the little cafes, the cinema – but the beach was growing on her and the sea air invigorating. The spindrift in the wind was gentle on her skin and she reveled in the elements before pulling her hood over and moving to a nearby bench. A group of women were coming out of the sea after a swim. Bella watched them with grudging admiration – how could anyone survive freezing cold water on a day like today? Two ladies had wet suits on, but most only had costumes, their skin red-raw. They were laughing and chattering away as they rubbed themselves vigorously, all shapes and sizes without embarrassment as to who might be watching.

Looking out over the water, Bella played last night over in her head. She had hangxiety, a palpable fear that she had made a great, drunken faux pas. But she hadn't. They'd had a good time and snogged, nothing else. She remembered singing in the bar like idiots. Thankfully she knew no one, and no one knew her, so she may have been under the radar. Unlike Iain, who was friends with everyone in the pub. She remembered his kiss on her lips, Iain's beard rough against her cheek, desire springing up inside her. Bella enjoyed playing over the memory; it had been good spending time with a man, flirting and having fun. Over the years she'd missed having a significant other in her life – the warmth and support of a relationship, someone there just for you. Chinner MacBain. Crikey, he wasn't married, was he? He glossed over the question. Would he be out on a Saturday night if he was married?

'Morning.' Bella jumped as Celeste appeared and did her jog-on-the-spot-while-chatting routine. She wasn't in the mood for high spirits at close range; she wanted to be solitary with her cracking head and paranoia.

'I see you've invested in appropriate footwear. New fitness routine?'

Bella wished Celeste would bugger off; trying to focus on her bobbing face was proving painful.

'No. Just comfort.'

Celeste sat down beside her.

'Not going for a swim?' asked Bella.

Celeste looked out at the bathers on the beach. 'I'd love to, but I don't have the guts. I'm not a strong swimmer, either. They always look so happy and healthy, I bet it's wonderful. One day I'll pluck up the courage and run in. Do you fancy it?'

'Me? Noooo. It's mad. Won't catch me doing that.'

'Have you recently moved to Broughty Ferry?'

Bella couldn't ignore Celeste's friendliness. 'Got a job here for a bit before I move to London.'

'I've moved from London and am looking for a job. Not finding it easy though.'

'It was hard, but I eventually got a sales assistant spot locally. You'll find a job; you've just got to keep trying.' Bella got up. The wind was pinching and she was over her early-morning commune with nature. Time to return to base.

Celeste stood up, too. 'Have a good day, Bella.' She ran off, the neon pink sports jacket fading into the distance as she got into her stride.

'You too, Celeste.' Bella called after her, too late and lost in the wind.

Later, Bella was in the garden showing off her handiwork to Amina, waiting with trepidation for the verdict.

'I love the Harris Tweed,' said Amina. 'Where did you find it?'

'Red Cross. I snapped it up.'

'You've done a fabulous job, an excellent finish and the stitching under the seat is so neat. You've even got protective bases on the legs – and got rid of the dent, or am I missing it?' Amina twirled the chairs around, scrutinising them. She sat down on one and, flipping her shoes off, put her neatly pedicured feet on the other. 'Comfy.'

'It's incredible what you learn on YouTube. It's my main viewing these days. Do you think they would sell?'

Amina appraised the chairs like an expert. 'Yes, I can put them on. You should get at least £250 for two and we should sell them as two pairs – not separately.'

'What about your commission?'

'I won't take commission; make me more of that wicked rocky road you handed in last week.'

'I will. But you also need to take a fee. Business is business and you've helped me out so much. Fifteen percent?'

'Mmm. Ten percent and we're on. I'll take photographs and put them on my stories as well and see what the response is.'

Bella was confused.

'You need to download the app, Bella!'

'I will, I will.'

'You may as well leave them here as part of my ten percent. I can be around for couriers more easily than you.'

'Thanks, Amina. I appreciate it. There's another seven chairs stuck in the shed, and two armchairs. I'm going to do those next. I'm watching all these upholstery videos; it's important to find the right fabric.'

'Oxfam is your best bet for cloth.'

Bella did a quick mental calculation. 'If I sell all the chairs, including the armchairs, it could be another £1500 at least – more than I can save in a month, anyway. I have to stop spending what I'm supposed to be saving doing up the cottage. I must focus.'

'Let's get these on Insta and see what happens.'

'I'm getting through your books, getting things in order.' It was taking Bella longer than initially envisaged; there was a tendency to go off into daydreams, or worse, stare at figures for ages in a foggy haze. Even with the self-medication, she had to haul what she was looking for from the depths of her brain, and her concentration was dreadful. She had to get on the ball otherwise a return to her career would be impossible even if she had the money to get down there. Please let the chairs sell.

CHAPTER 21

'Compliance?' Bella squeaked the word out. She was on an early-morning video call with Shirley, discussing her prospects.

'I think it would be the quickest way to get you into the job market. You would study all the financial regulations and sit an exam. You have a brain like a treasure chest, hoards all info, always has done. They're crying out for compliance people. In fact, I'm sure I could get you a job here.'

'Wow. Do you think so?'

'It'll be like old times. I'm so looking forward to you coming down. It's been getting a little quiet here of late.'

'What happened to Dexter? You not seeing him anymore?'

'Nah, too boring, wanting to stay in, eat curry and watch Netflix all the time. I like going out, remember.'

Bella did remember. There was no stopping Shirley; she'd be out every night if she could. Part of the business was looking after clients, in a very upmarket, expense-account kind of way, and Shirley enjoyed the perks.

'How do you do it? I'll need to get into training for coming down, I'm such a lightweight these days.'

'Not on Saturday night by all accounts!' Shirley laughed. Bella had told her about Iain.

'But I do think this is the way forward. You pay to take the exam; it's only £1,200 plus VAT. I'm going to send you links to the stuff, you'll soak it up. The exam will be a cinch for you.'

Bella gulped at the extra expense, and the confidence Shirl had in her doubtful abilities. 'I've been out of it for such a long time. I have to say my brain is definitely not what it used to be—'

'Then this is the answer. You've plenty of time to study and exercise the grey cells. It brings you up to speed, gives you a certificate to show you understand the regs and you keep everyone on the straight and narrow. Easy.' A doorbell chimed in the background. 'Oops, better go. It's Rudi, he's popping round to discuss a new client.' Shirley gave a huge cartoon wink. '*Ciao*, Bella! I'll send the deets.' And she was gone. An exam? Bella felt sick.

***

Precariously balanced up a ladder, Bella was restocking traditionally bristled scrubbing brushes. She sniffed them like an expert and ran her hand over the wood appreciatively. There was a loud beep and she fumbled for her phone. Amina had sent a link, and there were her chairs online. She almost did a little dance up the ladder but brought herself down to terra firma first instead.

She texted Amina: *They look great. So professional! I'll text with any news x*

Bella had everything crossed. Even with a free place to stay, if she was going to pay for this exam, she needed more money. Bella totted figures up on her notepad. Once sold, she'd give Keren a date.

A loud ting heralded a customer.

'Jem! What are you doing here?'

'I need to buy screws. What are you doing here? Is this where you're working?'

Bella went pink. 'It's a stop gap till I return to London. Can I help you with something?'

'Screws?'

The bell tinged again and another customer came in.

'I'll look around.' Jem moved off down one of the cluttered aisles while Bella's heart thumped like a sixteen-year-old's.

'Erm, excuse me?' A tremulous voice from a tiny woman. 'Can you help me? I need light bulbs.' The woman's hand was unsteady on the stick she was holding.

'What kind are you looking for?'

The old lady shakily handed her an empty bulb container; it was vintage, but the strength and size were still legible. 'Bayonet Cap?'

'Aye...'

'Do you want to have a wee seat here?' Bella brought a chair out from behind the counter.

'Aye...' the woman sat down gratefully.

'How many do you need?'

'Seven. I counted them afore I left the house.'

Bella went off to get the bulbs and could see Jem peering into shelves loaded with fixings.

'Here you are. I've chosen LED ones; they'll last much longer. Have you got someone to put these in for you?'

'Ehm. No.'

Bella wondered how long the woman might have been in darkness. 'I can do it for you when I finish work.'

'How much would it cost?'

'It's a free service we offer. Don't be worrying about any charge.'

'Are you sure? It's awfy good of ye, lassie, thank ye.'

Bella wrote down the address the woman gave her. 'Do you want me to bring them when I come, save you carrying them?'

'Aye. Please.' Bella saw the woman to the door. 'See you later.' She tottered out.

Jem reappeared from the aisles.

'All part of the service?'

'I couldn't bear the thought of her sitting at home in the dark. I wonder how long she's lived without them. She needs seven.'

'You forgot to charge her, too.'

'Damn. I keep getting distracted. Being an apprentice costs me a fortune.'

'Let me pay.'

'No. You can't.'

'Yes. Please. I insist. For the old lady. I'll take this pack as well.'

'OK. Thanks. I'm sure she'll appreciate it.' Bella rang the sales up and Jem handed over his card. It was a private American bank she recognised.

'Dad's house needs a bit of an overhaul, but I'm starting small.'

'You can't beat a good-quality screw.' Bella blushed again as she handed over the card and receipt. Jeez Louise.

The door tinged once more and this time it was Mr Mirza.

'It's lunchtime, Annabella. Off you go and have your break. I'll see to this gentleman.'

'Oh, it's all sorted. He's a...he's...' Bella looked at Jem. What was he?

'He's an old friend,' said Jem.

'Aah. Come to take you to lunch. Off you go.'

Bella, flustered, retrieved her belongings. 'I'll be back in an hour.'

Jem held the door open for her as they left.

CHAPTER 22

Outside on the pavement Bella fumbled putting her coat and backpack on.

'Do you want to go for—' Jem started.

Bella raised her hand. 'Look, you don't have to—'

'We can go for lunch, can't we?'

Bella smiled. 'You're right. Yes, we can.' They set off, Bella conscious of Jem's closeness as they bumped up against each other on the busy High Street.

Ten minutes later they were seated inside Visocchi's, having headed there automatically, and after placing an order, an awkwardness filled the air.

'How's your dad?' Bella tried to break the ice.

'He's OK. I mean, he's slowing down with a heart condition and can't overdo it. He was a smoker for years, if you remember, so there's emphysema too.'

'I'm sorry. Must have been such a worry for you in the States.'

'Yeah, it's too far. Dad loved to come out to New York so he spent weeks at a time at home with me. But he can't make the trip so often these days. Dundee's too far away to properly look after him, and Ben, my son, he's almost finished college...'

Bella's stomach tumbled. 'You have a son?'

Jem brought his wallet out. 'Yeah. He's twenty! I've got pics on my phone, but I love having the photos to touch. I miss him.'

Bella looked at the collection of photographs showing a growing boy with a marked resemblance to the young Jem she once knew, minus the freckles and milky-white skin.

'He's so like you! He looks strong and happy.'

'He's a good boy. His mother and I ... we didn't last long, but we made the best of it for Ben and he's turned out perfect!' Jem smiled proudly. 'He might come over later in the summer, loves his Scottish Grandad, but I'm still trying to persuade Dad to come to the US. Did you have children? I remember you—'

'No.' Bella butted in. 'I had my career. I loved it and I, well, it didn't happen; I didn't really want...' She was saved from saying more as the waitress arrived with the drinks and sandwiches. She had wanted children, with Jem. Once they'd split she'd never met anyone else who brought out a desire to have a child. Not even Sam. But she remembered nights at the house, when she would curl into a ball, feeling her last fertile years draining away, hugging her belly, lamenting to her innermost self that she would never be full.

Another photo fell out of Jem's wallet of his son with – she could only assume given the age of Ben in the photo – Jem's ex-wife. Even with the tiny picture, it was clear she was a beauty. Jem scooped everything up and tucked them in his wallet. Bella wondered if there was a current woman in his life.

'Anyway, I'm here to care for Dad.' There was an attractive transatlantic twang to his voice she hadn't noticed before. 'A bit like you coming home. Dorothea was a woman to be reckoned with, though.'

'Always. When she had the first stroke, it seemed the right thing to come home. I didn't have a plan; I wasn't thinking it would be a particular length of time. Naively I supposed she might get better. But she needed a lot of care – lack of mobility – she couldn't do much for herself at all. Frustrating for her, sad to see.'

'It must have been hard, Bella. The way Dorothea treated you; I remember she could be so cruel.'

Bella's chin wobbled. Jem knew more than anyone what her mother had been like and his sympathy moved her. She couldn't speak and a single tear rolled down her cheek. He brushed it with his thumb and suddenly she was in the past.

'It's over. She can't hurt you anymore,' he said.

Bella leaned away and retrieved a laundered handkerchief out of her backpack. 'This is Fergus's; can you give it to him? From the funeral.'

'I think he'd want you to keep it. He loves handing them out to damsels in distress. I'm lucky. Fergus will be a much easier patient for me.'

A mobile rang loudly and Jem fished his out. 'Speak of the devil. Hello.'

Jem listened. 'I'm having lunch with Annabella. I'll get it, it's no problem... I will. See you later.' He slipped his phone into his pocket. 'I retract what I said – he's going to be very demanding. He wants a pie.'

Bella smiled into the warmth of Jem's eyes.

'Your smile is the same,' he said. 'When I saw you at the party, I recognised you immediately.'

'You recognised me?'

'Yeah. As soon as you came in with the tray.'

'You saw through the wrinkly, dishevelled waitress disguise?'

Jem chuckled and Bella giggled. If he was only being polite about recognising her, she didn't care.

'What's the job like? A world away from Beers Brooks, I imagine.'

'It is.' How did he find out about Beers Brooks – the company she worked for before she and Sam set up together? 'I'm going back to London. Soon. When Dorothea died and Roddy and his family moved into the house, I came here. I wanted to be independent. When I saw the job advertised... I've always liked an ironmonger.'

'I remember you used to like making things. Always good with your hands.' Their eyes met again and a frisson of excitement ran through her. Bella was heating up, in more ways than one. A slick layer of dampness broke out on her brow and moisture trickled down her spine. She casually slipped off her jacket and managed to resist using the menu to fan herself, taking a good swig of water instead. Jem bit into his sandwich and Bella surreptitiously mopped her forehead and neck with the napkin.

'It's a stopgap. I need to sit exams, bring myself up to date and I'll be off. I can't wait to get there. I loved living in London.'

'Funny, I always thought you'd follow a different path in the end ... the business degree was to please Dorothea.'

'No. It was what I wanted to do.' Bella's response was crisp. As if she didn't know her own mind.

'Remember those?' Jem indicated two large Coke Floats going past on a tray. 'We used to drink those all the time, didn't we? How do we have any teeth left? The summer we spent at the beach – it was sublime. Or is the summer always sublime when you remember the childish stuff?'

Childish. Did Jem remember their love as childish? She supposed they were children when they first met, although teenagers never saw themselves as such. The invisible wall had created a distance between them once more.

Bella's phone pinged. Amina had texted: *1100 likes! They're getting attention.*

'Jeez.' Bella was thrilled.

'What is it?'

'I renovated vintage chairs and my neighbour's put them up on Instagram for me. I hope they sell; it'll help with the London fund.' Bella had been uncharacteristically frank. 'I mean, it's a bit of fun.'

'Let me see.'

She leaned over and showed him the chairs Amina had put up. Jem took the phone from her, and their hands touched. Tanned. Strong. Bella wished there wasn't still such a physical pull towards him.

Jem enlarged the pictures and flicked through them. 'These are fabulous. They're like those Wishbone chairs – mid-century design?' She nodded, not surprised he knew. He'd always loved design and he would enthusiastically introduce her to magnificent buildings in various parts of the country. Architecture was what he'd been studying when he dropped out. He'd become passionate about the combination of design, tech and storytelling in the fledgling games world and had left architecture behind. Jem had seen what the future could be before many others did. She didn't have his vision and thought he was selling himself short.

'And Renaissance?' Jem's question broke into her thoughts.

'I have to set up my own account for the other ones I'm going to sell and I came up with Renaissance – seemed fitting.'

Jem continued examining the chairs. 'They look like new; have you got before shots?'

Bella's body tingled as he leaned closer and she showed him the earlier images.

'You've done an amazing job – and a lot of work.'

She glowed. 'What about the games company? What happens while you're here?'

'I'm still CEO but there's a managing director and various creative directors and vice presidents of numerous departments. They always have such high-fallutin' titles in the States. I was ready for a challenge away from the games world when Dad had his heart scare. I suppose I'm enjoying not doing very much at all. Out of the rat race.'

'When I first came home, it was good to take a break…' Bella's voice tailed off. She was still looking at his hands as he cupped the coffee mug, remembering a time when she knew every inch of him. Jem's sleeve moved slightly when he lifted his coffee, and she saw his watch. She gave a sharp intake of breath. It was a Timex she had bought him, all those years ago.

'It's still going strong.' He'd noticed her looking and held his wrist up. 'I've only ever replaced the strap.' He smiled at her, but Bella couldn't move, rooted to the spot. He wore the watch. Memories flooded her mind. Bella fumbled in her backpack and laid her set of keys on the table.

Jem dangled the keys and laughed. 'You've got the penknife I gave you the same weekend…'

The weekend they'd pretended they were on a school trip so they could go camping on their own. To sleep together for the first time. God, it had been a wonderful two days. They'd cycled over the road bridge to Tentsmuir beach, with an ancient tent she'd found in the garden shed. The weather was atrocious, but they were oblivious to the pounding rain and buffeting winds as they huddled together inside. Their passion mirrored the clamour outside, as hands and tongues and mouths became familiar with each other's bodies. She wondered if he was thinking of their first time together too, how close and loving they had been, leaving their innocence behind and taking their relationship into the adult world. The passion continued all through the years of their relationship; she always wanted him and he wanted her. It had been so difficult to understand why he'd slept with someone else. *Remember what happened, Bella McCaa. Remember what he did to you and how it ended, for God's sake. Don't be a fool a second time.*

Bella broke the gaze. 'I should go.' Leaving a half-eaten sandwich, she pulled her belongings together. 'I'll get the bill.'

'I'll get it. I invited you, remember?' Jem went off to the cash desk and they were soon on the street.

'It was good to see you.' Bella was business-like. 'I hope your dad keeps well.'

'Sounds like it's all going to work out for you going to London.'

They stood on the pavement, occasionally catching each other's eyes as pedestrians sidestepped around them.

'Thanks for lunch. Bye then.' Bella turned away, her head all over the place, forcing herself not to turn and look. She hurried on.

'Bella!' Jem was striding towards her. 'Here's my card if you fancy a coffee? It would be good to catch up properly...' His voice tailed off, he sounded unsure. 'I've written my UK number on it.'

She looked down at the card. 'Thanks,' was all she could say. He turned away and this time she did watch him, and his long-legged gait, until he was lost amongst the High Street shoppers.

CHAPTER 23

Bella stepped out early the following morning with her new trainers on; she might be able to march away the blues she'd woken with. Heading along the deserted lane, peaceful in the early light, she was soon at the beach and tried, what she hoped, were professional-looking stretches. Unsure what to do next, she sat down on one of the seats and watched the flow of the sea. Only two swimmers were bobbing in the waves. She had reason to celebrate; Amina had come round last night with news the chairs had sold for £1300, twice what they'd hoped for. Sold to a local dealer who was paying cash but when they'd looked at the page of who'd messaged her, it was a local man with a van. Amina suggested he'd bought them for one of the antique shops in Perth. Who cared? It gave her such an unexpected thrill that someone had bought what she'd created, and her bank balance was growing – she'd be able to set a date for London.

Despite the joy of the sale, she'd barely slept, disturbed by dreams on the cusp of consciousness. Jem had been in them – elusive scenarios mixed with snippets of their time yesterday leaving her full of longing for the love they'd once had. The feeling was so strong she could almost touch it. The phone rang – it could only be Shirley at this ungodly hour and, as she picked it up, her friend's face came into view.

'Get yourself ready, babes, there's a job here coming up soon! Maternity cover for our compliance person who's leaving in six weeks and the department boss is interested in you. He remembers you from his Warder Park days – Chris Jones?'

Excitement – or was it fear? – burst through Bella's body, bringing her heart to her mouth. Her move to London was becoming a reality.

'Bella?'

'I'm here. So quick. I can't believe it.'

'Thank God you've got Keren's flat; it makes it all so much easier. You just need to sit the exam. How are you getting on with the manuals?' Shirley's face bobbed in and out of view as she walked through London to work.

'Getting there.' Bella put on a positive smile – she'd yet to open a page of the package Shirley had sent. It made her queasy even to think about it.

'You'll pass easily. Didn't I tell you it would work out?' Shirley beamed.

'I'm so grateful, Shirl. Thanks so much. I can't believe everything's coming together so well.'

'You deserve it, my friend. About time things went your way. Catch up later, I can't see where I'm going. *Ciao!*'

The screen went blank but Bella sat immobile, staring at it. 'Six weeks...'

She was still staring at the screen when the phone rang again. Iain.

'I thought you might be an early bird! Have you recovered from the other night? Think I'll stay out of The Ship for a while, but there are plenty more pubs we can misbehave in.'

'We were singing the school song, for God's sake.' Speaking to Iain immediately lifted her spirits and she giggled at the memory.

'Fancy dinner this week? More than a packet of crisps and dry roasted nuts...'

Bella laughed. 'I'd love to.'

It had been a fun night with Iain, and a bit more fun might take her mind away from Jem and the past. She had to look forward not back. She was going to London.

'Saturday night? There's a great French place down here I can book.'

'Mmm, yes please, sounds fabulous.'

'Pick you up at seven?'

'Yes, I'm looking forward to it.'

Heavens, it was only 7.15 am and she had a potential London job and a second date.

Bella totted up all the numbers in her head while she drove out of Broughty Ferry towards the West End. If she cracked on with the chairs and managed to sell them, plus what she could save from her salary and the tiny bit of savings she had left, she should have over £3000. The £1,500 for the exam was a bit of a blow, but she would need to invest to win the job. Having free accommodation made it all possible. *Thank you, Keren.* Her mind was working overtime with a tummy full of jitters as she contemplated the move and this second chance. Life was going her way. Her head full of plans, she turned into the driveway without thinking and parked in front of the house. No cars in sight. It was a chance to pick up bits and pieces she'd left behind.

'Anyone home?' She stood in the hallway listening for signs of occupation, then crept upstairs to her mother's bedroom.

Pushing open the door, she was met by an expensive refurbishment. The walls were painted and papered, with new carpet and furniture. She understood Roddy and Lorna would have wanted to re-decorate, but it was unsettling. There was nothing left of her mother here.

Bella went downstairs and into the small bureau off the hallway. The shelves had been emptied of their files but Dorothea's desk was still there and she sat in her mother's chair. The stroke had rendered Dorothea's left side useless, but she'd been right-handed so could write and work away on the business. It was her mother's domain and Bella was entrusted to clean it. Once settled at the desk, she would leave her to get on with her calls and other business.

On one side was a photo of her father in a romantic Hollywood hero pose, idly dangling a cigarette. Next, a picture of herself and Roddy, aged about eight and sixteen. He was bending down to wrap his arm around Bella, crushing her to him, and both were smiling happily at the camera. She'd seen these pictures every day but hadn't looked at them closely for a long time. They appeared so happy together, and she remembered being ecstatic in the arms of her big brother. On the empty shelf was a photo of Bella with her mother taken the day she married Sam. They stood slightly apart, each holding a champagne glass. Her mother's hand was resting awkwardly on her daughter's shoulder. They looked straight at the camera with small, uncertain smiles celebrating detente for a day.

Bella opened the oak desk drawer – pens and pencils, letter opener, old cheque books and her mother's small notebook were still inside. Dorothea would write a to-do list every evening and work through it the next day. She flicked through. *Women's Guild*, calls to friends, shops, Aunt Nettie, Roddy – all scored through efficiently as the tasks had been completed. Bella was filled with sadness, presented with this evidence of her mother making plans, unaware of how little time was left. She came to the last page and entry: Aunt Nettie was at the top of the list, next the butchers (2lbs of stewing steak), then Dali's name: 'Dali – call'. It was odd, she thought Roddy always dealt with Dali. Then 'solicitors' and 'shares' and at the bottom, 'Annabella'. Underlined twice. Bella was moved to think she had been on her mother's mind so close to the end of her life, before she had become unwell. She quickly flicked through the notebook and saw no other mention of her name. 'Annabella'. Underlined twice.

Bella pushed the chair into place. She no longer wanted the bits and pieces she'd been thinking of and crammed the photos into her backpack.

She was half-way to Broughty Ferry when she remembered she was supposed to be visiting Aunt Nettie and whipped the car round. It wasn't clear why she was mentioned in the notebook, but Bella believed Dorothea planned to tell her about the house. It gave her comfort – her mother was thinking about her and wanted to bring Bella into her confidence. But why had she been in touch with Dali?

CHAPTER 24

Alone in the shop after a challenging afternoon meeting the ironmongery needs of the local populace, Bella was pondering a range of questions. Like how did she manage to have such a busy weekend ahead, and how would she fit it all in? She examined the list in her notebook:

Saturday night Iain
Amina's accounts – finish
The chairs – ditto
Study compliance!!!!
Aunt Nettie
KY Jelly
Condoms!

They had snogged the last time. Was sex on the menu? Did she *want* it to be on the menu? He was good looking, entertaining, considerate – why not? Iain had called the night before and they'd been decidedly flirty, with ridiculous double entendres making them snigger. Hence the KY jelly; it'd been such a long time, and she was going through the menopause – would it all work properly? What if she had massive sweats mid-bonk? What if she had a hot flush during orgasm – her head could explode.

God, men had it easy. She added 'Beard Trimmer' to the list.

By the time Mr Mirza arrived she was happily swishing the feather duster around the shop.

'How's business today, Ms McCaa? Have I made my fortune so I can retire?'

'Not yet, I'm afraid, but we did sell two of the handwoven sweeping brushes – the large deluxe versions? And three radiators. You may want to order more of those.'

'Ah, Annabella, you have good service here; the customers like you and you can sell. I'm very happy with your work indeed. Are you enjoying your change of career?'

'Yes, of course.' Bella changed the subject, 'We need more paper bags, though.' Mr Mirza had to be told she was off to London, but first she would speak to Celeste and see if she might be interested in the job. It would be good to find a replacement and she wouldn't worry about letting Mr Mirza down quite so much, but she didn't need to think about that quite yet. Bella hid her discomfort by pulling her coat and bag out of the cupboard ready for her lunch break.

'Why don't you take the afternoon off? I want to see where I am with stock and place orders. I'm sure I'll be able to cope with the customers, too. Go on, off you go and enjoy the sunshine.'

'Thanks, Mr Mirza. I've got so much to do for some reason. See you tomorrow.'

Bella popped into the chemist: beard trimmer – tick; condoms – tick; KY Jelly… Hmm. There seemed to be such a choice of lubricant: water, oil, silicone… Things had certainly moved on over the last ten years. Or maybe she'd never paid much attention until she had to. Bella went for the most natural-sounding water-based one, then swiftly added in one of each kind, and to cover all bases seized a triple pack of the tried and trusted KY as well. The lube was followed by a face pack promising to make her skin dewy and youthful in fifteen minutes. Bella's optimism knew no bounds.

'Fancy meeting you here.'

'Iain!'

Don't look in the basket, please don't look in the basket. Bella hoped telepathy would save her from the embarrassment of him seeing her shopping. Her mind had gone blank.

'Erm, how are you? Caught any robbers lately?' Oh gawd, how lame. 'Sorry – stupid joke.'

'Hold on, I did catch two robbers! They'd stolen a pile of jewellery from the Oxfam shop. You're standing in front of a hero!'

'The streets are safer with MacBain on the prowl.' They smiled and Bella shifted the basket to behind her legs, hidden away.

'I've booked La Folie. Still OK for seven? We could have a little aperitif beforehand?'

'I'll be ready for that.' Bella waved weakly as she reversed away, hiding the basket.

Iain looked bemused as he smiled at her. 'See you Saturday.'

Thankfully, there wasn't a queue at the checkout and she paid for her purchases, stuffing them out of sight.

Should she investigate HRT again? Last time her doctor had determined her perimenopausal state was over and that symptoms would stop, supposedly making HRT redundant. But the various features of the menopause she was dealing with told her emphatically that it was ongoing. Negotiating a love life was difficult at the best of times but when your body had a mind of its own... The idea of being intimate after such a drought – and at her age – was nerve-wracking. Nevertheless, Bella had a little spring in her step as she headed to the cottage.

She didn't waste her free afternoon, making headway with Amina's accounts and the studying thanks to full-bodied Red Bull and Pro Plus. The unhealthy combo cleared the brain fog and gave her hope for the future.

Her attention was taken by the envelope of cash sitting on the TV. She needed to stash it in a cupboard or take it to the bank. Amina had brought it round the night before and they'd giggled while it was counted out, numerous times. Bella was delighted to give Amina her commission and it was good timing as she was off to Glasgow for the weekend. Things were looking so positive, a stark contrast to a few months ago. She'd found a job, made a home out of what had been a hovel, had a new friend in Amina, and had found a hobby she enjoyed. People actually wanted to buy her handiwork. It gave her a sense of achievement she hadn't had for a long time. Thanks to Keren she had a place to stay – and if she managed to glue information into her foggy brain, she could pass an exam and have a foot in the door of the finance world. Not to mention she had a date for Saturday night. What a difference to her life of the last ten years. She wanted to celebrate her good fortune and started to text the girls through their chat group, then realised it was too late to go schlepping to the other side of town; they would be settled for the evening. Bella looked outside. It was dry, and still light. She'd celebrate with a fish supper.

CHAPTER 25

Bella wandered along the beach and turned into Gray Street. Live music was booming out from The Anchor and Bella recognised the sound. She looked at the poster outside. The Danfans were playing! She couldn't believe the old hometown favourites from her student days were still going strong. She hesitated; she'd never gone into a pub on her own without a plan to meet a friend. Taking the plunge, she pulled open the door, thinking she'd order a soft drink and find a quiet corner.

The pub was a heaving sea of grey and bald heads, peppered throughout with unnatural blondes and brunettes. Half the crowd were singing along to the band, the other half weaving rusty dance moves in the tight space. Bella burrowed through and eagerly waved her money at a barman. 'Pint of Snakebite, please,' escaped her lips. Jeez Louise, where had that come from? Drink in hand, she was forced back into the throng and, trapped in the crowd, she swayed with them, joining in the singing until a voice shouted in her ear.

'Of all the gin joints...'

Jem.

They grinned at each other. Too loud and cramped for anything else, they clinked glasses and returned to enjoying the band. Warbling at the top of her voice, Bella was amused she could remember every single lyric but barely an iota of financial data when it was needed. She and Jem were pushed tightly together, moving with the music as they'd done in their student days. He got another round, laughing when Bella asked for a Snakebite – a half this time; she wasn't completely stupid. When the band played its number one hit, *Astronomica*, they waved their arms and sang along. For an encore, The Danfans launched into a frenetic reel and the audience performed as expected, whirling and staggering around the bar, Jem and Bella included as they linked arms and spun each other, trying to save their drinks from spilling. Another rendition of *Astronomica* followed and Jem put his arm around Bella, hugging her to him, and they belted the song out to each other, lost in the past.

The band finished, unpersuaded by the crowd's hopeful chanting for them to play on, but Bella and Jem stayed close. He bent down and kissed her, the sensation charging through her body as she melted against him and their kiss deepened. Time fell away as Bella was transported to the past, his lips as familiar now as they had been thirty years ago.

'It's past time! Please!' the barmen called. Bella was jolted away from Jem as the overhead lights came on and they were swept up in the crowd reluctantly making their way outside. She turned for home and Jem tripped along beside her.

'How many pints have you had?' Bella smiled at his loss of composure.

'Three! Can't take the Scottish brews anymore,' he laughed. 'I'll be fine. I'll walk you home.'

The beach was quiet as they ambled along companionably, but Bella's mind was working overtime. Should she invite him in? What might happen? Did the kiss mean anything? Did she want to go there? How drunk was he? They arrived at her turn off to Long Lane.

'Do you—'

'Belle.'

'What?' She smiled at him; he looked so serious.

'Don't you think you owe me an explanation?'

'What? What for?' Bella was confused. What was he talking about?

'Why you ended our relationship? Suddenly it was over; you wouldn't see me, didn't return my calls. I never understood what happened.'

'What?' Bella recalibrated her brain. This was not what she was expecting. 'Don't you think it's you who owes me an explanation?'

'Like what?' Jem had raised his voice to match Bella's.

'Like why you slept with Sandra Drummond? Why did you sleep with her? We'd been going out for years and suddenly you decide to sleep with another woman?' Decades fell away and Bella was in the devastated place she'd been all these years ago. Why had he been unfaithful?

He looked confused. 'I never slept with Sandra Drummond.'

'Oh, for God's sake, if you're not even going to be serious about it, there's no point.'

'But I didn't. Why would you think I did? Why?'

'Really? You're going to do this?' Bella came closer. 'That weekend when I couldn't come through to Dundee and you, Keren and Dali went to the party. Keren told me you got off with Sandra and she was bragging the next day about having slept with you. Keren saw you snogging her! Did you think I wouldn't find out?' Bella didn't care who heard her shouting.

'I did not snog Sandra Drummond. This is crazy.' Jem paused and swayed slightly. 'I can't even remember who Sandra Drummond was, but I didn't sleep with her. You were the only woman I'd slept with until I went to New York.'

Bella hesitated.

'Did you say Keren told you?'

'Yes. Why?' Bella snorted. 'Are you going to tell me she was lying?'

'The Keren who calls you Windy? Which you hate. Who delighted in making a fool of you much of the time and years later is still at it by getting you to waitress at her party? That Keren? I never got your friendship. You believed her over me?'

'Why would she lie?'

'I don't know. Because she's always been jealous of you?'

'Of me?'

'Of us and what we had. And of you. Keren was Miss Popular. But so were you – although you never could see it. People would come to you with their problems;

you were so kind. You smoothed over any friction caused by Keren. You thought you needed her, but she needed you more – you made her more appealing. People knew they could count on you, and if Keren was a friend of yours, they accepted her too. And because you and I were a couple and Dali wasn't interested in making it a foursome.'

Bella opened her mouth to speak but Jem ignored her.

'You believed I would be unfaithful? You didn't even ask me. You didn't want to hear my side of it? I never heard from you again. No one would tell me anything and you waltzed off to London. In today's terms, you ghosted me. I had to come to the bank to find you in your fancy-pants job and you couldn't spare me the time; it was like you were embarrassed to see me.'

'You broke my heart,' Bella wailed.

'And you broke mine!' Jem shouted.

'It doesn't seem to have done you any harm. You married, had a child and now you're Mr bloomin' Successful, so why are you even standing here?'

'Yes, I made a life for myself. So did you.'

Had she? 'I don't believe Keren would lie. She's my oldest friend.'

'But you think I would? Ask her. Why didn't you give me a chance? Why didn't you ask me?'

'I was so hurt. It took me years to get over you.' She whispered. The fight had gone out of Bella. Had Keren lied to her all these years ago?

'I can't believe this is what you thought of me. All these years I went over and over what it might be. I was too poor; too gauche; not in the right career; not smart enough; you fell out of love. And that was it? You believed a lie. You couldn't even speak to me on the phone! For a long time I hated you—'

Bella interrupted, holding her hand up. She couldn't listen to any more. 'Keren wouldn't lie to me.' She turned abruptly, scurrying away with '*Are you sure about that?*' ringing in her ears.

CHAPTER 26

Bella unlocked the cottage door with shaking hands and slammed it shut, putting the snib up and ramming the bolt and chain over. She dropped her head against the door and stood in the darkness.

No. Keren wouldn't have lied, wouldn't have deceived her in such a way. Why would she? She 100% believed her friend. But why would Jem say it was untrue? After all these years it would mean nothing to him if he had.

Jem had called after the weekend and she'd got Keren to say she wasn't there. He'd called again and again and she'd stood, listening to his messages as he spoke into her machine, frustration, anger and hurt in his voice. Within days she was off to London. Somehow, he'd tracked her down to the bank. Shirley had come into their office and said there was a Jem Adam to see her and Bella had looked out the window of the office they shared. Jem was standing in the reception area, looking out of place in his jeans and trainers amongst all the suits. He'd looked up and seen her and she'd crept away, asking Shirley to tell him she wasn't in. Bella went to the loos and sobbed, only coming out when Shirley informed her management was looking for their new intern.

She sat in the dark for a long time. As the early summer dawn light came up, and crawling into bed fully dressed, she drifted in and out of a tortuous sleep. She was wide awake at six-thirty, admitting to herself that twenty-two-year-old Bella may have believed her friend, but fifty-two-year-old Bella no longer did. What Jem had told her had a ring of truth about it. Why Keren had lied was beyond her, but she believed Jem. She could hear the hurt and anger, suppressed for thirty years, in his words – saw it in his face.

He'd hated her.

Bella texted Mr Mirza and pleaded illness; she couldn't face anyone. Turning her mobile off, she burrowed under the duvet and hid from the world.

Rising in the afternoon, she flung her clothes off and ran a bath. She lowered herself into the tub and allowed the scalding water to distract her from the pain inside. The tectonic plates of her world had shifted. An intrinsic belief she'd held for so long had been untrue. Hidden under the duvet, Bella had examined her friendship with Keren from a fresh perspective. She knew Keren had often been less than a friend to her, and she'd allowed the dynamic to continue through the years. The barbed comments, the little jokes about her life and relationships – Bella had let them pass, had allowed herself to be bullied into things she didn't want to do for the sake of friendship, to not be seen as a killjoy, grateful to be part of the gang. Keren had shown herself capable of being a good friend often enough that it almost balanced out the less pleasant side to this woman who had been part of her life since she was five years old, when she'd taken Bella under her wing and made everything terrifying about school and meeting strangers manageable.

When Bella had first returned to Dundee, Keren helped her find the care agency and invited her whenever the girls got together. As Bella's freedom to socialise was curtailed, it was natural the invites would fall away. Bella was able to venture out less and less as her world got smaller and smaller and she had nothing to say, nothing to share except for the mind-numbing repetition of her life week in, week out.

She had to confront Keren with what Jem had told her but she would wait, wait until she'd stopped trembling with rage.

Bella retreated to bed again, unable to face anything else, and tortured herself with what a life with Jem might have looked like. She was disorientated, as if a rug had been tugged from beneath her feet and she could no longer find steady ground.

She rose as dawn lit the sky and headed off down to the beach. There was no one around and she settled on a bench listening to the waves lapping into shore. They would have married and had children, she was sure. She might have become a grandmother, like Keren. She imagined their wedding, the humanist service in a romantic Highland glade they'd talked of as students. Would she have gone to New York with him? Given him the child he loved so much? Bella curled over, the yearning for this parallel life a physical pain inside. What kind of person would she have become if she'd had Jem's love all these years? Not the broken, depressed woman who'd given up on life and spent the last years directionless, trapped and alone, with the acres of love she had inside to bestow wasted and lost.

Seeing the early morning swimmers arrive at the beach brought Bella out of her reverie. Sick with trepidation, she knew it was time to confront Keren.

CHAPTER 27

Texting Mr Mirza, Bella apologised and asked if she could take another day. He was only concerned for her health, racking Bella's guilt quotient up another notch.

Jangling with a couple of hours' worth of coffee and energy drinks, Bella got in the car and headed to the West End, heart pumping. Keren had a Pilates class at 9.30 on Fridays and Bella wanted to catch her before she left, before she had any grandchild to distract them.

As Keren answered the door, Bella immediately brushed past her, heading to the kitchen.

'Windy! I'm leaving for a class, as you can see?' Keren indicated her leggings and vest.

'Why did you tell me Jem slept with Sandra?'

'What? What are you talking about?' Keren started to fuss with the kettle but Bella sent it sailing along the countertop, forcing her friend to face her. 'What is wrong with you?'

'*You* told me Jem slept with Sandra; you saw him kissing her. I've spoken to Jem and it was a lie. All a complete lie. Why would you do that?' Bella tried to keep her anger under control but her voice was raised.

Keren started putting things in her gym bag. 'Of course, Jem would deny it, what else is he going to say? You can be such a fool where men are concerned.'

Bella grabbed the gym bag and flung it into the neatly stacked crockery on the dresser, causing cups and plates to smash on the floor.

'What are you doing!' Keren moved to pick the bag up but Bella wasn't having it and she kicked it away.

'No! *Answer me!*' Bella yelled and Keren retreated under the loud blast, but Bella moved forward. 'Listen to me. You lied. I know you lied. Why would you want to hurt me like that? I'm your oldest friend. What were you thinking, Keren?'

Hands on hips, Keren looked straight at Bella. 'I didn't do it *to* you – I did it *for* you!'

'What?'

'Oh, what am I going to do...' Keren put on a whiny, simpering voice. 'I don't want to live in Dundee but Jem's dropped out and taken a job there. We're supposed to be together.' Her face was contorted in her mimicry. 'What should I do, Keren? I love Jem and he loves me. On and on and on. Jem did this for me, and Jem did that. Mr Perfect Boyfriend.'

Bella was shocked at the vitriol.

'I did you a favour. Did you really want a life with Jem? A tea boy? Oh, yes, he made good, but he got lucky. He got lucky for the very same reason you had a brilliant career – going off on your own. Look how successful you were. And at last Dorothea was no longer giving you a hard time. You should thank me.'

'But your lies altered the course of my life. Our lives. You don't have the right to play with people. It was years before I was ready to have a relationship, until I met Sam.'

'My point exactly. Unfortunately, I wasn't around to help you swerve another one, Windy.'

'Stop!'

'What?'

'Stop calling me Windy. I hate it. I've always hated it and I've asked you so many times to stop. My name's Bella, or A*nna*bella.'

'It's a joke, for God's sake – you call me by my nickname!'

'*Keren*! You swapped an 'a' for an 'e' in your name so you'd be like Keren in Bananarama! Can't you see what your lies did to us, how it changed everything?'

Keren bent over to pick up her bag, revealing a backside no amount of Pilates was going to save.

'You don't care, do you? I'm not sure what I expected, but not this. I never want to see you again, Keren; I don't want you in my life. I certainly don't want your friendship.' Bella headed for the door. 'And you can stick your London flat up your arse – it's big enough.'

She opened the kitchen door to reveal Pam and Jean standing there, also in their gym clothes. They jumped out of the way.

'The front door was open...' Pam put an arm out to Bella but she brushed past it and carried on.

'Bella!' Jean followed her to the door. Ignoring her too, Bella slammed the front door so hard the glass popped and shattered on the ground. She got in the car and drove off, only to squeal to a halt around the corner and pummel the steering wheel.

Keren had done it. She had lied. And she didn't give two hoots about it. Didn't care how it had altered the course of Bella's life – and Jem's life. She cringed inside with shame at the way she had treated him, seeing it from his point of view and imagining how confused and hurt he must have been. No wonder he'd hated her.

It was so easy to not be in contact in those days – no mobile phones, no social media – if you didn't have a landline number or an address, it was hopeless. Unless you found out where a person worked and came five hundred miles to see them, as Jem had done.

Why hadn't she given him a chance? She'd never doubted what Keren said for one minute. She'd been so crushed by the hurt, Bella couldn't face hearing Jem make excuses, didn't want to hear his apologies, knew she could not live with his infidelity. It was all a lie – years of heartache and lack of trust in relationships, believing herself worth less than – until she'd met Sam and his irrepressible confidence and way of looking at the world swept her off her feet. Before Sam there'd been years in the wilderness; she'd certainly kissed a lot of frogs along the way. Bella started up the engine and drove off, aimlessly turning left and right, not sure where she was going until she found herself up The Law.

She couldn't wait to get to London and put everything behind her. Be independent. She'd been under her mother's thumb all these years, and it turned out she'd been under Keren's, too. It was time to do what she wanted to do. No more existing under another's influence. Jem would leave for New York and there was no point in thinking about what might have been. Or what might be. He'd hated her, was still so angry after all this time. There was no future. Please God, let her get to London, away from everything, away from the past. Keren offering the apartment and the loan now seemed insidious rather than generous. Did she want to get rid of Bella to London – again – away from Jem and finding out the truth? The sooner she was away from Dundee the better.

CHAPTER 28

Early next morning, Bella sat on the promenade and waited. The haar lifted, revealing dull grey cloud and the dark sea at high tide. Despite the inclement weather the swimming party were bobbing about on the water as usual, happy as Larry in what must have been frightening temperatures.

At last Celeste came round the corner and joined her on the seat.

'Morning. Good run?'

'Yes. Such a great start to the day.'

'I've been waiting for you. I have a proposition.'

'Oh? Do tell.'

'Have you got a job yet?'

'No. I'm looking but no luck.'

'What did you do before?'

'I was a medical secretary, many moons ago – thing is, I haven't worked for twenty-five years.'

'What?'

'I was a stay-at-home Mum. I married my boss, a doctor, and well, anyway, it was easier not to work. I had my hands full. Twin boys. I've no experience, you see. At all. What's the job?'

'It's Mirza's the ironmonger. Where I work.'

'With you?'

'Not with me because I'm moving to London, and to be honest handing in my notice might be easier if I've already found a replacement.'

'Right. I've experience of spending money in shops over the years. Do you think I could do it?' Celeste frowned. 'I did volunteer for a while in a charity shop but I had to give it up.'

'See, there you are. You do have experience.'

'It was only a month.'

'But you handled money? You'll have managed your housekeeping, so loads of experience.'

'A bit, my husband and I, we did it together. It's not for me; an office might be better, at least I can remember how to file.'

'Celeste, it's not difficult. The hardest part is remembering where the stock is around the shop because there's tons of stuff. It's all priced by Mr Mirza. Or he leaves out a note so I can do it. It's helping the customers, dusting, keeping the shop tidy and of course, taking the payments – mostly by card.'

Celeste looked doubtful. 'I'm a bit scared after so long out of work. I want a job. I need a job, but getting one terrifies me.'

'You've brought up two boys. I always think bringing up kids must be the hardest, and twins even more so. Are they in London?'

'They're at Durham doing medicine. Doing well, I think.'

'You think? Don't you see them?'

'It's complicated. I left my husband you see, and...' Bella listened while Celeste told her story of an overbearing, controlling husband and how one day she decided she had to leave. The twins had left home for good; they hated the strained atmosphere. She didn't have a plan. She looked at the money accrued in the housekeeping account and emptied it, got an overnight bus to Dundee, and managed to get a bedsit in Broughty Ferry – where she'd once come on holiday as a child. Her husband would never look for her here.

'I've been surviving on benefits and can't get out of the rut.' Celeste bit her lip. 'I had a bit of a breakdown when I moved and landed up in hospital. But I'm glad I left. I couldn't stand it any longer. He wasn't violent but everything had to be done his way... I was dying inside, or possibly already dead. I've left messages for the boys, and they've texted but I know they feel caught in the middle. It'll take time.' They sat in a companionable silence until Celeste said, 'OK. I'll come and meet Mr Mirza because I'm middle aged, broke and bored and it would be stupid not to.'

Middle aged, broke and bored – Bella could identify with that.

'Sorry, oversharing.'

'Don't apologise. Look what you've achieved already – you moved away, made a new life for yourself. Takes a lot of guts.'

'Just as brave as you going off to London. What will you do down there?'

'Try and pick up my career where I left off. I spent ten years looking after my mother, who had had a stroke and needed care, but she died a little while ago.'

'I'm sorry, that's so difficult for you. A big sacrifice to give up a career to care for her. And sorry your mother has passed. You must miss her.'

'We had a terrible relationship so mostly I fight the happiness I feel about being free, knowing how it came about.'

'It's a big thing, losing a parent, whatever the relationship.'

Bella blew her nose. 'Sorry. My hormones are all over the place. Here's me blubbing when you've got your own sad tale.'

'I think many middle-aged women have their own sad tale; we're the care-givers and the career-losers, and the world leaves us behind. What I've done isn't easy but at least I'm being true to myself. When I do get a job, I'll see the boys and explain, hope they understand. They're good, kind boys. Men. Young men.'

'Shall I mention you to Mr Mirza? I can say you've had experience in the charity shop; we can be a bit economical with the truth there, and I think you'll like it, be good at it. No guarantees, of course. It's up to Mr Mirza.'

They exchanged numbers and Bella would text Celeste once she'd spoken to her boss.

'When I woke up this morning, I felt it was going to be a good day – and look what's happened. Thank you. Thanks for listening. I hope we can be friends, even for the short time you've got left before you go.'

'Yes. Friends. I'll be in touch.'

They got up. 'Can't persuade you to come for a run one morning?'

Bella laughed at Celeste's persistence. 'I don't think it's for me; makes my breasts ache, no matter how many bras I wear.'

Bella walked home, thinking about Celeste and her bid for freedom. She was a good person, she could feel it, and Bella was full of confidence she could recommend her to Mr Mirza. Jeez Louise. She was going to hand in her notice – a massive step closer to the life she wanted.

CHAPTER 29

'Ah, Annabella. You're breaking my heart, telling me you're leaving. You're wonderful in this job. Why do you want to go to London?'

'I came home to look after my mother. Now she's gone I want to try and pick up where I left off. An offer has come up ... unexpectedly.' Bella fiddled with her overall to hide the lie. 'I'm so sorry. I appreciate all you've done for me.'

'But if you're going to leave Broughty Ferry with its bonny beach and all the lovely ironmongery, what will I do?'

'I know someone who'll make an excellent replacement. It's an older woman, like me. She used to work in a charity shop in London, not long ago.' Bella mumbled through the last bit. 'But she's trustworthy and keen to learn and will work with me for free for a day or two so you can test her out. She's so keen.'

'Who is this person? Is she local? Who is her father? I knew your father. We had a connection.'

'You can meet her. She can come to the shop, and you can give her an interview. She's not from Dundee but she wants to make her life here.'

'Argh, Annabella, why do you have to leave? You have your happy life here. A job, a place to live, good friends. Why go to London? People are not happy in London.' Mr Mirza was not taking the new plan very well.

'I miss my life in London. I miss my job and the lifestyle and all my friends down there.' Saying 'all my friends' aloud reminded Bella most of them had made their money and decamped to the suburbs, or they were mutual friends with Sam she hadn't kept in touch with. But she'd soon make new friends and join in with Shirley's busy social circle, too.

'I understand you want to go to London. But I think you're making a big mistake, Annabella.' Mr Mirza shook his head as if the world were ending.

'Would you like to meet Celeste?'

'OK, OK. Text your friend and ask her to come in at 1 pm on your day off. Oh, this news is making me sad.'

Bella felt rubbish. Mr Mirza had been so good to her, paid her well and left her to get on with it. She would have been lost without the job, and she did enjoy it, the simplicity of it. There was no pressure – if she remembered to collect payment from customers. But she'd always planned to leave; it was just sooner than expected.

Mr Mirza put his jacket on and, with a dejected wave, left the shop. Bella was relieved he'd agreed to see Celeste; it alleviated part of the guilt. She sent a text to her about the interview.

She took a deep breath. She'd done it, handed in her notice, and in four weeks she would be loading up the

Mini and hitting the road to London, come hell or high water.

Saturday was a busy day – screwdrivers, mousetraps, paint rollers, plugs, curtain wire… all swept out the door in the keen DIY hands of the Broughty Ferry-ites. The doorbell was constantly tinging and it kept Bella's mind away from Jem, from thinking about what might have been.

She'd almost forgotten about the date with Iain and considered cancelling but decided to keep moving forward. She'd had years in solitary vegetation in front of the TV – this was her new life. Iain was a lovely man and she was going to go out with him. She hadn't had a date in a decade and what better way to get one man out of your head than to go out with another?

By 5.30 pm Bella was home and sinking her tired feet and legs into a bath sprinkled liberally with scented oils. The heat and potions seeped in and Bella dozed, the bath so small there was no danger of her sinking. Woken by her delicate thermostat overheating, she clambered out. Had it been this difficult and uncomfortable when she was going through puberty? The first change heralded the future – and the menopause? A lot of discomfort, pain and depression over a long period of time.

Letting herself drip dry, she readied her toolkit and, selecting the razor, she got to work on legs, underarms and other nooks and crannies left unattended for years. Next up was the twelve-times magnifying mirror, allowing her to hone in on the spiky chin hairs sprouting daily. Bella flinched in horror when she saw up close the state of her eyebrows and moved in for an attack on them, too. She washed her hair at the sink with the ancient jug. Last and not least, she picked up the beard trimmer; jamming the batteries in and choosing a No.2 setting, she tackled the pubic hair she'd left to grow wild and free. No way was she shaving the lot off, and she had to admit Jean's pain-free method had its merits. It all felt a bit naughty. Who knew what might happen, or what she wanted to happen, but like the good Girl Guide she once was, she would be prepared.

She was liberal with the scented moisturiser, dried her hair and finished the rituals with minimal slap. She'd discovered that the more make-up she caked on trying to hide the wrinkles the more obvious they were, so she kept to basics – tinted moisturiser, liner and mascara. She'd invested in underwear – definitely not pre-loved. She'd bought a decadent, lacy underwire bra of the correct cup size with ample support that reduced spillage. And French – yes, French – knickers to match, bought for a shocking amount from the unexpectedly busy lingerie shop on the High Street. The silk and lace design neatly covered her slightly saggy bum cheeks.

The notion that sex might be on the menu thrilled and frightened her in equal measure. It had been so long, which brought her mind to Jem. They'd been good together, and as they learned about each other, making love became more passionate and intense. Her ex-husband Sam had been a surprisingly gentle and considerate lover, far removed from the cocky city broker he displayed at work, and it was one of the reasons she fell for him.

Now, after years in the desert she wanted sex, to feel vital again. She banished Jem and Sam, remembering instead the mindless sex she'd had in her late twenties. Short-lived affairs and one-night stands, much of it unsatisfying. Her body buzzed in anticipation, and she was surprised to find lust buried underneath the hot sweats and flushes, and the general war her hormones were waging against her. There was life in the old dog yet – hurrah!

She debated what to wear – a fine pink cashmere jumper she'd found or a light blouse. The cashmere was sexy, the knit so soft and tactile, and the colour complimented her skin tone; the blouse was sheer and even though she'd need a little vest top underneath it, she was less likely to overheat. It was May and there had been sunshine, but in Scotland, it could turn freezing without notice. She googled the weather – nine degrees; wind chill factor five. A cool draught came in through the skylight. Right, she would dress for fresh Scottish sun and wear the pink jumper. She loved the softness of it, and although it showed off the podge tyre, there was no point pretending that, when the clothes came off, she had a six-pack underneath. Jeans and boots next and she was ready.

Bella tidied the study manuals out of the way and grimaced. From tomorrow there would be no more distractions. Full steam ahead preparation for the exam. Tonight, she'd concentrate on having a good time.

At 7 pm sharp there was a knock on the door.

'Excellent timing.'

'We aim to please,' Iain joked. 'I like the jumper.'

Bella pinked with pleasure and knew she'd made the right decision. 'Thank you.'

'Fancy a wee cocktail in The Gunners before we go to eat?'

'Well, we can't return to the scene of the crime!' They laughed and set off along the lane.

They spoke simultaneously. 'How's your week?'

'You first,' said Bella. 'Your week is bound to have been more exciting than mine.'

'I'm not sure – speeding tickets, a couple of drunk and disorderlies, missing juveniles; very common. Paperwork, paperwork, paperwork. A contrast to my daughters, they sound like they're in *The Sweeney*.'

Bella laughed. 'Have they even seen it?'

'Oh yes, they watch all the old detective series. There're channels devoted to ancient cop TV. How's the shop doing?'

'I like it. I suppose I didn't expect to, but I love dealing with the customers. I'm like an agony aunt when the oldies come in and need help. It's becoming a public service.' She didn't tell him she'd handed in her notice.

'Can't be bad. Shall we sit outside? Not too cold?'

'No. Very European.'

'Fancy a mojito?'

'Yes please.'

Bella had read that it was better to drink spirits than wine when menopausal – the grain didn't heat you up so much. Cocktails included. Being outside was good; the sun still blazing in the sky but the wind made her glad she'd chosen the sweater.

Pleasantly squiffy after a couple of drinks, it was time to head off to eat.

'Let's go inside, shall we? It's going to get colder.'

Bella looked wistfully at the outdoor diners as they went in and were shown to a table.

'They've got a fabulous rosé here, what do you think?'

'That sounds lovely.' All plans to stick to spirits went out the window. 'Been entertaining here a lot?'

'Truth is it's usually my daughters if they're home. Or my buddy Vince; he's another singleton.'

'Have you been divorced long?'

'I'm not ... it's... It's a long story. I...' The waiter returned with the wine and, with an exaggerated twirl of the bottle, poured, waiting for Iain to taste.

'*Parfait, merci*. That's all the French I have. And *omelette*. Oh! *Gateaux*...!'

Bella laughed, enjoying the silliness. They talked about languages and places travelled. The wine was delicious and flowed easily. The starters were yummy: duck in a savoury jelly.

'Jelly.' Iain wiggled his brow.

'What?'

'Did you get everything you needed in the chemist the other day?' He gave an exaggerated wink.

Bella was mortified, but they giggled like naughty schoolchildren and scooped up more of the fabulous crisp, light wine. She was tucking into the main course, a bubbling chicken casserole – oh, why didn't she go for a salad – when the inevitable eruption sprang from her core. She stopped eating and drinking to see if she could ride it out, but it was too late. Making her excuses, she dashed off to the loo. Once inside the tiny single ladies' room – always a solitary cubicle – she tore her jumper off and pushed her jeans down to her ankles. Gasping for air, she placed her hands on the wall, hugging the cool surface in a fugitive stance.

'Excuse me?' A voice accompanied a rap on the door.

'Won't be long.'

But as Bella jolted upright her bum hit off the hand dryer blasting its heated air into the confined space. Bloody hell. She bashed it to make it stop but a little too harshly and it fell off the wall – still throwing out heat.

'Everything OK in there?'

'Give me a break!' For god's sake, can you not give a woman peace? The dryer stopped. Using loo paper, she mopped her face and neck as things cooled down and she shook with cold while rearranging her clothing. She managed to replace the dryer on the wall and it blasted out again, making her grateful for the warmth as she washed her hands. She unlocked the door and trying to look casual, smiled at the impatient young woman at the head of the small queue.

Just you wait.

'I've ordered more wine. Do you want any water? Sorry, I couldn't wait.' Iain indicated his plate; he'd demolished his steak frites and all the wine.

'Oh, yes. Queue at the ladies. The usual. Water would be good.' They shared a pudding and finished off with port. Iain insisted on paying the bill with a '*You can get the next one*'. They sailed into the night, refreshed by smir in the wind as they headed towards the cottage and Iain followed her in.

'What would you like? There's beer or Prosecco?' Bella had stocked up for the occasion.

'A beer would be good.' She brought the drinks from the kitchen and, as she was pouring, Iain came up and put his arms round her.

'I've been wanting to touch you all night. Especially in this gorgeous jumper.' He placed their beer bottles on the dresser and cupped her face. 'Can I kiss you?'

Bella wasn't as drunk as their last passionate kiss, but she had a buzz running through her. She enjoyed his lips on hers, the softness of his beard and the strength of a man's arms around her. Iain kissed her neck and held her close. She moved against him as she felt his hand reach under her jumper and stroke her bare skin. Iain whispered in her ear. '*Voulez vous coucher avec moi?*'

'You are positively fluent. *Oui.*'

Iain kissed her again as he guided her towards the staircase.

They were lost in the passion of it all when Iain accidentally backed into one of the chairs and landed hard on the seat.

'Aaaargh. Ooooooh.'

'What's wrong?'

'My hip.' Iain grimaced in real pain, holding his hip and breathing heavily.

'What can I do?'

'I'm sorry. Aaaaargh.' He pushed his leg straight out in front of him. 'It's so sore. I'm getting a replacement but, if I move the wrong way, it gets stuck. I shouldn't be doing this.'

'What do you mean? Have you been told not to have sex?'

'Noooo. Aaaaaargh.' He stood up and hobbled around.

'Let me get you painkillers.' Bella set about getting water and tablets. 'Here, take these. Ibuprofen?'

'Yes, it's the inflammation. It'll ease off. I'm sorry.'

'Nothing to be sorry about. Come on and sit here.' She led him hobbling towards the sofa.

'I'm out of practice, I suppose.'

'Is it not long since you and your wife separated? I didn't want to pry.'

'I'm not separated. My wife ... she died.'

'Oh, Iain, I'm so sorry. What happened?'

'She had MS for a long time, since the kids were born. It got worse and worse and she passed fourteen months ago.' Bella clasped Iain's hand but he was up again, limping about, trying to shake the agony away.

'I'm sorry Bella, I'm a right old crock.'

'No, you're not. You can't help a bad hip. I'm sorry about your wife. Fourteen months isn't long, not when you've spent a lifetime together. I'm going to make you tea and we'll sit here and have a cup.'

She busied herself in the kitchen, sorry for Iain and thinking about best-laid plans as she handed the hot drink over. Iain sat down gingerly on the sofa.

'It's Black Cohosh. Good for inflammation. And for 'women's issues'. Which is what was wrong with me earlier this evening.'

'I wondered you were away so long. I remember when Rosie went through it. Nightmare. You should have said but I get it's embarrassing.' Iain smiled. 'Look at us. Me with a bad hip and you with your flushes. Time's passed right enough, hasn't it?'

'It has. C'mon, drink up. It'll do you good. Fancy watching a film? There's excellent schlock on at this time of night.'

'You're a woman after my own heart.'

With a bit of flicking they settled on *Tremors*, which they'd seen before but were quite happy to sit through one more time.

The sun had been up for over an hour when they woke. They'd fallen asleep, full of wine, good food, Black Cohosh and biscuits Bella had bought for her aunt. They got up, creaky and slow after a night on the sofa.

'What are we like?' Iain smiled.

'How's the hip?'

'Better, thanks. It needs a bit of exercise. Promenade?'

'Yes, but I need to freshen up a bit and I've got a spare toothbrush you can have.'

In the bathroom, Bella peeled off her clothes. The pink jumper lay in a moist lump on the floor, followed by the jeans. She'd had a night sweat without even waking up. Was wine the answer to a good night's sleep? She examined herself in the mirror. Perhaps not. Hair greasy with excess perspiration, she had bloodshot eyes and could go shopping with the bags underneath.

Stepping out with Iain into the lane, Bella could see a figure running towards them through the early morning light.

'Jem!'

'Bella.'

'Erm, you remember Iain, don't you? From school.'

'We used to be on the same running team, remember?'

'Iain? Iain MacBain? I remember.' Jem held out his hand and Bella watched the two men give a firm shake.

'I heard you were home – and you're still running! How're you finding it, bit of a change?'

'It's good. Catching up with people – banging into old friends in unexpected places.' He smiled at Iain and ignored Bella.

'I'd better let you get on with your morning stroll. Good to see you.' Jem nodded briskly at Bella and set off again on his run.

Bella was angry at Jem for ignoring her but couldn't resist looking after him. Jem did the same. He stopped and raised his arm in a wave before disappearing into the mist.

'No dodgy hips there. He looks so damn fit and healthy, doesn't he? He didn't get those teeth beside the Tay, either. That's the US for you.' Iain stopped and looked at the road. 'What's he doing jogging along this ankle trap of a lane? You'd think he'd be down at the beach.'

Bella thought so, too.

CHAPTER 30

Bella sat staring at the laptop screen wishing she could phone a friend like the contestants on *Who Wants To Be A Millionaire*. She was wading through all the compliance regulations but as soon as a page was finished, she could barely remember what she'd read. There was a short questionnaire at the end of each section and if she was able to answer one question, she was lucky. What was wrong with her brain?

She got up and made herself a coffee, hoping the caffeine might help. There had been a time when she would have got very excited about the ins and outs of new legalities; she loved the fine print and it was what had stood her in good stead throughout her career. These days her head was a mush of refried beans. Could she have early-onset dementia? This couldn't be normal, even for females of a certain age. Or was it just the blooming menopause and if so, how long would it go on for? She couldn't be like this in work meetings.

Get a grip, she admonished herself; virtually all women had to go through it, it was natural, it would pass. Surely it would pass. Thank goodness Mr Mirza was rarely there when she was looking after the shop, standing in an aisle like a robot as she dredged up what she was looking for. Was it fair to recommend Celeste when she hadn't worked for twenty-five years and had only done a month in a charity shop? *Concentrate!* Bella focused on the screen and read on, religiously taking notes and reading each one aloud afterwards.

Hours later the text on screen was blurring and it was time to call it a day. Bella had got through loads and was confident at least a percentage of it had stuck. The phone rang and Shirley appeared on screen.

'Hey Bella – how are things?'

'Going well. I've completed a full day of studying – and I've handed in my notice.'

'Fabulous, babes. A step closer to your triumphant return to London – and you've got somewhere to stay.'

'Not anymore, but I'll find a place. I'll explain later over a glass of wine, or three, in London. If you hear of anything—?'

'I'll put the word out. Big news: the exam is set for a week on Tuesday. Not long to go.'

Jeez, a week and a bit left to prepare. Bella wanted to vomit. 'Brill! I'm delighted. Can't wait. Thanks, my friend.'

'No problem, babes, you can buy the Shirl girl copious cocktails when you're here – where you belong. Right. I'm off out to dins. Have a good one. *Ciao!*'

'*Ciao!*' Bella gave a weak wave as Shirley switched off. All would be fine. *Look forward, not back. Think positive.* As soon as she had a work contract she could get a loan or an overdraft. She could sell the car for at least £1000.

After checking in with Aunt Nettie and catching up with her news, Bella decided to crack on with the chair refurbishment. She needed them to sell more than ever.

Pulling up a little stool in the garden she got to work with the sandpaper, rubbing rhythmically on the wood. The repetitive action calmed her mind, her hands working away, enjoying feeling the grain coming through. Amina poked her head over the wall, and they caught up with their lives until the gloaming became darkness and it was too cold to stand outside.

As Bella set the alarm and fell into bed, Jem came into her head again. She missed him, which was ludicrous. How could you miss a person who hadn't been in your life for such a long time? But there was a hollow inside, especially since Jem had told her the truth of what didn't happen the night of the long-ago party. Seeing him had evoked so many memories. When he'd kissed her in the bar – it had touched places Iain's kiss hadn't on Saturday night. They had never seemed to lose the thrill of being together. One evening in first year at uni, she'd returned to her shared rental in Edinburgh to find Jem cooking up a storm. Everyone else had gone home; the place was theirs. He'd created all these wonderful dishes and they'd spent the weekend together, no need to venture out to the shops; they barely left the bed. He introduced her to the exotic tastes he'd created, full of spices and herbs. They made love, and lay together, and talked about the future. A future where they would travel and have three children and live a mad, bohemian lifestyle in exotic locations, speaking a multitude of languages. She missed the intimacy they'd had, and she'd never found again, not even with Sam.

Things became difficult between them in her final year when she wanted to pursue a career in finance and Jem dropped out to join the games company, but they would have found a way through their differences, wouldn't they, before Keren's dreadful lie had led her to an alternative future. She had to make things right with him before she left. But perhaps he didn't want to see her, was quite happy, now he knew the truth, to put it all behind him and forget her existence. But why was he jogging along her uneven cobbled lane when there was a whole stretch of promenade to run? She didn't want Jem to think she was going out with Iain. But would he care? Why did it matter? It wasn't going to make any difference. Bella switched off the light and tried to sleep as her thoughts circled madly round her brain.

***

Celeste didn't limit the neons to her sportswear; her orange T-shirt was blinding and clashed with her multi-coloured midi skirt, but Bella had to admire her individuality.

'Found this in PDSA.' Another charity shop aficionado. Celeste put on a bright pink overall. 'People don't like the neon colours so much but I spent too long in Jaeger beige and browns to care.' She spent the afternoon learning the ropes and serving customers, only needing help when she jammed the card reader. Bella managed to reboot and hoped they hadn't caused any lasting damage to Mr Mirza's bookkeeping. By the end of the afternoon Celeste had the hang of it and was beside herself with excitement at the prospect.

'I won't let you down. Thank you; thank you so much.'

'Wait till you've seen Mr Mirza, he's the one who'll decide. Fingers crossed. If I don't see you before, good luck. You'll do a fantastic job.'

Once Celeste had gone, Bella cleared up for the night, set the alarm and left. Her spare time was filled with study, looking for accommodation and refurbishing the second set of chairs.

She was still working on the chairs on her day off when Celeste appeared at the door, brandishing two bottles of Cava.

'I got the job! I hope you don't mind; Mr Mirza gave me your address.'

'Come in, come in. Fantastic – congratulations. He's a nice man, isn't he?'

'He thinks you're the bee's knees and according to him, you'll be a hard act to follow.'

Bella's butterflies swooped and soared as London drew a little closer. She had cut the safety net of job and income. She led Celeste through to the garden and they sat on a couple of the chairs and opened the Cava.

'Did I hear a cork being popped?' Amina's head appeared over the wall.

'Come on over. This is Celeste – Celeste, my neighbour, Amina.' Amina clambered up the wall but needed help to get down their side, which had them all laughing. They toasted Celeste's success. Numerous times. Amina told them about a collaboration with a designer to research vintage and waste sari fabrics to recycle for a collection. It was a big deal for her influencer brand, so needed to be toasted, too.

'I take my hat off to you, putting yourself out there on social media. It can't be easy. And you're so young. I'm not being patronising; I think it's wonderful.' Celeste clinked Amina's glass. They clinked for Bella moving to London and they talked and clinked until rain dampened their celebrations. Amina was hoisted back over the wall, their sozzled movements making them cackle like hens as they pitched her into the garden. As Bella waved Celeste off down the lane, she noted that it was too late and she was too full of Cava to do any studying and climbed up to bed. Five more days until the exam and three-and-a-half weeks until she went to London. The countdown was on.

CHAPTER 31

She was tossing and turning in the early hours when there was a loud knock at the door. Bella looked at the clock. 7.30 am – *who the hell?* Grabbing a shirt she'd managed to save from Amina's clutches she tottered down the stairs, feeling every last drop of the Cava she'd drunk last night. When would she learn to say no?

She opened the front door to see Roddy standing in the rain. He brushed past her.

'I've been emailing you with no response and Dali tells me you're away to London soon,' he said. 'Thanks for keeping me up to date.'

Dundee was indeed a small town.

'Good morning and how are you?' She was shocked by his appearance. 'You don't look well, Roddy. Is everything OK?' *Gaunt* came to mind.

'What? I've been off my food. Don't change the subject. You've got to understand – this place needs to be on the market.'

'Can you think of nothing else?'

He ignored her and appraised the décor. 'I must admit you've made an excellent job. I could get a decent price for it. Apart from the kitchen; that needs to be done.'

'Can't it wait until I go?'

Roddy was agitated and unable to settle. 'It won't sell immediately, and it's always six to eight weeks before all the paperwork is done. Plenty of time. There's no point in hanging around. The investment will be useful.'

Bella was unsettled at the thought of strangers moving into what had become her home.

'You have to understand the position I'm in,' he said.

He looked so stressed she took pity. 'Why don't you sit down and I'll make you coffee and a toasted bagel? I need to get to work but you can have breakfast while I get ready?'

'I can't, I can't. I've got to get going. I'm going down to the site and there's a load of legal stuff to get through.'

'Can't you get Dali to help? He's so good at what he does and he'd defer any fees if he did charge you at all.'

'No! No. I don't need Dali. I'm completely capable of managing this on my own, thanks. It's fine. It's all fine. When are you going?'

'Not long.' Bella sat on the sofa. 'But hey, don't worry, I'll be sure to keep you up to date,' she added with a sarcastic tone.

'Good, good. It'll all be fine.' It sounded like he was telling *himself* it would all be fine. 'I'll be in touch.' Roddy let himself out and Bella used her foot to close the door, catching his heel in her haste to see him gone.

'Ow!'

'Sorry.' Bella slammed the door as he retreated.

Did he care at all about her going to London, or what she was doing? They hadn't had a great relationship for a long time, but they were never as bad as this. She looked at the photo of them together that she'd hung on the wall and wished Roddy had seen it. She wanted him to remember that they'd once been close. Bella sniffed loudly. She was hungover. So what if he wanted to sell the cottage? She would be gone. Off to London and away from him and his useless property deal – her life to do as she pleased. Celeste would be working in the shop, Amina would have her fashion contract and she would be in an office, wearing an expensive, well-fitting business suit with a large desk and matching salary. She needed to focus because it was all coming together and she mustn't get distracted.

CHAPTER 32

Mr Mirza seemed to have been placated by Celeste as a replacement but continued to lament Bella's departure.

'But London? Edinburgh, or even Paris, I could understand. It's not called the Big Smoke for nothing, young Annabella. I'm worried you might regret this move.'

'No, I'm looking forward to it. It'll be great. I love it there. So busy. Exciting. Fantastic shopping. Buzzy. There's a great buzz!'

'Well...' Mr Mirza remained unconvinced.

At home in the evening, she studied. Early in the morning, she studied. Over the weekend she checked in on Aunt Nettie and studied. She drank loads of coffee, copious amounts of Black Cohosh and extra caffeine tablets – all to keep her mind as sharp as possible. Bella even had professional Zooms with Shirley: catching up on what companies were doing what, who exactly she might be working with, what her salary would be. Jeez Louise – to have money again.

'You'll be fine.' Shirley's face loomed in and out of sight as she settled herself on a sofa with a glass of red.

'It's compliance, I guess. Out of my comfort zone as an analyst. I used to enjoy looking at companies, assessing them, working out strategies. It'll be full-on concentration of the rules and regulations.' It was the night before the exam.

'It's a way in. Once you're down here and get your head round the business again, you'll be invited to join the finance team in no time!'

'You're right, of course, and I appreciate everything you've done.' Bella hoped her smile hid her apprehension.

'Have you got all the log-in stuff?'

'All sorted. Two-hour exam from 9 am, an interview at 11.20 am. Phone off, radio off. It's peaceful round here if the seagulls behave themselves.'

'It'll be easy peasy for you. Then we can celebrate.' Shirley lifted her glass and tapped it to the screen.

'The strongest I'm having is the miracle menopausal tea.' Bella brandished her mug. 'I haven't been out. Studying. Eating. There's been a lot of cheese. It's supposed to help your brainpower. Not so good for sleeping, though.'

'Is it not fish?'

'What?'

'Gives you brains. Don't think cheese has any special properties. Nightmares? You should lay off it tonight.'

'Too late! I've already eaten so much cheddar I might throw up. At least it'll soon be over.'

'You'll be fine. You were always an excellent sponge for facts and figures.'

'I think my age is against me.'

'Nonsense. It's the best thing about us. Our age, our experience.'

'Do you never get brain fog?'

'No. HRT.'

'I think it's too late for me,' Bella grimaced. 'I'd better go to bed, I want to sleep as long as I can, if I can. Oh God, it's like being at uni. Exams. Yuck. I'll text you after. And thanks. Thanks for everything. I owe you big time.'

'No, you don't. Just get yourself down here. It'll be so good to have a friendly face around.'

'I hope mine isn't the only friendly face you see?'

'No, but sometimes ... people are busy with their own couple-y shtick, no place for the singlies. But soon you and I can hit the town – like the old days. Good luck! You'll be fantastic. *Ciao*, babes.'

Bella was left staring at her image. A *singly*. She stuck her tongue out and switched off.

CHAPTER 33

Bella didn't miss the alarm clock because she hardly slept a wink, thrashing around all night. She was a wet rag, weak and dehydrated. She couldn't get her hair to sit; the weird, wiry texture had returned, making it stick out at odd angles. She should have put more highlights in; it helped the texture last time. Too late now.

Her outfit was all set out. She wasn't going anywhere, but wearing her old suit made her feel professional, channelling her career-woman past. The trouser zip didn't quite close but no one would see when it came to the interview. Her blouse was fine and the jacket didn't need to fasten. By 8.50 am she was sitting at the dining table with her laptop, a litre of water nearby, a large packet of crisps even closer and her notes and books piled high beside her.

She opened the windows; it was going to be a muggy day. The heaviness in the air didn't stop the seagulls screeching relentlessly. Bella logged on and waited for the clock to count down. At nine o'clock the screen revealed the examination paper. Bella pushed her sleeves up to her elbows, all business, filled in her details and read the first question.

There was a loud bang at the door. Bella ignored it and focused on the screen. She heard a key rattling in the lock.

'Hello?' Bella went over to the door, clutching her unzipped trousers. She opened it to see three workmen.

'We're here to do the kitchen. From McCaa Properties?'

'What? He didn't tell me!'

'It's all booked in for today and tomorrow, a quick refit.' Bella was left holding the door as the men waltzed past. Immediately she was on the phone.

'Roddy, what's going on? You didn't say anything about workmen?'

'Yes, I did. Remember I told you the kitchen needed done? I can't believe I managed to get them so quickly – they had a cancellation. They were round the other day to measure up.'

'What? You can't be letting people into my home without asking. I've got an exam online today. It's incredibly important to do with the London job. I need peace and quiet.'

'It must be done, Annabella. Can't you go upstairs? It's so difficult to get workmen.' She looked at the time – 9.20 am. 'For God's sake, Roddy!' She ended the call and picked up her papers and laptop.

'Where's the water pipe?' One of the men poked his head out of the scullery. 'We'll need to switch off for a bit, but not right away.'

'It's in the cupboard. Look I've got work to do, I'm taking it upstairs.' Trying to keep her dignity, she clutched her trousers and dashed upstairs. She settled on the bed and spread out, relieved to see she hadn't been logged out. Half an hour had gone already. The first question was easy and boosted her confidence. Multiple choice next and she motored through, making up time. By 10 am she was halfway, according to the little icon at the bottom right-hand corner. Heat was building up under the eaves and she opened the window as wide as it would go and removed her jacket.

The radio came on downstairs and a loud voice sang along – badly. Bella stuffed tissues in her ears but jumped out of her skin when banging started, the noise grating down to her bones. By the sound of it, they were hammering tiles for removal. Of all days for this to happen. Bella focused on the screen as her internal thermostat struggled with the close weather. Questions swam in front of her and she had to read them repeatedly before they made sense, then scrape the recesses of her brain for answers. The rain started and pelted the roof, increasing the humidity. She whipped her clothes off and replaced them with the Duranie T-shirt. Panic rose as she saw it was 10.30 am and she still had 45% to go; her head vibrated in unison with the banging below. Sweat ran down her forehead. It was too much.

'S*top*!' She jumped up and ran halfway down the stairs. 'Jeez! You have to stop! I can't hear anything. *Please*!' She grabbed chunks of hair, crazed with frustration.

'We won't be much longer.'

'No! You have to leave now, for God's sake! *Get out!*' she screamed at the top of her voice.

Three scared faces stared up at her – a bawling mad woman in a see-through Duran Duran nightie. The men swiftly sidled out, closing the door behind them. Bella viciously disconnected the radio; not caring she sent it whirling across the floor before resuming her position in front of the laptop. It was 10.37am and she still had 45% to go. She stifled a sob and got down to it.

She typed out the answers as quickly as she could. Her fingers flew across the keyboard. There was no time to look at her notes, no time to consult the books. Question. Answer. Question. Answer. On and on. No time to think. Bashing away until the end with twenty seconds to spare. There was no point in trying to check anything; no time to reconsider her responses. She did a quick review to see if she'd left any questions blank in the last section. Apparently not, and at 10.59 and 56 seconds she clicked the large red submit button.

Bella collapsed on the bed. What a mess. A total pile of pants. Two minutes later she was in the bathroom, stripping off and running the cold tap. Nada – the water was switched off. She wiped herself down with a towel, re-did her makeup, blow-dried her hair with cold air and got part dressed. With only her knickers on the bottom half, she went downstairs, put the snib on the door and sat at the table.

At 11.19 am she clicked on to the Zoom interview and over the next twenty minutes discussed compliance in what she hoped was a professional and practical way with the young woman on screen. She stumbled over a couple of questions initially but using the tried-and-tested method of repeating the question before she answered and writing down a one-word clue, Bella made sure she found her thread whenever she lost it. Coherent speech miraculously came out of her pickled head, and by 11.43 am it was over, no doubt in more ways than one.

CHAPTER 34

Bella quickly changed to jeans and T-shirt and headed to the beach. The rain had stopped and it had become a warm Scottish summer's day. She slowed to an amble, letting the fresh air wash over her.

The beach was already busy and she could see a variety of shapes and sizes toasting on the sand; no Dundonian wanted to waste sunshine. The soundscape of screams and laughter lifted her spirits and she stripped off socks and trainers and rolled up her jeans, exposing her milk-bottle-white ankles and venturing a shallow paddle. It was icy cold. The water swished around her feet, occasionally soaking her jeans, but she didn't care – everything was going to work out. The release of tension blew away her inhibitions and she spread out her arms and whirled round and round, wading through the waves. She didn't care if she looked like a mad woman; her life was changing. She splashed in the water until the wild exuberance made her head spin and she stopped abruptly, facing the shore.

There was Jem, watching her from the promenade with an inscrutable expression on his face. Bella brought her arms down to her sides, frozen in the water.

Fergus appeared beside him and raised an arm in triumph. 'Way to go, Bella!'

Bella held her trainer aloft like a prize and Fergus moved away. Jem remained, staring at her, then he turned and steadied his father with an arm as he caught him up. She dropped the trainer in the waves but managed to grab it before it drifted away.

The whole Jem situation discombobulated her. She couldn't think of what might have been; she couldn't think about the kiss and must banish him from her mind. She'd hurt him terribly and he'd hated her for years. There was no going back, and each time he entered her head, uninvited, she would close down and think of something else, frightened to examine the depth of desire in her heart. It was time to think about the future, not the past. She left the beach and, putting the trainers on her sandy, wet feet, scrunched home.

Bella drove the route along the river and cut off onto the Perth Road until she found herself parked outside her mother's house. From the road she could see the view of the Tay and across the water to Fife. Lorna's car was sitting in the driveway, with no sign of the dent Bella had created. Roddy and Lorna lived there now with their children and it was the way it should be. Perhaps it would be a happier home than it had been for her. She hoped so. What had already been a strained household had become a cold mausoleum when her father died.

Jem had found her crying in the school gym shortly after her dad's funeral and had comforted her. She barely knew him but as he'd lost his mother only weeks before, they had an instant deep connection. Grieving brought them together; they were going through a life-changing experience none of their peers understood. A memory flooded in of being with Jem at his house after school. He'd set the table for dinner and was cooking as his father came in from work.

'Oh, son, your mother would be so proud.'

Jem started to cry at Fergus's words and his father wrapped him in his arms.

'Ah ken, ah ken, we both miss her so bad.' Bella had watched with envy until Fergus raised a welcoming arm. 'Come here, you'll be missing your dad, too.' They hugged and cried until they noticed the food was burning and then they laughed and went out to the chip shop instead.

Lorna came out of the front door, locked it and made for her car. Not wanting to be seen hanging around like a stalker, Bella shot off.

She was in good spirits by the time she was outside her aunt's door, and less out of puff than in the past.

'Come away in.' There was a lot of clattering going on in the kitchen and Bella gave her aunt a questioning look.

'This is Michelle. Michelle, this is my niece, Bella.' A young woman poked her head out of a cupboard and waved gloved hands to say hello. 'Spring cleaning.'

'She's doing a fantastic job.' Aunt Nettie ran her hand along a countertop.

Bella hefted the shopping on the kitchen table and admired the gleam. 'She certainly is.'

'I'm getting positively ancient and when you add up all the time spent cleaning one's house, I decided there were better things to do.'

'Can't argue with your thinking.'

'Would you like a tea or coffee?' Michelle asked.

'Would you? That would be lovely. I'll have tea and you want a coffee, Bella?'

'Yes, please.' She'd been anticipating cleaning and organising when she got to her aunt's; this was a welcome surprise.

'You go sit down and I'll put a tray together.' Michelle busied herself and Aunt Nettie led the way to the living room.

'Isn't she great? It's only been three weeks and I'm thinking – why didn't I do this years ago? Besides cleaning, she does the odd bit of shopping, too. You see, you've no need to worry about me.' They sank into armchairs on either side of the fireplace. 'How was the exam?'

Bella groaned. 'I got through it – no thanks to Roddy though. He sent workmen round without telling me and they were banging away like crazy. They did leave, eventually.' The less said about that episode the better.

'How is Roddy? I haven't seen him since they were all round for lunch a month or so ago. Is the business going well?'

So much for her brother's plans to look after Aunt Nettie. 'He's fine. Busy, busy as usual but it's all going fantastically well.'

'Is it? That's good to hear. And you'll be fine. You were always academically gifted.'

'I'm not so sure. It was a tad stressful.' Bella's eyes watered.

Aunt Nettie got up and embraced her niece.

'I don't understand it. I'm getting what I want but I'm like a wet rag.'

'Remember what's going on. So much change in your life, including *the* change. When it happened to me, I thought I was going mad, and I was so depressed. It was awful. Why don't you stay here tonight? We can order in; there's a new Chilean restaurant opened and I've got a menu. Then we can download a movie?'

Bella looked at her aunt. 'How do you do it?'

'What?'

'Manage to stay so up to date with everything.'

Her aunt laughed. 'Movies and food are easy but remind me to write a cheque for Michelle before she goes. I'll get the menu.'

Aunt Nettie was one of an endangered species who still liked paying people by cheque, hating online transfers in case she made a mistake. Bella would make sure the accounts were 'ticketyboo', as her aunt called it, by reconciling them every couple of months. She'd be able to continue the service from London.

Bella sipped the coffee. She supposed recent events would have an impact. Dorothea dying, the house, the lack of funds, moving to the cottage, meeting Jem again, Keren, the job, Iain, the exam. More had happened to her in the last three months than in the ten years she'd looked after her mother. Not to mention her hormones: the rages, the mood swings, the temperature fluctuations, the sore breasts, the night sweats, the brain fog, the wiry hair. A dried-up old singly so angry she vandalised cars and shouted at old codgers and workmen. She bashed her head with her knuckles, trying to rid herself of the desperation and hopelessness that had crashed upon her from nowhere. By the time her aunt handed her the menu, Bella's head was ringing, but the violent self-flagellation had done the trick. She might be in pain but was much calmer. A relaxing evening with her aunt was what she needed.

CHAPTER 35

The ping of text messages coming in brought Bella gently round the next morning and she stretched luxuriously on her aunt's large sofa, reveling in the fact she'd slept through the night. There was plenty of time to get to work so she relaxed and flipped through messages.

Iain: *Fancy a movie this week, or at the weekend? How did the exam go?*

She'd put him off before, citing swotting as an excuse, but she had to get the chairs finished this week. She liked Iain but wasn't sure it was anything more than friendship. And she was going to London.

Amina: *Don't forget you've got an Instagram tutorial tonight. Over dinner?* xx

Ah yes, Amina had promised lessons. She sent a text in the affirmative and threw back the covers to start the day.

Her underwear had dried overnight and a work overall would hide where her T-shirt had been subjected to last night's dinner. No make-up, and her hair was a fright, but Bella was so refreshed from the long sleep she didn't care. The worst was over, the exam done – only the agonising wait for results to endure. Bella gave her aunt a grateful hug, promising to come over at the weekend.

Soon she was unlocking Mirza's, where she was followed in by an agitated customer looking for nails and a claw hammer. The number of hammers she sold in the Ferry made her worry whether it was safe to go out at night. The early customer heralded a busy day with the doorbell constantly tinging, and Mr Mirza had left lots of stock for her to add to the already bursting shelves. It made the day go fast but every so often Bella couldn't resist squeezing in a scan of her emails in case the results were in.

Every day Bella checked, double-checked and checked again. No news. At night she fretted over the prospect of failure. What would she do if she botched this chance? She couldn't cope with no place to stay and no job.

The chairs were finished and ready for sale, and Amina had given her tips on taking pics on her phone and building the Insta account. It seemed pointless when she was going to London but she understood that Amina didn't want to put them on her own carefully curated feed again so soon. She loved the name *Renaissance*; it worked for the furniture and herself – surely she was going through a renaissance, too? Bella wasn't keen on having a profile pic but Amina styled her in jeans and a floral blouse tied at the waist and she sat, legs akimbo on one of the chairs the wrong way round. Amina handed her big 80s sunspecs and a pair of dangling earrings to top it off. Bella loved the look – cool, retro and blessedly incognito. When all was set up, Amina did one post, sending followers Bella's way with an image of a chair and on the expert's advice, she found designers to follow and was thrilled when they reciprocated.

Two chairs went on the first night to a buyer in Glasgow – it was all so exciting. The rest were sold to the cash buyer from before. A dealer in Perth; a dodgy dealer, considering all the cash, but Bella wasn't complaining. The price they reached was fantastic – she'd hit the market with mid-century furniture at the right time and would love to see them in the showroom. She might take Aunt Nettie there before she left if she could find out which one it was. Amina would organise the couriers again.

Bella had also created a range of recycled bags she'd run up from charity shop finds. By the end of the week these were all sold too and she went off to the Post Office at lunchtime with the packages.

Standing in the queue, her phone pinged with an email – it was the news she'd been eagerly awaiting and dreading. She balanced everything as she struggled to read; this was her future.

In relation to your examination with yadda yadda yadda we have had blah blah blah – Bella scrolled down. Pass! She'd passed. She'd passed! Yes! She punched the air, her packages went flying and by the time she'd reorganised and re-taken her place in the queue she had a chance to read on. Her initial excitement was seriously dimmed when she saw the score: 51.04%. Jeez Louise, 51.04%! She didn't think she'd ever had such a low mark for anything. Would they want her? But it was a pass...

She was trudging to the shop when Shirl phoned and demanded she find a quiet spot. Bella found a corner in a car park she was passing.

'OK. I'm here...' Oh God, was it going to be a no after all this?

'I'm with Chris in the office and you're on speakerphone.'

'OK.'

'Hi, Bella. How's it going? Nice to hear you're returning to the fray. We got the results and...' Bella held her breath. 'It was lower than we'd like, but you made a good impression on the interviewer and—'

'Did I? I was so worried. I'm sorry about the result; the day was a nightmare with the unexpected kitchen fitters.'

'Shirl told me,' said Chris. 'But you passed and the devil you know—' Hmm, he didn't sound incredibly positive.

Shirl piped in, 'What he means to say is he wants you here in two weeks' time. What do you say?'

'Thanks so much, Chris. I won't let you down. I—'

'I know you won't. Get yourself down here.'

'Thanks, I will—' But the call had ended and Bella was left speaking to the ether.

Jeez Louise. This was happening. She had a job in London. She sat down on a wall and, gulping in air, gathered herself. Two weeks. *Two weeks*!

In the shop, Bella got on the phone to Aunt Nettie to pass on the news.

'I'll miss you so, but I'm delighted, my darling.'

'I'll come home more often than before. And you can come to London once I've got a place sorted.'

Bella had a sneaking suspicion that employing a cleaner was her aunt's way of paving the way for a guilt-free exit. Aunt Nettie had been so kind, offering support and encouragement when home life was hard and she was deserting her.

Nettie would have none of it. 'If you stayed here because of me, I would move to London. This is your time, take it; take all the good things coming your way. You deserve them. I've got a busy life here, I'll be fine. I've got Michelle, too, of course. She makes such a difference.'

Things got too busy for more calls, so in between customers she texted the news. First Roddy, to tell the ratbag he could have the cottage all to his damned self. She texted Pam and Jean, and Jean was immediately on the phone.

'You've done so well. Congratulations. We need to get together to celebrate. Not Keren, though. I understand. We don't see her anymore. It was too awful; we overheard everything. We're so sorry. I never knew, Bella, and neither did Pam, please believe us.'

'I do. It's still a shock but going back to London will be good for me. I was thinking I might have a farewell do?'

'Oh, yes, let's have a night out. Pam and I can organise it. Text me when you decide what night is best and we can take it from there. It's been far too long since we've been out together.'

At closing time Bella rolled down the shutter and locked it, anticipating a relaxing night, but Jem appeared beside her.

'Hello. Do you need more DIY?' Bella indicated the shop.

'No, I... Fancy a drink? Have you got time?'

'The Ship?' They headed down the road.

'No extracurricular DIY tonight for your old ladies?' he asked.

'Not tonight. I must admit I love helping them out – word got round and Mirza says sales are up because of it. It's now a bona fide service we offer.'

Bella sat at one of the tables outside, she needed the cool breeze.

'Pint of Snakebite?' Jem asked.

Bella laughed. 'A bottle of Bud will be fine, thanks.'

Returning with the drinks, Jem sat down across from her.

'Jem—'

'Belle, let me... I'm sorry for being angry with you, for shouting at you. I don't know what came over me. Seeing you again after all this time and then being at the gig...' He took a long drink from his bottle. 'It's like I'd time-travelled to all those years ago, still wanting to understand what happened between us.'

'I'm sorry I believed Keren. I hurt you and—'

'I was drunk. I shouldn't have lost it.'

'But I was wrong; I didn't give you a chance and it had such an impact on our lives.'

'It was thirty years ago. So long ago, but weirdly it doesn't feel it. I imagined all these various scenarios, but not Keren lying.'

'I should've come down to see you that day, at the bank – whatever I believed I shouldn't have ignored you. I was so hurt. I'm sorry, I'm so sorry.' Bella looked into Jem's face, seeing her pain reflected there.

'It haunted me for a long time, the not knowing. But I wouldn't have gone to New York, worked so hard to prove myself – and maybe you wouldn't have been so successful in your work either, if you hadn't taken the internship and gone straight to London?'

'Keren said that – said she was doing us a favour.' Bella gave a bitter laugh and shook her head.

'You've seen her?'

'Yes, and never will again. She has a lot of broken crockery.'

Jem laughed. 'I wished I'd been there.'

'I reverted to an age much younger than twenty-two.' They were both leaning over the table, folded arms touching, so close. 'It's hard not to think of what might have been.'

'Yes, I've been thinking about that a lot, too.'

Bella took in the angles and curves of his face, his five o'clock shadow, his denim blue eyes – a face she would have known blindfold. Her fingers ached to reach out and trace the contours.

'But I could never regret whatever path brought me my son,' he said.

'Of course. I understand that.' Bella pulled away and fidgeted with the beer bottle. 'For a long time, I had a wonderful life too. We worked hard and travelled so much; it was exciting, being constantly on the go. I was happy.'

'What happened with your marriage?'

'Business problems; one big deal too many and we lost the company – the lack of solid ground revealed how precarious our relationship was. I think part of me was glad to come home, despite the circumstances.'

Jem finished his drink. 'Dali told me you'd come back to Dundee to look after Dorothea. One time when I was home, I saw you outside your house. I was going to say hello, but you got a call and turned back into the drive.'

'No doubt an imperious command from the mothership.'

Jem smiled. 'Dali said you got the job in London?'

Bella was surprised. 'He did?'

'I swear he must have paid informants.' Jem said.

'It must've been Roddy. I'm leaving in two weeks.'

'That's what I want to talk to you about. Do you want another beer?'

'It's my turn. Same again?' Bella got up and went to the bar. What did he want to talk about? Did he want her to stay? Was it crazy to try to recapture their past?

'Lady – do you want a drink or not?' Dragged to the present, Bella placed her order, thinking about another possible future as she carried the beers outside.

'What do you want to talk about?'

Jem examined his beer label. 'I want Dad to come to the US with me. I think he'll get better treatment and it'll be good for him, especially when Ben's home, but...' He glanced up at Bella. 'He has this mad idea you and I will ... you know, rekindle something, be a couple again, if we stay?'

Bella looked directly into Jem's eyes, finding it difficult to breathe.

'Would you come for dinner and tell him about the London job and that us getting together isn't on the cards? He'll believe it from you.'

Bella felt she'd been sucker-punched.

'Dad is so fond of you and he's got this bee in his bonnet but... I mean, I've been telling him, it's been too long and you can't go back, can you?'

Bella felt Jem's eyes on her, waiting for an answer.

'No, of course not. What a notion to have.' She glugged her beer. 'And I'm definitely London-bound.'

'I know.' Jem finished his beer. 'And I want him to have the best care.'

'I understand. I'll come. When?'

'Tomorrow night?'

Bella nodded.

'Thanks, Belle. It means a lot.'

She concentrated on a young boy, flapping across the empty road in flippers and scuba mask, rubbing his arms in the weak sunlight. 'What will you do in the US? Another game?'

'I don't think that's for me anymore.' Jem smiled. 'I've been drawing a lot, and painting; classic middle-age pastime, but it's so … meditative, peaceful. I'm lucky, I don't need to work. I think I'll build up the charity over there. Do you still draw?'

'No.' Bella had forgotten she used to enjoy sketching. 'I loved refurbishing the chairs though; it gave me such a thrill when people bought them. To think my handiwork had value. I'll keep it as a hobby.'

Jem stood up. 'So 6.30?'

'What?'

'For dinner? Dad likes to eat early.'

'Yes. Of course.'

Jem placed his bottle on the table. 'I'll text you the details.'

'You don't have my number.'

Jem handed over his phone and Bella added it in, all fingers and thumbs.

'Thanks for doing this, Bella.'

'I want the best for Fergus, too.'

Jem leaned over and kissed her cheek. 'I'll see you tomorrow.'

She watched him walk away through a blur of tears.

CHAPTER 36

What an idiot she was. Jem had texted the address and the following night Bella marched to their house to tell Fergus she was moving to London and to get all romantic notions about his son and her out of his head because it was stupid. Stupid, stupid, stupid. Bella was not in love with his son. It was a lifetime ago and there wasn't going to be any rekindling of anything. So don't be a bloody fool. She would temper her words for Fergus, of course.

Bella re-read Jem's text of the address on her mobile. This was it: a large, detached villa right on the front and at the opposite end of Broughty Ferry from her cottage on Long Lane. There would be uninterrupted views across to Fife and she could tell loving hands had encouraged the glorious tea roses in the garden. Bella dipped her nose to take in the scent. Gorgeous.

Fergus opened the front door.

'Is this your handiwork?' she asked. 'They're wonderful. You've still got green fingers; I remember your blooms from years ago, they always had such a heavenly perfume.'

'I'm not so able to do everything these days, but I still like a bit of pruning. Come away in, Annabella.' He gave her a cuddle as she came through the door.

A wide hallway with various doors leading off and a curving staircase to the upper floor showed how large the house was.

'It's huge.'

Fergus laughed, 'But it's still smaller than the other ones Jem wanted to buy me. It's great for having my bowling mates over. The whole team fits in and there are three bathrooms for all the ancient bladders!'

Jem appeared wiping his hands on a towel, looking hot and bothered.

'Hey, Bella. Thanks for coming. Let me take your coat.'

Bella dropped her bag and shrugged out of it. She was conscious Jem was looking at her and was glad she'd made an effort. She had on black jeggings and boots and had gone for the sheer top Amina said showed off her curves. She looked up as she handed him the coat and Jem quickly looked away; Fergus was watching them with a huge grin on his face.

They settled in the front room with the large bay window overlooking the garden and the water. 'Jem's in the kitchen cooking up a storm. He's been at it all day. Thanks for the flowers, Bella. I'll get a vase.'

Fergus went off and she looked around the room. It was full of photos: Jem's Mum; Fergus and his wife; the three of them together. There were others of Jem on his own at various stages of life, and lots of Ben, from a chubby, chortling baby to the young man she'd seen in Jem's photos. In the centre of a cabinet full of bowling trophies was a picture of Bella and Jem, arms round each other, smiling widely at the photographer, with Bella sporting a 21 badge. She bent down to look more closely.

'A grand day, wasn't it? You two were so happy. I could never bring myself to put that photy away.' Fergus placed the vase on a table in the window, showing off the cheerful sunflowers she'd brought.

'It was a lifetime ago.' There'd been a staid lunch with her mother, Roddy and Aunt Nettie in a hotel in town but later she'd gone to find Jem and his place had been festooned with balloons, birthday messages, and a massive cake. Their friends were there, too, and Fergus had taken photos to mark the occasion. A happy, joyful celebration. 'Jem bought me that dress – I loved it.' Bella straightened. 'It wouldn't fit me anymore.'

'Och, away you go. You could get into that fine if you still had it. And you were always a bonnie lassie, Bella.'

Jem came in. 'Food's ready if you'd like to come through.' He looked so hassled it made Bella smile, his top testament to the trials of cooking.

'Smells delicious.' Bella's mouth watered as she followed the men to the large dining kitchen. 'And it looks fantastic.' The table was heaving with a variety of dishes.

Fergus sat down. 'He's been at it all day – wouldn't take any help from me.'

'There's chicken tikka masala, samosas, dahl, Nan bread, pakora. It's ages since I've cooked anything like this. I went a bit mad.'

'He wanted to do a special meal for you, Bella.'

'Dad! I wanted to see if I could still do it. Sit down – I'll get beers.' Jem handed bottles of Kingfisher out and joined them at the table, taking a slug of beer and wiping his forehead with the towel. He looked like he'd had a long day.

Bella lifted her bottle. 'Cheers!' She didn't know where to start as she took in the feast Jem had prepared. She loved chicken tikka masala – loved everything in front of her, in fact.

'This is like old times, isn't it?' Fergus said, smiling paternally over them.

Bella and Jem glanced at each other and she felt it was her cue. 'It is. It's nice to be able to celebrate with you before I head to London. I got the job I was going for, Fergus.'

'Naw, are ye really going to London, Bella?'

'In two weeks' time. I can't wait.'

'I ken ye came home to look after your mum, but is it no time for something new?'

'I want to take my chances while I can. I'm not getting any younger.' Bella laughed. 'I'm keen to get on with my career.'

'There's no one special you're going to leave behind?' Fergus nodded in Jem's direction.

'Bella's going out with a policeman. A guy from school.'

'No, I'm not.' Bella looked at Jem. 'Iain's a friend, we're not together.'

'I thought—'

'But won't you miss your friends?'

Bella turned to Fergus. 'I will, but I miss my friends in London, too.'

'Still...' Fergus sipped his beer, looking dejected.

'Bella has plans; she's returning to her career. You've got to look forward, not back. C'mon. Let's eat before the food gets cold.' Bella watched Jem hand the dishes round, surprised to hear one of her own recent mantras coming from his lips.

As mouthwatering as it all was, Bella soon had to admit defeat. She'd tried everything on the table and was completely full, thinking fondly of the skirt with the elasticated waist. She'd savoured the flavours, appreciating how each dish complemented the others. Fergus was right, it was like old times, with Jem cooking up delights for her, and they would make love afterwards. How did they manage after so much food? She shouldn't be thinking about sex, but it was difficult with Jem opposite in his soft T-shirt showing off his strong, wide shoulders and tanned arms. *Woah!* The Kingfishers had gone to her head.

'Give me a hand through, Bella,' said Fergus. 'I'm so full, I think I'll fall over.' She escorted Fergus to the front room while Jem started to clear. 'I didnae mean anything about you going to London, Bella. I want to see you happy. I just always thought you and Jem were made for each other and I wanted this to be a second chance.'

'It's all in the past, Fergus. Far in the past. There's nothing between us; it's all too long ago.' She looked up and saw Jem standing at the door, watching her.

She helped Fergus settle in the armchair, he was looking tired.

'You're going off to the US with Jem to get tip-top treatment, and you'll be so much better.'

'Aye. I suppose so. But I'm gonna miss mah buddies.' Bella released Fergus's hand and Jem covered his father's knees with a rug as he dropped off to sleep.

Bella hovered awkwardly. 'I should hit the road but I'll go to the loo first.' The beer was calling. 'Where—?'

'Just down the hall, on the left.'

There were a lot of doors. The first one Bella tried was a bedroom and she quietly retreated. She opened the next one along, a large utility room with evidence of Jem's recent artistic efforts. She was about to retreat when something made her look again and she opened the door wide. There were her chairs. All of them. Ranged in rows against the wall, still in their cling film protection – including the two sold to Glasgow. Jem had bought the chairs. Her insides curdled. All the money she had left to go to London was from the chairs. Is that why he'd bought them? To send her off, help her on the way? She heard movement behind her and Jem joined her in the room.

'*You* bought the chairs?' Bella shook her head in disbelief. 'What was it? A pity buy?'

'No, Bella! I love the chairs. I bought them because—'

'Because you could. But why pretend?' Bella moved towards the door. 'I don't need your money, Jem. I can look after myself. I don't need anyone's help.'

'Belle!'

'I've done what you asked and you can go off to New York. Say goodbye to Fergus for me when he wakes up.'

She got her bag from the hallway and left.

CHAPTER 37

Bella stalked off along the front, clipping a fast pace home. She'd forgotten her coat when she'd flounced out and there was a nip in the air. And she was bursting for the loo. Why had he bought the chairs? She'd been so excited they'd been appreciated, believing people admired the craftsmanship. Ye gads, she was sick of people interfering in her life. She knew it could have been a kind gesture, but why do it in such an underhand way? It hurt to think he'd bought them to hurry her off to London. A pity buy for poor, broke Bella who needed a hand. '*Fuck off!*' she shouted to the empty shore.

Bella arrived at her front door in record time, crossing her legs as she burst inside then tanked upstairs. Thank God it wasn't long until she was leaving, breaking away from this emotional rollercoaster. She would live life at an even pace, find a good place to stay and a steady relationship. She wanted a secure job wearing a nice suit in a big office where all the numbers worked out and if there was a mistake, it could be found and easily rectified.

Bella lay down on the bed in the dark but knew she wouldn't sleep. Jem's cash lay in a pile on the dresser. The money had lost its lustre; her joy in selling the chairs had diminished and she imagined stuffing the notes through his letterbox.

Shirley's face popped up on the mobile and she propped it against her pillow.

'I'm sorry it's late, but I have a surprise. I've got you a place to stay.'

'What? Where?'

'It's in Belsize Park and it's through a guy at work so he's only looking for one month's deposit and a month's rent in advance, which is brill. It's a super cool studio, near the underground. Bijou. A month there and you can move on. I've sent pics, can you see them?'

Bella found the email and peered. 'Hmmm. I see what you mean about bijou – where's the bedroom?'

'It's a studio! The bed pulls out from the wall. Cute, yah? See the bathroom? Uber chic or what?'

Bella could see a small wet room with black tiles and chrome fittings, including a chrome toilet raised on a pedestal. The sink was in the shower, with a pull-out mirror. 'It's very stylish. How much does stylish cost?'

'It's £2k a month to you. One month deposit and one in advance, so £4k and it's yours. Didn't I tell you we would do it? Nice building, too.'

Bella gulped. Four thousand pounds. Virtually all her savings. There would be a couple more weeks' pay and no more. Thank God she had the car to sell. She'd been hoping for a room in a house, for a lot less. In fact, she'd seen a possibility the day before. A room in a decent-looking three-bedroom house in Shepherds Bush – half the price including deposit. But Shirley had gone to all this trouble, had got her the job – Bella didn't want to let her down.

'*Hello*? Earth to Bella?'

'Sorry, sorry, I was looking at the pictures. Brilliant. It's all coming together.' She hoped she sounded positive. 'When do I need to pay?'

'Because you're an old mucker of mine, if you do a transfer by the end of next week, Alvin will be fine. I'll put you two in touch, OK? How's it all going? Are you organising a farewell do?'

'Yes, next week. I didn't imagine when I first moved, but I'll really miss things here. The cottage, Amina and Celeste, Aunt Nettie – even the ironmonger's shop. But it's time.'

'You've blossomed, Bella, in recent months. Your mojo's back. You look fab; I love the hair and if you weren't in Scotland, I'd say you were sun-kissed.' They laughed.

'Thanks, Shirley. It has been sunny-ish. It's all the beach walks – and I ate too much spicy food tonight – that's given me some colour.'

'With Iain?'

'No. But I'll see him this week. He's been away staying with one of his daughters, and I've had a lot on, too. It's good I'm sorted with a place to stay; everything's in place. I finish work next week, night out to celebrate, and down to London on the Sunday. Goodness, I'll be working a week on Monday!' Bella laughed. 'I can't believe I'm saying this but it's been so mad up here I'll be glad to get to the quiet of London.'

'I can't wait. Sweet dreams, Bella.'

'And you, Shirl. Thanks for everything.'

Bella padded downstairs, filled a glass with water and sat in the garden. There would be no stuffing of cash through letterboxes – she needed every penny even if it narked her that she could only afford the studio because of Jem's money. She winced at the thought of him paying over the odds, making sure she went to London so Fergus would go to the US. She retreated inside and had started upstairs when she heard a noise outside the front door then footsteps. Bella stood and listened, tiptoeing to the front door she opened it quietly and looked out. No one. But her coat was hanging on the door handle and in the pocket was a bunch of beautifully scented tea roses.

CHAPTER 38

'I'll miss you, Bella. It's always been on the cards, you going away, but I didn't think it would happen this quickly.' Bella was sitting outside The Ship with Iain. 'We never really got started, did we?'

'Bad timing for us.'

'What are you going to do with all your sex stuff?'

'What?' she giggled.

'I saw everything in your basket. I'm a detective, remember.'

They laughed, enjoying each other's company. 'I'm taking it to London. They have long sell-by dates – I checked.'

Iain roared.

'You'll come to the night out next week?' she asked.

'You bet.'

Bella had also met Pam and Jean in a café on the Perth Road, one of their old haunts. They were still shocked at what Keren had done, the things she'd said.

'We could've been there for you much more than we were; I'm sorry, and now you're off and we won't see you,' Pam said.

'It's only London. Come and visit once I'm settled. Like you used to years ago.'

Jean had booked the tapas restaurant for the night out. It would be strange with no Keren, and without Dali as well. Bella was still intrigued that Dorothea had him in her notebook, but it would be awkward to contact him and not invite him to the night out or invite him without Keren.

'Roddy and Lorna are coming – shock! You'll meet Amina and Celeste, my chums in the Ferry – and Mr Mirza. Iain MacBain. Aunt Nettie, of course.'

'No Jem?' asked Pam.

Bella looked away. 'Nah. Too much water under that bridge.'

Jean squeezed Bella's hand. 'Are you sure?'

'I'm sure. Oh, I've thought about it.' Bella gave a weak laugh that barely hid a stifled sob. 'I've been here, there and everywhere like crazy thinking about it. But I'm fifty-two, not twenty-two, although I behave like it sometimes. Thirty years. Truth is we're not the same people; we're strangers to each other after all this time. I'm going to London with a job and a place to stay. But what makes me happy is being here with you, still friends after all these years.'

'Stop it. You'll have my mascara running,' said Pam.

Hardest had been the private goodbye to Amina and Celeste.

'When you said it was all sorted, a big part of me wished you wouldn't go, even if it meant not having the job,' Celeste said.

They were sitting in the garden, having an impromptu party. It was cold and they were wrapped up to eke out the summer while it was here.

'I'll miss you too, Bella. We've had super fun. Not to mention my accounts and business set up is all in order, thanks to you. This influencer is a limited company!'

'Woohoo! Congratulations!' Bella said as she filled their glasses and they all glugged the Prosecco. 'I'll miss you both as well. I was lost when I first moved and you both helped me so much.' Bella's voice wobbled. 'Listen to us. It's all good. We're embracing the changes in our lives.' Swooping seagulls cawed loudly above their heads. 'I'm even going to miss the Evil McSneagulls and their damn squawking!'

'That's going a bit too far,' said Celeste sensibly as she opened another bottle.

Bella was doing yet another mental tot up of her finances and losing track. There was enough, she didn't need to keep going over it, but she did: deposit paid; first month's rent paid; money to live (very cheaply) for a month; car to sell.

Her mother had liked Bella working in London. 'Opportunities I never had,' was a constant refrain when she came home. Those visits were pointless; her mother was always in meetings with Roddy to discuss the business or out with friends. Bella rattled round the house alone and saw more of her friends and Aunt Nettie than she did her mother, who apparently only had time for a morning coffee. Bella would wonder why she bothered and vow never to return, then Dorothea would complain and the well-rehearsed dance would start again.

She'd sorted what she would take and what to leave behind. It would be a wrench to leave the cottage; it had become her home and when she flicked through the photos of when she'd first arrived, Bella could see what she'd achieved. Broughty Ferry had grown on her: she'd mooched the charity shops like a true connoisseur, loved the little galleries and, of course, the beach – she would miss the beach most. She hadn't become a runner like Celeste but she was a walker, wandering at night and early mornings, the long summer days of Scotland a balm for those who didn't sleep well. Bella decided to head out.

The seaside was empty at 6 am and she beachcombed along the sand, picking up shells and bits of driftwood, watching the early morning swimmers. She looked up and saw Jem jogging along the promenade; he cut off and ran towards her.

'Can't sleep?'

'No. You too?'

'I've got into a habit of waking at six and going for a run. I guess it's harder to leave a routine behind than you think.'

They fell into step along the shore.

'Bella. I'm sorry about the chairs. I wasn't thinking how it would appear. I didn't mean to be underhand...' He looked at her. 'It was only … after everything we had, everything we went through, I wanted a part of you to take home with me. A happy part, something to take away the bad feeling from the past. You working on them, creating beauty out of what they were – I loved it. How you brought them to their former glory, so they could be cherished and appreciated again. I could have them in my house with me… I wanted them. It wasn't a pity buy.'

Bella caressed his cheek, and he moved his head to kiss her palm. 'It was a lovely thing to do. I'm sorry for how I reacted. I'm being hypersensitive and we need to stop apologising to each other.'

Jem encased her hand in his. 'You're right. No more apologising.' When he released her, she missed the warmth of his touch.

'When do you go?'

'Next Sunday. I'll miss this beach, listening to the waves.' Bella indicated the expanse before them.

'It's kind of got to me too. Must be all the sea air.'

'When will you and Fergus leave?'

'A couple of weeks; I need to get things organised.'

They stood quietly together, comfortable in the silence, then Bella said, 'I'm having a leaving party, food and drinks – do you … do you want to come?' The invite had popped out, unplanned. 'It's on Friday, we're going for tapas – Jean's organised it but there's room. You'll know most of the others. From before.' She was rambling.

'I'd love to come.' They smiled at each other.

'Eight o'clock.'

'Where is it?'

'I'll text you the address. It's near the front.'

'OK. Thanks.'

'I'd better be going – work.'

'I'll see you at the night out.' Jem turned and jogged off then called over his shoulder 'Renaissance. It's an excellent name, if you ever think of a second career.'

Bella watched him until he was out of sight.

CHAPTER 39

Bella had gone through her limited wardrobe umpteen times. In the end she wore one of the original tops Amina had found. She needed a camisole because it was see-through, but the fine fabric aided the all-important temperature regulation. She paired it with lightweight black trousers and the boots – she must buy new footwear when she had a salary again.

Regarding herself in the mirror, Bella had to admit she didn't look too shabby. She remembered the night of Keren's party and realised how stressed out and lost she'd been in comparison. There was a knock at the door and Amina poked an arm round, holding a cocktail shaker.

'Margarita, anyone?' she called as she came in. 'I made this as a little pick-me-up before we go in case you're feeling on edge. Leaving do and all.' She whipped two margarita glasses out of her bag – a recycled one Bella had made her – and poured.

'Mmm. Very tasty. You make a mean cocktail. Woohoo.' Bella reacted to the zing of the alcohol hitting her bloodstream.

'The place is so chi-chi. You've given it a super makeover.'

'I think it's sold. Roddy's tight-lipped but he's been showing people round while I was at work and it's no longer on the estate agent's page. I'll miss it.'

'You'll make another home – wherever you go. But it won't be the same without you.'

'I'll miss you, Amina. You've been a true friend and guru. Thank you. Not to mention what you've done for my hair. Your potions certainly keep the wire under control.'

They downed the rest of the cocktail. 'Mmm. Lovely. Shall we?'

They floated out into the night, sailing along on the punch of the alcohol and, thinking they'd arrived in good time, were surprised to see everyone already seated with jugs of margaritas lined along the table. They greeted her with a huge cheer.

'I made sure we were here early; a bit of detective work with Mr Mirza got me Celeste's number. Sorry, Amina, we knew you would come together so couldn't tell you.' Pam made sure Bella was seated at the top of the table and as she took her place she noticed the empty chair. Jem hadn't come. Disappointment settled in her stomach – at least they'd parted in friendship. Bella smiled gamely thanking Jean and Pam and they all toasted, tapping everyone's glass while making eye contact. They looked crazy. Aunt Nettie joined in with a tiny measure.

'There's an empty chair. Everyone's here, they must have miscounted. Waiter, would you mind—?' Pam was in organiser mode but she stopped mid flow and Bella turned to see Jem striding towards them, casually dressed in jeans and T-shirt, his battered leather under his arm.

'It's for me, I think?'

Bella's heart soared. Along the table she was aware of Pam and Jean nudging each other.

'Come and sit down, Jem,' Pam called.

On his way to the chair he stopped and kissed Bella on the cheek. 'Sorry, I'm late – unexpected work stuff.'

The party started to swing. Food flowed out from the kitchens on large trays twirled flamboyantly by the waiters and were placed on the table. Hungry hands stretched out for the tapas. The jugs of margaritas were replenished, as were jugs of water, but only Mr Mirza and Aunt Nettie were sensible enough to drink much of it. They got louder and laughed more; even Roddy was joining in, pink in the face and smiling inanely as Amina brandished her mobile towards him, scrolling through her images, no doubt educating him into the world of the influencer.

Aunt Nettie stood up. 'Bella, darling. I think it's time for me to go, and Abid is very kindly going to take me home.'

Abid? Mr Mirza – of course.

'Thanks for coming.' Bella hugged her aunt and the guests queued up to kiss her too.

'Stop it. Or I'll never get home,' she laughed, loving every minute of it.

'I'll see you both before I go,' Bella called after her aunt and Mr Mirza. They settled again and Bella found herself next to Jem.

'It's a great night, lovely seeing Aunt Nettie after all these years.'

'You must be keen to see Ben?'

'Yeah, I miss him a lot. Of course, he doesn't miss his old dad. His life is too full. Not sure how much he studies but he gets good grades. He's found a job for the summer in LA while he decides what to do next.'

'What about you? What will you do next?'

'Stay away from work. Get a clear head to think about the future, and about Dad. Concentrate on his treatment and looking after him.'

'*Let's all go dancing!*' Iain bellowed down the table. The party jumped up as one and before anyone knew what was happening, they were out on the street.

'The bill! We've done a runner!' Pam shouted. 'Come on – quick!'

'No, it's all sorted. Will and I did it earlier,' Jean slurred. Bella was overcome with alcohol and gratitude.

'I love you guys.' She flung her arms round them both and tottered slightly.

'Follow me!' Iain had his hands raised in the air and they weaved along the street behind him, like a bunch of tourists. He led them to a bar with a late licence, a DJ and a tiny dance floor, and Iain ushered them in like a traffic cop. 'Come on, come on, let's be having you.'

The DJ gauged the age of the group falling in the door and laid on the vintage tracks. As one they hit the dance floor. Culture Club, Wham, Pet Shop Boys, Cher – they gave it laldy. Amina, a true retro devotee, did not let the side down and danced as if she'd been there the first time round. Bananarama sang out from the sound system and Pam, Jean and Bella did the moves like old times. Iain arrived from the bar balancing a tray of tequila shots and they slammed them down. A collective madness had overtaken the group as they got lost in the music of their youth. Queen's *Don't Stop Me Now* came on and Bella danced wildly.

'Don't. Stop. Me. Now,' she sang as she let herself go. She was going to London and she was with all her friends and Jem was here. Jem. The DJ slowed the music down with Tracy Chapman's *Baby Can I Hold You Tonight*. Bella swayed to the music, and Jem appeared beside her, taking her hand, pulling her close, and she moved into his embrace. Catapulted to the past, Bella remembered dancing to the track with Jem at a party, about six months before they broke up; before her life went off track and she got hurt and lost. The lyrics resonated, full of meaning for what had been between them. Jem was holding her tonight, and years had gone by but it felt like no time – his body against hers as they danced, immersed in the music and each other.

No sooner was the dance over than they were out on the street, those travelling into town ready to get into waiting taxis. Celeste and Amina dived into a cab and Iain stood at the cab door. 'We're going to a club in the centre, Bella. Do you want to come?'

'I've had an amazing night and I'm going to end it here. Thanks, Iain.' She gave him a big smacker on the cheek.

Soon all the others had gone and Jem and Bella were left standing together on a deserted street. They turned towards Bella's cottage and she could feel Jem beside her with every inch of her being, their hands occasionally touching. When they got to the front door, Jem leant down and kissed her lips. Too briefly. They stared at each other for a long time. Bella didn't want to breathe, to break the spell.

'Good luck, Belle. I hope all goes well.'

'For you, too, and with Fergus.' And still they gazed until Bella opened the door and Jem followed her inside.

They moved towards each other. Jem's lips crushed down on hers and he kissed her in a way she hadn't been kissed for a long, long time. She could feel Jem's warm, sweet breath on her neck, his lips as he suckled into her. They undressed each other, peeling away the years. Bella's skin electrified under his touch and he carried her upstairs, where they made love as if they could make up for the time they had lost.

They woke in the smallest hours, ravenously hungry and thirsty. Jem whipped up a pasta dish with ingredients Bella had forgotten were in the cupboard. He pulled Bella onto his lap as they shared the plate of food, feeding each other, savouring the closeness. There were whispered conversations, remembering happier times – nothing of the intervening years between their tragic separation and this night. Later, in bed, Bella's body exploded with a tumultuous hot flush and Jem rushed to open the window, fanning her with a magazine until she cooled down – enough to make sweet love once more.

CHAPTER 40

As Bella slowly came to, she tried to work out what the noise was. It was her phone, and she had the feeling it had been ringing for a while. The clock read 6 am as she unwrapped herself from Jem and rustled around in her bag beside the bed. Roddy. She croaked out, 'Hello?'

'Annabella! At last. It's Aunt Nettie. She's had a fall. You need to come. I'm at the hospital, she's in the operating theatre.'

'What? What happened?' She could feel Jem stirring beside her.

'It's all the info I have. Phone me when you get here.' Roddy clicked off.

'What's wrong?' Jem asked.

She jumped out of bed with no regard for her nudity. 'It's Aunt Nettie. She's in hospital. I have to go.' Bella turned full circle, trying to pull herself together.

'I'll phone a taxi and come with you.' He got up as she threw clothes on and ran into the bathroom, returning after quickly washing and brushing her teeth.

'You can't come with me. You've got your dad to think about; I'll be fine, don't worry about me.'

Jem held her hand. 'We need to talk.'

Bella could only think of her aunt. 'I have to go.'

In the lane, the taxi appeared as Jem drew her close. He kissed her lips and held her cheek. 'She's in the best place for whatever's happened.'

Bella nodded and broke away from him, sinking into the rear seat of the cab, head clanging, the remnants of tequila swilling around her brain. 'Ninewells hospital, please.' She made sure her purse was in her bag and prayed her aunt wasn't badly hurt. Looking at her phone, she saw she had missed calls from Roddy and an unidentified number. It was probably the hospital, Bella thought, as she gritted her teeth and willed the taxi faster.

She found Roddy in the waiting room he'd directed her to. 'How is she? Is there any news?'

Her brother looked dreadful, hair all over the place, his face blotchy and unshaven.

'No, she's being operated on. She fell and hurt her head so it's cause for concern.'

'What else did they say?' Bella's hand shook as she pushed her hair out of her face.

'Nothing else.' They sat side by side in silent vigil. At one point Bella got up to find water and Roddy gulped his down gratefully. An hour passed, then two.

'I should've made sure she got home safely,' Bella blurted out. She'd been turning events over in her head – how much had Aunt Nettie had to drink? Surely it was the one tiny glass. She'd been so caught up with Jem and downing margaritas she didn't think about anyone else. Her phone beeped – Pam.

Well?!!! It beeped again. *Did you and Jem....?* followed by salacious emojis.

Bella switched the phone off and went in search of news. As soon as she was out of theatre, the doctor would come and speak to them, the nurse told her. The siblings paced the corridor, no longer able to sit, Bella occasionally wiped frantic tears as her innermost fears spilled out and Roddy was clearly agitated. At last, a doctor arrived and they looked to her for comfort.

'Your aunt had a nasty fall. She's fractured her skull and had a brain bleed. We've managed to stem it, but we won't be able to assess what the damage is until she wakes up. She's heavily sedated and will be for twenty-four hours; it protects the brain from swelling, giving her the chance to heal as quickly as possible.'

'So we won't know until tomorrow?' Bella's voice broke as she asked.

'It could be a couple of days, longer. We have to be patient.'

'Did her neighbour say what happened?' Roddy asked.

The doctor's pager beeped and she glanced at it. 'I understand she fell going into her flat; when her neighbour came home he saw her on the floor. He called the ambulance and came with her.'

'She could have been lying there for ages.'

The doctor looked at her notes. 'Annabella, isn't it?' Bella nodded miserably. 'Look, your aunt's in the best place; we've stopped the bleed and nurses will be checking at regular intervals. Why don't you pop in and see her, she's in a private room off Ward 12. There won't be any updates for a while so you should come back later instead.' The pager beeped again. 'I'm sorry. I have to go.'

They thanked her and made their way to a small room off the ward where Aunt Nettie lay, a tiny figure hooked up to numerous wires and machines beside her bed. A nurse was writing up notes. The patient was as pale as the bandage covering her head, and a metal brace confined her neck and shoulders. Roddy placed his hand on Bella's shoulder.

'She's strong, she'll pull through this.'

The nurse whispered, 'I'm sure your aunt will be fine; she'll need a lot of care when she gets out and you can shower all your love on her then.' Bella stroked her aunt's hand. 'For the next wee while it's good to let us do our job and take care of her.'

Bella and Roddy kissed their aunt goodbye and left.

'We should go to her flat. Make sure it's secure. I've got her key.' Bella fished around in her bag while a taxi sped them up the road. They opened the front door with trepidation and saw a pool of blood in the hallway.

Roddy blanched.

'You go and sit down; I'll clear this up.' There was a small rug in the vestibule and Bella thought this may have been the cause of her aunt's fall. She rolled up the rug and washed the blood away. She gathered nightdresses, a toiletry bag and her aunt's favourite hand cream. 'For when she wakes up.' Roddy stared into space. Bella was worried about him; he looked truly dreadful. 'Let's go down to the house and have a cup of tea. We need it.'

***

Lorna made the siblings hot drinks and served jugs of water while they updated her on Aunt Nettie's condition. She then served up a full Scottish breakfast Bella thought she couldn't face but wolfed down. More tea followed and Bella felt more human, her body rehydrated.

'I suppose your London plans are adrift, Annabella,' said Lorna.

Bella sat up straight. London and what might happen hadn't entered her head. There was no way she would be travelling this weekend. She'd need to ask for time off – already.

'I mean, she'll need long-term care and I can't do it. I have the children and a husband to look after. Roddy is far too busy.' Her brother sat at the end of the table and said nothing, a useless lump.

'But she'll recover,' said Bella. 'She'll be fine.'

'I'm just saying, you might have to rethink London. You have responsibilities here.'

Bella got up, plunging her hands in her pockets to stop her from grabbing Lorna's hair and birling her around the kitchen with it.

'Annabella will be able to go to London. We'll look after Aunt Nettie.' The zombie had spoken, shocking both Lorna and Bella with his response. Jeez, had her brother found a heart?

'C'mon, Roddy, let's go to the hospital.'

***

They met the doctor outside Aunt Nettie's room.

'There's encouraging signs of healthy brain activity, but it'll be morning before we can assess properly. You can sit and talk quietly, let her know you're here. I'm a firm believer in the subconscious sensing loved ones' presence, so it can only be good for you to stay a while.'

She left them to it and Bella sat and stared at her aunt's chest rising and falling, while Roddy scrolled through his phone. Bella remembered the clothes and toiletries she'd brought and packed them into the bedside cabinet.

'You'll need to leave the cottage,' Roddy said quietly.

'What?'

'The missives are signed, the sale's going through. You can come and stay at the house until we understand what's happening with Auntie Nettie and you know what you're doing.'

'But it'll be weeks until the move-in date.' Bella whispered. Roddy's recently-found heart had retreated under its stone.

'There's work that needs to be done that we agreed for the sale and it'll be much easier if it's empty to complete it in time. I'm only keeping you in the loop.'

Bella rubbed her hands down her face. 'For God's sake, Roddy, can you not give me a break? And I know what I'm doing – I'm still going to London – but Aunt Nettie needs to be well, first.' She looked at her brother. 'You look awful. Why don't you go home; I'll stay and update you with any news.' She wanted him out of there, to be alone with her fears.

'You don't exactly look a picture yourself – have you looked in a mirror today?' The whispering between them was getting louder.

'I don't think this was the kind of subconscious presence the doctor was referring to!'

'Right, I'm going. Make sure you've got your phone switched on.' Roddy's whispering was becoming a shout.

'Shh! Heavens, Roddy, get a grip, think about Aunt Nettie.' The response was the swinging of the door; he was gone. What was wrong with the man? One minute fine, the next a maniac. You'd think he was menopausal.

Bella looked at her phone; it was switched off. Truth was she didn't want to speak to anyone. The thought of moving into her mother's house made her sick – sick and tired. Jem flitted into her mind. The passion of being with him had been so powerful – it scared her to examine the strength of her feelings. She pushed the memories of them together out of her mind and focused on her aunt, willing her to recover, praying she would be all right. Let the octogenarian, once so full of joie de vivre, return to them. Bella lifted her aunt's hand and held it.

CHAPTER 41

Bella jolted awake, disoriented. A nurse was monitoring her aunt and updating the notes.

'What time is it?'

'It's 4 am and Henrietta is doing fine. She's coming round and the doctor will be here soon. Why don't you soak one of these little sponge sticks with water and run it across her lips? She'll be moving a little bit, but don't worry, we've got her head well supported.' The nurse left and Bella gently used the sponge.

As dawn crept into the room, her aunt moaned and looked around.

'You're in hospital, and you're being well looked after.' Bella stroked her cheek.

Another doctor came in, read the notes, and shone a tiny torch into the patient's eyes.

'Thirsty.' A whisper, coming from her aunt. Bella moved in from the other side and pressed liquid into her aunt's mouth from the sponge as the doctor examined the dressing.

'You've had a nasty fall and banged your head, Ms McCaa. Do you understand?' The doctor placed a gentle hand on her forehead, his voice over-loud in the still room.

Aunt Nettie nodded slightly.

'We're monitoring you, so we'll be in often. Rest is best.' The patient gave another small nod and dropped off to sleep. The doctor moved toward the door and motioned Bella to follow him. The door swung gently behind her.

'What do you think?' she asked.

'It's an excellent sign she's been awake and can take in her situation.'

'How long do you think she'll be here?'

'It's early doors but up to a week. Probably residential care before she goes home. The worry is whether the head injury plays with her balance and impairs mobility. Does she have anyone at home?'

'No, she lives alone and she loves that, the independence.'

'Let's not jump the gun. You should go home and come back this evening. She'll be well looked after here and will sleep most of the day I think.'

The doctor went on his way with a swish of his white coat.

'Can the residential care be a private nursing home?' Bella called.

'Yes, it can, as long as they're set up with good systems in place for those who are in medical recuperation.'

'Thanks, Doctor.'

Bella went back in, surprised anew how frail her aunt looked. 'I'm going home for a little while.' She spoke softly, moistening her aunt's mouth with the sponge before leaving the room, out into the bustle of the ward.

During the long taxi ride home, Bella switched her phone on and looked at messages. All her friends had been in touch, initially about the party night, but when they'd had no response, wondering if she had alcohol poisoning or escaped to the south already. There was a text from Jem asking how her aunt was and if she needed help. Two voicemails from Shirley. *London.* She was going to have to deal with the job and her absence today. A week and residential care – could she leave for London before her aunt got home again?

Bella reluctantly video-called Shirley; she couldn't put it off any longer.

'Are you not on the road yet?' Shirley, dressed in a kimono, had a pen and document in hand.

'Oh Shirley. It's—' Bella swallowed, finding it hard to tell her friend the news.

'What is it? What's wrong?'

'My aunt had a fall and we've been at the hospital. She hurt her head and needed an operation.' Bella blew her nose. 'We're not sure how it's going to affect her yet; could be days. Or longer. I can't leave until I know what's going on. I'm so sorry. Do you think Chris'll wait a week or so?'

'God, Bella – I'm sorry. What does the doctor say?'

'Her mobility might be impaired. I can't leave her—'

'I don't know about Chris – Abigail is on maternity leave already.'

'I'll email him today and tell him. There's no one else to take care of her. Roddy means well but he's useless.'

'Be careful, Bella. I don't want to sound cruel but please don't give up this second chance to be a carer for your aunt. It's premature to say, but you must think about yourself.'

'It won't be like Dorothea. I just need to know she'll be OK. My aunt always wanted to move into a particular home anyway and was talking about it at Christmas. But it's horrible talking about homes and care, even for a short stay. I can't leave Dundee yet. What a mess.'

'I'm sure Chris'll understand. A week, two weeks max, and you'll be here. Remember, your aunt is strong.'

'She is. She's also eighty-four. I better go and email Chris to warn him. I can phone him tomorrow to explain more fully. I'm sorry, Shirley.'

'Nonsense, don't apologise. Life. Life is what happens when you're making plans. Keep me up to date and take care of yourself, too. *Ciao*.' Shirley was gone. Despite the encouraging words, Bella sensed her disappointment and hated letting her down. Her phone chirped. Jem.

How's your aunt? Will you postpone London? It would be great to see you, to talk. Are you around for a coffee/drink later? X

Bella was digesting the text when the phone rang. Roddy.

'What's the news? Are you at the hospital?'

'At home. The doctor thinks she might be in for a week or so then residential care. But it can be private

– remember she always wanted to go the Tides on the beach front? I'm going to call them.'

'It needs to be a place with full medical care. No point wasting money when there're NHS places that can do the job.'

Bella fumed. 'She has the money, for heaven's sake.'

'When are you going to London?'

'When she's better. I told you.'

'Why don't we visit at separate times? I'll go at three o'clock – why don't you go at five? Makes sense. I've got stuff to do this evening. And we need to confirm a date for you moving out, whatever happens.'

'Fine. Bye.' Bella clicked the phone off, sick of her brother. She'd check out the Tides anyway. If her aunt couldn't go home, it would be nice for her to be where she wanted to go, where she had friends already. Aunt Nettie had plenty of money; it wasn't going to cost him. What was wrong with the man? She switched the phone off and threw it on the sofa. 'Let me go to London!' she shouted.

Running a bath and pouring in aromatherapy oils brought a welcome calm and she sank into the heat, letting the scents do their therapeutic work. The water soothed her aching muscles, and she relaxed, allowing herself to think of Jem. It had been wonderful to make love, to be touched and held; to be desired, to desire. Her body had melted against Jem's, his touch filling her with a long-suppressed need, a sexuality she'd feared had gone. Bella's temperature rose as she remembered how uninhibited they'd been with each other and she lay daydreaming until the bath cooled and the chill brought her out of her reverie.

Bone-weary, she crawled into bed, still a tangled mess from Friday night. As she pulled the duvet around her, she could smell Jem and crushed the scent to her as she fell into a deep, rejuvenating sleep.

***

When Bella arrived, Roddy was coming out of the ward.

'How is she?'

'She's been awake. Wanted to know if her flat was locked up, so she's on the ball. I think she's going to be OK. How long will you stay?'

'Till they throw me out, I suppose. I'll text you with any news.'

Roddy, a more amiable version of his earlier self, ambled off.

The invalid was sleeping and Bella sat beside the bed. She spent the time composing a draft email to Chris. She also sent a holding text updating all as to what had happened and saying she'd be in touch. Next she texted Jem. She didn't want to make any arrangements until she knew for sure about her aunt, but it would be good to see him. Could they rekindle what was there such a long time ago? Her heart told her she wanted to see him again. Would he want to? He seemed keen to meet. But Jem had his son and his life in the US to return to – and she was moving to London.

Aunt N not out of the woods yet but getting better. Am at the hospital. What else should she say? Bella dithered and then got bored with her infantile behaviour. *Will know more in a couple of days.* She added an *x* and pressed send.

'London.' A soft voice croaked from the bed and Bella was up and giving her aunt water. She placed the straw in her mouth and the patient had a grateful sip. 'Thank you.' Her aunt licked her lips, opened her eyes slightly. 'This mustn't stop you going to London.'

'I'm staying until you're on your feet. You gave us such a fright. All's fine in London; the job'll wait. Please don't worry. How's your head?'

'Tender.' She gave a weak smile.

'Concentrate on getting better and getting out of here, and you'll be home again in no time.'

'I hope so,' her aunt whispered and closed her eyes. Bella stayed the night, drifting in and out, making sure her aunt had water to sip, or to moisten her lips. When Bella came to in the morning the original doctor was on duty and her aunt was awake.

'How's my patient?' She lifted her aunt's dressing and scrutinised the wound. 'You're healing well.'

'How long…?' It was an effort for Aunt Nettie to pull out the question.

'How long will you be in?' Her aunt nodded. 'I think a couple more days at least and we'll talk about putting a care package in place. We need to see you up and about first; residential care may not be needed. We're strict round here and we'll have the physio with you this afternoon to make you work.' The patient smiled wanly. 'The nurses will be in soon to organise a bed bath so you've got a busy day ahead. I'll look in later.'

Bella followed the doctor.

'Is she going to be OK? And home soon?' Bella's guilt erupted asking the questions, hating her selfishness in thinking about her own plans.

'I think she's coming on. Tests and exercises will be done today and I'll have a report then, but I'm pleased with her progress. We need to see her walking and check how her balance is. You should go home, too. Your aunt will be busy and in between will need rest.'

'Doctor, thanks so much for looking after her. I'm sorry, I didn't catch your name.'

'It's Dr Jardine.'

'Thank you; we appreciate it.'

Bella stood in the corridor. Could she go to London and leave her aunt while she was still recovering? Was two weeks enough time? The care package; Michelle; she could get Roddy to pay for a nurse if he and Lorna were going to be too busy. He did seem happy about her going to London. Surely it would be alright to stay in the cottage until then?

CHAPTER 42

'It does sound hopeful about your aunt.' Bella and Amina chatted over the garden wall. 'Brill they're going to wait for you in London.'

'I could tell they weren't happy. It's going to be a pain for them.' Bella had been making calls about the job – Shirley, Chris, personnel. 'At least the studio's all paid for but it means I'll only have two weeks to find an alternative once I'm down there.'

'You'll make it work; you're so close to getting everything you want.' Amina looked at her watch. 'Right, I must fly. I'm styling a photoshoot today for The Sunday Post – success at last!'

Bella smiled. 'Fantastic. Hope it goes well.' Amina went off and Bella was conscious of her tummy growling; she'd hardly eaten over the last twenty-four hours and a full Scottish was what she needed.

She headed out, taking the beach route towards sustenance. It was barely warm, but hardy Scottish children ran in and out of the water, screaming their heads off – it would be Baltic. She couldn't stop her head flitting between her aunt, London, Jem and her job, and then settling on her aunt again.

It was the woman she noticed first – tall and willowy with wide palazzo pants and an expensively sloppy jumper. She flung her arms around her male companion's waist, whispering in his ear, and whatever it was made him laugh. With a gut-wrenching twist of her insides she registered that the man was Jem and he saw her at the same time. There was nowhere for Bella to hide as they walked towards each other.

'Hi.' At least Jem looked uncomfortable. So here was the reason she hadn't heard from him since her text. No one spoke. The woman disentangled herself from Jem and shot her hand out with a friendly, open smile. 'Cassie. I've been looking forward to meeting Jem's old buddies.' Bella shook Cassie's manicured hand, marveling at her confident manner and distinctive New York accent.

'Bella. Jem and I were at school together – a long time ago.' What else could she say?

'How's your aunt?' Jem asked.

'Better thanks.' She looked at her feet; she didn't want him to see what was inside. 'Enjoy your time here.' She directed this at Cassie and stepped aside to let them pass.

'I will. Jem's giving me the tour – it's good to see what's been keeping him away.' She linked in with Jem as Bella stuck an empty smile on her face, looking at Jem as he walked on – but he couldn't meet her eye.

What an idiot. Of course, there would be a woman in his life. Of course, it would be a tall, glamorous, attractive woman. She seemed lovely, with a genuine warmth about her. Bella had been utterly foolish letting her imagination run riot. The pain was physical, twisting her heart. She wanted to run away as far as possible and immediately came off the beach straight into Long Lane, and as she went over one of the crossroads, she saw them again stepping into the main road, this time apart. Darting out of sight, Bella retreated and took the long way home.

She went straight into the garden, gulping air into her constricted lungs. Thank God she was moving to London. She'd let herself get carried away over one stupid interlude. She'd been so grateful for Jem's touch she'd read far too much into it. It was only sex. They'd used each other to relive their youth. Bella lay face down on the grass and welcomed the damp, cold earth as seagulls screeched overhead. Her breasts were tender underneath her, but she couldn't move. She wanted to lie there and never get up again.

A warm splat on her hand brought her out of the fugue. Seagull shit. Bella stared at it. She'd never believed the bullshit that birdshit was lucky. It summed up her life – crapped upon, from a great height. Fuck Jem, and her foolishness. She was a middle-aged menopausal cliché. It was a drunken one-night stand of no consequence. London was happening, a job and new horizons beckoned. Plenty more fish in the sea.

She heard her mobile ringing and was tempted to leave it until she remembered it might be about her aunt. Inside she looked at the screen. Jem. He could flaff off. She ignored the ringing and washed the guano off her hand. A text pinged in. Jem again:

I'm sorry. I wanted to explain but didn't get the chance before Cassie arrived. Can we meet? X

Bella's fingers rattled across her phone:

You don't owe me any explanations. It was one mad night down memory lane. Hope it works out for you with Cassie.

She was going to put a kiss but it stuck in her craw. She pressed send and switched the contraption off.

***

Bella drove to the hospital and, over the next couple of days, focused on her aunt getting better. There was much improvement but her balance was impaired and she needed all of Bella's support to walk around the ward. The doctor didn't think this was permanent, but Aunt Nettie's confidence had gone. It was agonising seeing her so unsure of herself and Bella hoped that, once home and in her own territory, her confidence would return. The care package was coming together and she would be out in a couple of days, with no need to go into a residential home for further recuperation. The rest of the time Bella pottered, glazed over more rules and regulations and read the finance pages – which only made her doze off.

Avoiding the beach, she popped in to see Celeste who was loving being in work. Mr Mirza was pleased too, no longer missing his 'young Annabella'. She kept her other friends at bay with texted updates and was surprised to meet Keren coming out of her aunt's hospital ward one day.

'I wanted to see how she was doing and I hoped I'd bump into you. Do you have time for a coffee? Would you mind?'

Bella looked at her ex-friend. Rather than the usual pristine Keren, this was a dilapidated version, her hair uncombed and a stripe of grey showing thickly along her parting. No make-up. Bella was intrigued to hear what Keren might say and they carried takeaway coffees to the gardens.

'I'm so sorry, Bella. I'm dreadfully sorry – for what I did and how I behaved towards you. It wasn't because you couldn't decide about Jem, and I was helping you out – that was the version I told myself over the years. You moving to London and Jem to New York made it easier to push it out of my mind, and you never mentioned him again – and did so well in London I fooled myself it had been a favour.' Keren looked up at the sky as she blinked tears away. 'The truth is I was so jealous of you. You had it all, and at the party Dali was drunk and asking if you were coming through. I'd had a crush on Dali for years. *Years*. But he never noticed me because wherever we went, you were there too and I could see him watching you, wanting you.'

Bella frowned. 'Me?'

Keren looked at Bella. 'He told me, "I think I'm in love with Annabella." Jem came in with Sandra tottering behind him. Everybody was always fancying everyone else, through school and uni – but not you and Jem. You only ever cared about each other. Jem didn't even notice Sandra, hanging on his every word. And then Dali wanted you, too.' Keren blew into a disintegrating paper hanky. 'When I got to our Edinburgh flat the next day and you wanted to hear how the party went, I lied. It just came out. It was vicious and evil and I hated myself, but I couldn't withdraw it, couldn't admit to you what I'd done. I pushed you to the London internship because I couldn't stand seeing the results of my lies.'

Bella offered Keren a fresh tissue.

'I never saw Jem again, and I heard from Dali he'd gone. It was a couple of years later that Dali and I got together as you know, and as the years went by, I no longer worried about it.' Keren looked at Bella. 'When you came over and challenged me, I was horrible. Pam and Jean said they didn't want anything more to do with me. Dali came home and found the door busted and me crying and I told him.' Keren was sobbing freely and could hardly speak. 'He says he doesn't recognise me; he's disgusted I could do such a thing. He's moved out – he says it's permanent.'

Bella looked at her friend and found no joy in her unhappiness. If Dali had left she was paying a high price for those long-ago lies. But Keren had had twenty-eight years of happiness; she'd had children and a grandchild. A life Bella might have had if she and Jem had stayed together.

'Do you think you could ever forgive me?' asked Keren.

Could she? She was suddenly exhausted by it all – a lie told all these years ago was still impacting on her life so much today. More than ever she wanted to get to London, be the woman she was before, with her high-flying career and an uncomplicated life. Bella sat on the bench and Keren joined her.

'Does it matter?'

'It does to me.' Keren looked broken.

Bella took in the clouds speeding across the sky while Keren watched her. She was so, so tired of it all.

'I forgive you, Keren. We will never be friends again, but I know what it's like to love deeply and hopelessly.' She stood up. 'I hope you and Dali can work things out. He's a good man.'

Keren was making good use of the tissue as Bella left.

CHAPTER 43

Aunt Nettie got out on the Friday – was it only a week since the party? Bella would stay with her at the flat and carers would be coming morning and night. Her aunt was fretful, worried she wouldn't be able to look after herself anymore, and Bella tried to reassure her all would be well, but it might take a while.

'If you wanted to, you could go to the Tides for a short stay; it would help with your confidence and you'd get to see the friends you have there?' She would have twenty-four hour care, at least for a while, and be in good company.

'I'm not ready for that yet!' Her aunt said sharply before going into her bedroom and firmly closing the door. She didn't come out again until their Taiwanese food was delivered. They spent a quiet night together vaguely watching an instantly forgettable film. Bella expertly helped her aunt get ready for bed – years of caring for Dorothea enabled her to gently help her aunt undress and get into nightclothes; to guide her into the bathroom and make sure she was supported through the ritual of washing and brushing teeth.

Once Bella was lying on the sofa, deep sleep evaded her and she tossed and turned in a twilight zone between dozing and dreaming. On the threshold of waking, she was gripped with guilt and indecision about her aunt and London. When sleep did come it was full of her relationship with Jem in happier times, and then reality would dawn bringing confusion and hurt all over again.

She got up and looked out over the city's twinkling lights as the sun rose on her turbulent thoughts. She knew Aunt Nettie wouldn't countenance her staying in Dundee but could she desert her? Her aunt had been such a support all the years of looking after Dorothea. And why, when the Tides had always been spoken of enthusiastically, was she so angry at the suggestion? Was it because it was fine when it was a choice, but when it may be deemed necessary, even for a while, she was dead against it? Bella felt selfish, thinking about the Tides because of her own dilemma.

Closing the window, she huddled under the covers; an icy coldness had settled on her. In the core of her being she'd hoped more would happen between her and Jem. Sleeping with him once more had felt like coming home – and the pain of losing and missing was a tangible wrench, reminiscent of before. How foolish to think time could be reversed and they could be as they were – young and in love with their whole lives ahead of them.

Her aunt was up and about early, albeit wobbly; another reason to be impressed with her stoic relative. A good sleep in her own bed had fortified her and when the carer arrived, she helped with dressing while Bella made tea and toast. Despite her own bad night, Aunt Nettie's condition and spirit made her optimistic for the future.

Noticing she'd left her phone charger at the cottage, her aunt persuaded her she was fine to be left; an old friend was coming over and could take care of her if she needed anything.

'Are you sure you can manage?'

'Yes! I can look after myself, you don't need to be here, you've got things to get on with.'

Bella set out the tea tray and biscuits and issued strict instructions that the friend had to make the tea and carry it through. 'I'll leave the door off the snib so you don't have to get up. I'll only be a couple of hours and *no*! Not negotiable.'

As Bella got into the car and gunned the engine her phone rang – Chris. 'Hello.'

'Hi Bella. How's your aunt?'

'She's much better, thanks, big improvement. I can't tell you how grate—'

Chris jumped in. 'Bella, I have to tell you we've taken on another compliance person for the job. You'll be disappointed, but it was unavoidable. Problems came up last week and we needed to have a representative in the office. We've decided to stick with him. But when you come down, get in touch and we'll talk, yah?' She could hear a gaggle of children shouting in the background. 'Oops, must go. Bye, Bella.' He clicked off and she was left holding a silent phone, unable to process what had happened.

She was still staring at it when it buzzed again. Shirley this time. As much as she wanted to throw it out the window, she pressed the green button.

'Bella! Chris told me he'd called you. I'm so sorry. It all went tits up last week and I brought someone in and Chris got worried you might not have the experience he had to get us out of a hole and, well... Bella? Are you there? I'm so sorry.'

'Yes, I'm here. I understand. Don't worry. You'll have tried all you could. It was a shitty score – I wouldn't employ me. Look I've got to go and pick up my aunt. I'll call later, OK? Bye.' She clicked off, beyond caring about lying.

Bella took the car along side streets, upwards and onwards to The Law. The sky had darkened and soon big drops spattered the window and she flicked on the wipers. As she continued the winding drive up, several cars came down, the occupants escaping the weather.

Parking, Bella got out and, pulling on her coat, headed for the memorial. The place was deserted, the rain pelting down and the wind whipping it everywhere. Bella raised her face to the elements and sank on a bench. The wet seeped through her jeans, giving her a perverse enjoyment in being soaked. Jeez bloody Louise. She had no job, an expensive place to stay, and hardly any cash. She had her car to sell – for scrap. Her aunt was improving – a bit. And if she stayed? She'd have to move in with Roddy, or in with her aunt to look after her if she wasn't ready for the Tides. She could get a part time job, in a shop again, possibly save to get her own apartment in Dundee, rented of course. And put up with seeing Jem about town with the model girlfriend of the year before he jetted off to his New York idyll. The rain plastered her hair to her face but she didn't care.

Returning to London had been the unspoken desire for years. Whenever it reared its head, she would be racked with remorse – there could be no return to her old life while her mother lived, and she couldn't wish Dorothea gone. The days when thoughts of freedom flitted in she tried to banish them. When her mother's health deteriorated, and the doctor had made it plain what was coming, Bella had ramped up the care to compensate for the shame of thinking about her future.

She wanted to banish these wilderness years from her memory, make up for lost time, return to who and what she was – a decent job, her own money, her independence. Another company would need compliance experts. She could re-sit the exam, borrow money on one of these stupid high-interest loans but pay it off quickly. She would lose herself in the anonymity of the huge metropolis and live, rather than just existing. She remembered nights out with Shirley and whoever else was party to a particular negotiation; they would splash out on champagne and expensive restaurants, laughing at how they might have scraped through it but got there in the end. She wanted to be on a crushed underground train, part of the City commuter crowd – London teemed with life and she was so ready to be in amongst it.

A police car came into view, circled round the monument, and slowed to a crawl as it passed Bella, a solitary figure sitting in the pouring rain.

'Y'awright dear?'

Her brain screamed '*Bugger off!*' but she gave a wave instead – only a menopausal middle-aged woman sitting weeping in the rain, nothing to see here. Their appearance gave Bella the impetus to return to her car. She wrung out her hair, her hands as numb as her heart. She'd been boo-hooing so much recently it was a wonder there were any tears left. She thought again: 51.04%. A terrible result incapable of sparking confidence in any employer; no wonder Chris was keen to bring in a replacement.

Bella headed into town. Despite the pouring rain, the traffic was fast-moving and the Mini joined the stream of cars along the river front. She peered through the windscreen, visibility difficult even with wipers on full tilt. The car in front stopped at a set of lights and Bella rammed her foot on the brake in the nick of time. Close call. This was not the time to trash her Mini. She might be selling it for scrap but it had to be decent scrap. Bella sat taking deep breaths while her heart rate lowered to normal. She had to get a grip. It would be fine. Her aunt would be fine.

Wham!

Bella was catapulted from her seat as the Mini was lifted off the ground and rammed into the car in front. The seat belt pinioned her but not before her head had smashed against the windscreen, shattering the glass into a thousand pieces, and she was tossed against the door frame on return. Seconds passed; the sound of the rain receded; all was quiet. Then the driver in front was out of his car and shouting at her as the world returned full force.

She wrestled the handle back and forth but the door would not budge. The driver heaved from the other side, but no joy. Bella released her seatbelt and scrambled across the passenger seat, but when she tried that door it wouldn't budge either. The driver signalled for her to cover her face and she brought her hands up while he elbowed away the shattered windscreen, the glass ricocheting everywhere. She hoisted herself out of the seat and strong hands helped her over the bonnet, the glass remnants biting through her jeans and palms. With the rain crashing down like a tropical storm and horns blaring, she stood on trembling legs. The other driver was livid.

'Bandit! He's run away – bet it's stolen. Bastard!' Bella could see a figure hirpling into the distance.

'What's that?' He squinted at her, pointing at his own forehead. Bella put a hand up and explored a cut. She mopped vaguely with a tissue, but the blood was a constant stream and, mixed with rain, quickly soaked the paper hanky.

'I'm calling the police,' he said, but he'd been beaten to it – sirens wailed louder and louder through the busy traffic.

'Y'awright, dear?' Bella couldn't tell if it was the officer from before, but she was grateful they were on the scene.

He gently laid a large cotton pad on her wound and placed her hand on top to anchor it.

'Press down firmly; forehead bleeds always look worse than they are. The paramedics are on their way.' He ushered her into the rear of the police car and sank into the front seat.

'What a day! Climate change – right here, right now. I'm telling you.'

Bella had no intention of arguing. He noted her statement while his co-worker questioned the other driver, both huddled under a huge umbrella.

'Have you had alcohol today?'

Bella paused, suddenly unsure. Had she? 'No.'

'Are you sure?'

Bella nodded.

'How old are you?'

No hesitation this time. 'Fifty-two.' Tears joined the drips coming off her hair.

'Ach, come on. Fifty-two's not so bad. My mum's fifty-eight!' He dug into his pockets and brought out a pack of Simpsons tissues, passing them over as he keyed the information into the black breathalyser unit. 'Take a nice deep breath and blow as long and hard as you can.'

Bella complied, dizzy with the effort. She handed it over and the officer examined the result. 'See? All good. Zero.'

Another siren could be heard through the rain and intermittent car horns, and soon a paramedic was helping Bella out of the car and into an ambulance.

'How are you doing?' The paramedic looked under the pad pressed to her forehead. 'A nasty wee cut; not too deep though. How you feeling?' Her name badge identified her as Serena.

'My bag. My bag's in the car. The Mini.' Bella indicated the trio of vehicles fused together, with her own a crumpled mess in the middle.

'No worries.' Serena strapped Bella in and dashed into the rain to retrieve the bag while the policeman from earlier informed her that a recovery truck would come and pick up all the vehicles and assess the damage. They'd be in touch soon. He gave her a wet A5 card with all the details of who to call and what would happen. Serena passed over her backpack and jumped in as the siren whooped into life.

She pressed a clean cotton dressing against the cut and taped it in place. 'You'll live. They'll sort you out at the hospital, give you an X-ray, but you seem fine. You're fine, aren't you?' The paramedic lifted the dressing for another peek, then replaced it.

'Yes, I'm fine. It's all going to be fine.' She clung on as the ambulance cleared a path through the traffic.

Bella was pitched out at accident and emergency where she was looked after quickly and efficiently: details taken, head examined and X-rayed, wound cleaned and butterfly clips applied to the cut.

'Who's coming to pick you up?' The nurse handed her two paracetamol and a glass of water. 'You can't leave until you get picked up.' Saying a friend was waiting in the car park, Bella turned toward the exit.

'Not yet! You must have someone with you for twenty-four hours. Here's what to look out for.' The nurse handed Bella a sheet of paper. 'No stress and no contact sports.'

'I definitely will steer clear of contact sports.' Bella hobbled to the exit – stiff and sore and damp and cold – and was soon in a taxi to the cottage. She stripped off and ran a bath, allowing the warmth of the water to bring life back to her freezing core. She submerged under the welcome heat, shutting out as much as she could of what had become a cruel, calamitous day.

CHAPTER 44

Bella squinted at the spyhole when she heard the knock – she wasn't up for seeing anyone, but it was Iain in full regalia so she opened the door.

'I saw on the logs you were in an accident?' He gently pushed her hair away from her face and lifted the dressing. 'Ouch. Looks painful. Are you OK? An accident can give you such a fright. Why don't you sit down and I'll make you a cup of tea.'

Iain's sympathy brought Bella's emotions to the surface and unable to speak, she moved towards the sofa. He sat and put an arm around her while she made good use of his shoulder.

'Here,' he passed the tissue box and Bella had a good blow. 'The four-wheeler, the one that rammed into you, was stolen. Bad for the insurance, can be a real pain.'

'Can it?' Bella reached for another hanky. 'I don't seem to care. I suppose I'll have to do something about it, but not today.'

'First your aunt and then your car; you're not having much luck.' Iain stood up. 'Do you want tea?'

'I can't, I have to get back to my aunt's. I said I'd only be a couple of hours.'

Iain placed his hands on her shoulders and looked at her closely. 'Are you sure you should be going? I think you need a bit of looking after yourself, Bella.'

'I'd better, she's not ready to be on her own yet. I'll be fine.'

'If you're sure? Such a shame about your aunt. What a grand old gal she is. Do you need to ask for time off from the job?'

'They were great about it.' Bella got up. 'I'd better get over there. By bus, of course. Ha ha.' Bella laughed, unable to hide the slight hysterical pitch to it.

'I'll run you over. I've nearly finished my shift and there's not much doing. Even criminals hate the rain – apart from your car thieves and hit-and-run drivers.'

'I'd appreciate it; I don't feel up to bouncing about on a bus. I'll get my things; I'm staying there just now.' Bella set off towards the staircase.

'Saw Jem and his American bird the other day. A bit of a looker – have you met her? I guess being a multi-millionaire has its advantages.' Thankfully, Iain's phone rang so she didn't have to answer. In minutes Bella was ready to go.

'Still OK to give me a lift?'

He nodded. In the car, Bella asked about Iain's daughters, determined to keep him off the subject of Jem. His pride and joy dominated the conversation all the way across town.

***

Aunt Nettie was dozing, laptop precariously balanced on her knees, when Bella let herself in. The chat with her chum must have tired her out. Bella moved to take the laptop but her aunt laid a hand on her arm.

'What's going to happen to me? It's all gone.' She was awake but dreaming, unseeing.

'Relax, you need to rest.' Bella tucked a rug over her knees and Aunt Nettie drifted off to sleep.

The words echoed her own life. 'It's all gone.' No job. No car. And in a couple of weeks, either here or in London, no place of her own to stay. She would get the two grand deposit returned and surely some insurance money for the car, but compensation would take ages. And after? Roddy and his damned kitchen. If she'd been left alone, she would have done so much better – even with the brain fog. Bella sat, dismally going over her meagre options until the carer arrived and got her aunt ready for bed. She saw her to the door afterwards.

'Is your aunt worried?' asked the carer. 'She seems distracted and was asking if she could be forced into care. Has she mentioned it to you?'

'I mentioned it; probably shouldn't have, yet she's always talked about where she would like to go. I think she's worried about losing her independence, not being able to walk unaided.'

'Try and bring it up again, reassure her. The system's here to keep folks at home as long as possible, rather than in a home.'

'I will. Thanks.'

Aunt Nettie was tucked up in bed when she went in. 'You don't need to worry about me. I heard you whispering.'

'We were talking about you and your balance. The doctor told us it would take time and practice; it's only been a week. Why don't we take a wee spin out tomorrow with the walker? It'll be refreshing after being cooped up inside.'

'I am not using *that thing*!'

'OK. OK. No worries.'

'What did you do to your head?'

Bella had almost forgotten the reason behind the painful ringing in her ears and fingered the plaster. 'I was in an accident today and my car's in the garage. A little bump, not serious. Just one of these days.' There's an understatement. 'Need anything?'

'No thanks, I'm fine.'

'Sleep well.'

***

Come morning, Bella was so stiff and sore she had to crawl off the sofa – the after-effects of being tumbled between two cars. The doorbell rang and Bella shuffled off to let the morning carer in.

'God! What happened to you? You've got a right keeker.'

Bella looked in the hall mirror and grimaced. Livid bruising decorated her face from her cheek right up to her forehead and across her eyes. Her shoulder and arm continued the disturbing shades of blue and purple.

'I was in a car accident.' It was surreal. 'It didn't look this bad yesterday.'

'I'd better warn your aunt. I'm Wilma, by the way.'

By the time the carer helped her aunt from the bedroom, Bella had made an unsuccessful stab at breakfast. She'd burnt the toast and forgotten to boil the kettle. She slopped the milk all over the tray. 'Do you want tea, Wilma?'

'No, I'd better get off to my next lady, but thanks for the offer.' Wilma left with a cheery 'See you later'.

'Goodness, look at your face. You need looking after, not the other way around.' Her aunt carefully lowered herself into an armchair.

'I'm fine. It looks worse than it is.' In the kitchen Bella leant against the table, gathering herself. She felt dreadful; queasy, depressed and hopeless. Aunt Nettie hobbled in on the stick and Bella caught her as she swayed off balance. 'Oops. You need more practice, why not try the walker?'

'Stop it! I want to show you how well I'm doing so you can go to London.' Exasperation made her aunt raise her voice.

'But how can I go to London if you won't do what the doctor tells you?' Bella yelled. Aunt and niece were in shock at the outburst.

'I'm sorry,' said Bella as they comforted each other. 'They withdrew the offer of the London job, and the car accident—'

'Oh, Bella. It's all my fault.'

'It's not you, not the fall – I wasn't good enough and they needed an excuse. It'll be fine. I'll find another job. Life would be boring if it was straightforward, wouldn't it?' She tried to sound cheerful.

Her aunt wiped her face with a tissue. 'But you wanted the job. You were so happy at the party, and I don't want to be a burden.'

'You will never be a burden. You're getting better and, as you're always telling me – don't be hard on yourself, take things slowly.' Bella followed her aunt, ready to catch her as she tottered to her chair.

'Right, I'm going to make us a proper breakfast – scrambled eggs and mushrooms on toast?'

The landline rang and Bella left her aunt chatting happily. She went through the motions of making breakfast, but tears kept coming, dripping into the eggs and onto the toast. Every so often, a stifled sob broke free. Bella gulped in mouthfuls of air – she couldn't let her aunt see she'd lost the plot. She composed herself with deep breaths.

Bella laid the tray down with a weak flourish but neither ate much. The day crept by with her aunt unsettled, asking her to do bits and pieces around the house and becoming distracted. Bella wanted to go home and hide under a duvet for a week. Unexpected respite came in the afternoon when her niece, Heather, appeared at the door.

'Wow, your face is a mess.' *Gee, thanks Heather.* Bad news travelled fast; it must have been Lorna on the phone earlier.

'I'm here to look after Auntie Nettie. I've to stay the night.'

'Are you sure? She's unsteady on her feet, you'll need to be able to support and catch her.'

'I'm super fit, thank you very much. The exercise will make up for missing hockey practice.'

'Sorry. I appreciate it.'

'Besides, she needs demolishing at Scrabble, she beat me last time.'

Bella left them sitting at the dining table, sharing out the tiles, determined looks on their faces.

CHAPTER 45

On the bus, she sat as far away from the meagre number of passengers as possible, squashed into the corner, but it didn't stop one old wag observing, 'A right Saturday nicht oot you've hud, hen.'

Bella glared at the woman. Her phone rang and Shirley's name popped up. Reluctantly, she answered.

'Hello!' Rallying to sound cheerful, it was louder than intended.

'Listen, I've got an inspirational solution and I've spoken to Chris and it's 100% all sorted. Come and be a PA. We're always needing them; in fact, I need one – hint hint. The money's good, it's your foot in the door. What do you think?'

Bella didn't think her heart could sink any further, but it did – Shirley was her best friend, but Bella didn't want to be her PA.

'Amazing!' Bella scrunched her face at the thought.

'Isn't it? And if not for me, as … yeah, might be a bit weird,' Shirl giggled, 'Nick St Johnston needs a PA – remember him?'

Bella did; she used to be his boss, all these years ago – a right little wanker. Bile rose in her throat.

'Are you in the car?'

'Yes, so I'd better get off. But this is great news. I'll call later, OK? Thanks.'

Bella ended the call but before she had time to process this latest humiliation, Michelle's name appeared as the phone rang immediately.

'Is anything wrong?' Bella was confused – was Michelle supposed to be cleaning her aunt's house today?

'Yes, all good, thanks. Well… Not really. It's a bit embarrassing. I hope you don't mind me saying…'

'Yes?' What could it be?

'Your aunt's cheque bounced. And she forgot to leave one last time, too.'

'Oh no, I'm so sorry.' Her aunt would not let go of the cheque book. 'It keeps me right. I like it,' she'd say. There was no persuading her.

'I'm due another one on Wednesday, so I thought I should mention it.'

'I'm glad you did. How much is it?'

'It's £120 for the week when I did the spring cleaning, £80 for the week after, plus £37.42 for the shopping and then it'll be £45 up to and including Wednesday.'

'I'm sorry, Michelle, and you've been such a Godsend. Can you text me the full amount and your bank details and I'll do a BACS right away. I'll set up a regular transfer too. She must stop using cheques at long last.'

Michelle rang off. With a ping, her details came through and while the bus rattled on to the Ferry, Bella opened her bank app and transferred it over. She now had the princely sum of £317.46 to her name. Taxis, flowers, her aunt's shopping – it all added up. Or down. A text came in:

Bella, please can we meet? I'd like to talk. Jem x

Bella switched off the phone. She had no intention of mortifying herself by meeting Jem and listening to him talk about Cassie and relationships and how he didn't mean to deceive her. No, thank you. Only stopping to stock up on Diet Irn-Bru and a family pack of Caramel Logs, Bella was soon home. Closing the door behind her, she leaned against it and knew how much this little cottage had become a haven.

She relaxed into the Duran Duran T-shirt and her ancient pink candlewick, established herself on the sofa with her tuck and found a film. *Mad Max Fury Road* – brilliant. She chomped through the family pack of biscuits in its entirety and swigged from the can. Waking cramped and cold at 4 am, she found herself thinking, *Why would Aunt Nettie's cheque bounce?*

CHAPTER 46

Why would it bounce? Had one of the standing orders or direct debits she'd set up gone wrong? Her internal radiator rammed up to boiling and she threw off the dressing gown, opened the windows, and flung the garden door wide. Dawn was rising and the thick, cloudy sky took the bite from the breeze wafting in. Bella stood at the fridge and stuck her head in the freezer compartment, vaguely contemplating a business venture of menopausal ice caps.

Drifting over to the sofa she shrugged into the dressing gown, then closed the windows and door before logging on to her laptop. She entered the site in the Cloud where all her passwords and log-on details were stored and was soon in her aunt's bank account. There were various direct debits and all seemed in order. The state and work pensions were going in regularly and all of it should have been topped up with a standing order from savings and investments, but there was no trace of it coming into the account recently. She'd need to get on to the bank tomorrow and find out why it had stopped. Her aunt had made only small purchases recently: flowers from Bloomers;

food deliveries; films; books for her Kindle – but these expenditures shouldn't cause a cheque to bounce.

As she was about to click out, she saw that her aunt's savings were at £11.20. What? The savings account needed more security to get in; she could only see the total. With an authorisation choice between text and email, Bella ticked email, and downloaded her aunt's passwords. She felt like a spy and had to re-set her aunt's details to gain access. She'd tell her about it tomorrow and explain what she was doing. She clicked on 'Savings & Investments'. Yes, £11.20 in the account. The rest, a whopping £475,000, had been paid by cheque to … she clicked on payee … *McCaa Properties*.

Roddy. What had he done? Had he persuaded his aunt she should invest all her money into the new development? There was no way he could have stolen it; he couldn't have got in, not without the details. He must have done a number on her to get more money for the deal. Bella couldn't believe Roddy was capable of such chicanery. She remembered her aunt asking if the development was a good investment. She'd told her aunt it would be, not wanting to worry her and hadn't considered why she was asking. Alarm bells should have rung as her aunt never asked about the company – but she'd ignored it. No wonder her aunt was terrified about going into care – all her money had gone. There would be no Tides Home for Ladies on the beach because Roddy had taken it all. How could he? How could she have let this happen? She wanted to go there immediately and smash all the windows in his swanky Mercedes. It was part of being in business, taking risks and dealing with the results when things went awry, but her aunt shouldn't be part of it.

Bella paced the floor. She had a right to know what was going on – she had an investment in it too, didn't she? Half the house had been swallowed up in it. She wouldn't see him at home. She'd go to the office. This was business – not family. She paced faster and faster across the rug. If they hadn't been messing around with this stupid new investment, she would already be in London. Didn't she have rights? She hadn't even seen a will, for God's sake. Bella couldn't wait to confront Roddy, but it was only 6 am.

She showered and dressed for battle in her jeans, her Docs and the checked shirt she'd hidden from Amina's clutches. The old uniform was comforting and, unable to wait any longer, she set off to walk. The exercise would do her good and she could work out what she was going to say by the time she arrived. Roddy would be in at 8 am with his usual 'busy, busy'. It would be kept professional; she would approach it the way she used to in London when dealing with clients who had been a bit economical with the truth. A way must be found for her aunt's money to be replaced. They could sell the cars, the kids would have to come out of school, but it would take a lot more – these would be sticking plasters over a larger wound.

She hiked all the way from Long Lane to the centre of Dundee and into Whitehall Crescent. Bella spotted Roddy's gleaming Merc parked outside. Out came her penknife and, checking the empty streets, she created a deep and satisfying matching score to the other side.

Calmer, she ran upstairs to the offices and stopped in her tracks. *McCaa Properties*, the engraved plaque stated. She hadn't been here since her father had died and the sight of it blasted the wind from her sails. She regrouped and turned the large brass handle, making her way to her father's old office, flinging the door so wide it battered against the wall. Roddy jumped out of his seat.

'What the hell...? Annabella, what do you think you're doing? Heavens, your face!'

'What the hell do you think *you're* doing?' Very professional. 'I've been in Aunt Nettie's accounts and you've taken *all* she had. She's beside herself worrying she's going to land up God-knows-where because you've taken all the money she had for the home she wanted. What the fuck, Roddy? What the actual fuck? You have to put the money in her account right now. *Right now!*' The last two words bellowed out across the room.

This was an Annabella her brother had never seen – no one had seen.

'Calm down. It'll all be fine. It'll all be fine. You don't need to swear.'

'Swear? Is that what you're worried about? You cannot play with people's lives like this. You utter tosser!' Why did everyone else have to pander to his stupid deal? 'What have you done? Aunt Nettie – *our* Aunt Nettie, is sick with worry about her future and it's your fault. Shit, Roddy, what's happened to you?'

'I'm sorry. I just didn't want to lose the business for Father...' He ran his hands through his hair. 'It won't be much longer.'

'*Stop*! This delusion must stop.'

'But it can't stop – we'll lose the whole project.' Roddy stepped back and his chair rolled away from him. 'It can't, it can't.' He was panting, his face white as a sheet. 'Ugh.' He tried to sit down, but missed the chair and landed on the floor, clutching his arm, his mouth fish-like as he gasped for breath. He was having a heart attack! Bella dashed to the phone on his desk and dialled 999. 'Ambulance please. My brother's having a heart attack.' She rattled off the address and hung up.

She didn't know what to do. She wrapped her brother in her arms. 'Oh, Roddy, please don't die.' She laid his head on top of her parka and loosened his tie. He was groaning in pain but conscious. She tried to ease him into the recovery position, but his hand was clamped around his left arm and she couldn't get it off. The groaning was getting fainter.

'I'm sorry,' she said. 'I'm sorry for shouting.'

In the distance she could hear an ambulance and minutes later, feet were clattering up the stairs. Soon there were two medics, one pulling her out of the way as they assessed him. 'He's stopped breathing.'

'Defib.' A huge bag was opened and they ripped Roddy's shirt completely apart, standing clear as they used the defibrillator once, twice, and for a third time. Bella held her breath.

'He's stabilised. Let's go.'

One of the paramedics placed an oxygen mask over Roddy's mouth and they manoeuvred him gently on to a stretcher to carry him down the stairs. She got into the ambulance behind them and the ambulance took off, the siren screaming loudly while the medic gently tended to his patient.

'What's his name?'

'Roderick McCaa. Roddy. He's my brother.'

'We're going to do all we can for him.' The medic placed his hand on the patient's brow. 'Roddy. Roddy, can you hear me? We're on our way to the hospital.' Roddy didn't respond.

Bella tried to call Lorna but her hands were quaking so much she couldn't hit any buttons. The paramedic placed his hand on the phone.

'Wait till we get there. It'll be easier.'

Bella held Roddy's hand as the ambulance sped to Ninewells.

***

In the waiting room, she was hugging herself with worry when she heard her name called. She looked up and saw Lorna; her normally impeccable sister-in-law had no make-up on and her hair was uncombed.

'What happened? Is he OK?'

'Yes, the nurse has been – they've settled him and are running tests. They think he's going to be OK and you can go in soon.'

'What happened? Where were you?'

'I went to see Roddy at his office. We had an argument.'

'What about?'

'Money. He's taken all of Aunt Nettie's money for the deal. I said some terrible things.'

Lorna sat down beside her. 'He did what? Oh my God. He's been so stressed since Dorothea died. This property deal… He so wants it to succeed.'

'Mrs McCaa?' Lorna got up. 'You can go in and see him. One person at a time.'

'OK. I'll go in first.' Lorna headed off down the corridor.

Bella rested her elbows on her knees and dropped her head into her hands. What next?

After a while, Lorna rejoined Bella and gave her an update. 'He's stabilised. He's had an echocardiogram and they'll also send him for X-ray. He may need a stent put in. The doctor says they'll monitor everything for a couple of days.'

'But he's going to be alright?'

'Yes. You can go in and see him.'

'No. I can't.'

'Why not?'

'Because if I do, I may kill him.' Bella turned away from Lorna's shocked face. 'I'll go and look through the window.' She wandered along another hospital corridor and peeped through the room's small circle of glass, seeing another of her relatives hooked up to various machines. The McCaa family were certainly getting their money's worth out of the NHS these days. He looked dreadful, his legs white and spindly; he'd lost a lot of weight. A doctor was beside him writing up notes and came out.

'Are you a relative?' Bella nodded. 'You can go in and sit with him if you like.' The doctor went on his way and

Bella rested her head on the window. *Oh Roddy, when did you become such an absolute shitbag?* Eventually she trudged back along the corridor to the waiting area to learn that Lorna had organised private care to look after Aunt Nettie while Bella rested for a couple of days to get over the accident.

'Your face – I didn't realise it had been so bad. You must be exhausted, you can't be sleeping on the sofa while recovering from that.'

Bella could've hugged her. And then she did.

CHAPTER 47

At home, Bella opened her laptop and accessed her password and log-in file again. They were still there – the McCaa Properties details from her short stint as bookkeeper.

'You're supposed to update the passwords, Roddy.' Bella shouted happily to the empty room. She rooted around the company website and found she still had access not only to the confidential financial accounts, but other files, too. Roddy had bet the business on the building development, selling off the portfolio to get most of the cash and borrowing the rest. But he'd taken out a short-term high interest loan and, when the building work had been delayed, found he was in trouble, having to pay expensive penalties before the development was ready. Of course, he wasn't acting on his own; her mother's signature was all over the documents too.

They'd sold the portfolio their father had created, apart from the Long Lane cottage – owned by the company for sixty-five years – sale pending. She saw the family house re-mortgage money coming in, the money from her aunt – even the sale of office paintings. The loan repayments were horrendous and what Roddy was trying to do with her aunt's money and the house and the paintings was never going to stop an ever-widening gap.

Bella looked through years of company records, no doubt all uploaded to satisfy the chain of title. She tracked through decades of documents, mesmerised by her mother's confident signature accompanied by Roddy's smaller, more tentative scrawl. Then Annabella Winifred McCaa appeared, listed as a shareholder. What? She'd never been a shareholder. It was the year she was twenty-one and based in Edinburgh at university. Bella dug deeper – her email address was listed as secure on the site and she had no qualms about getting in and changing passwords to gain access to a variety of legal documents from when her father had died and Roddy and Dorothea had taken over.

Jeez Louise. After two hours of reading and downloading, Bella got up and paced the room, opening the door to stand in the refreshing cool air. *Annabella. Solicitors. Shares.* Is this what her mother's last notes had been about?

Bella sat in the garden for a long time, lost in thought. Retreating inside, she walked over to the fireplace, hefted up the poker and with steely determination smashed the pictures of herself with her mother and Roddy from the wall. They clattered onto the floor, where she continued the destruction until the photos and their frames were reduced to smithereens.

Sitting calmly at the table she made a call.

***

Bella sat in the expensive surroundings of Sharma and Daughters, under a huge list of associates. She didn't realise the practice had grown so big.

'Bella. Thanks for coming down.' Dali did a double take. 'What happened to you?'

Bella had tried to cover her bruised face with makeup. The black and blue had been replaced by varying purples and yellows.

'Car accident. It's only a bump. But Roddy's in hospital, he's had a heart attack.'

'I heard.' He saw Bella's look of surprise. 'Lorna phoned. Come away through.'

Dali led the way into a typical book-lined office, with a massive desk and comfortable leather chairs.

'Have you read all these books?' she asked.

'Sadly, I have. And I re-read them. For work, not pleasure. How is Roddy doing?'

'He's going to be fine. He'll need a stent op, but he's being well looked after.'

'Is this about McCaa's? I'm not sure if I can help – Sharma's don't represent McCaa's anymore. It's a London company – I do bits and pieces, and Roddy and I speak all the time as you know, but nothing formal.'

Bella brought out her laptop. 'This is about McCaa's but I want you to represent me, not the company. I'm not sure about the legalities of what I'm about to tell you.' She settled herself comfortably in the chair as Dali leant forward attentively.

'McCaa's is in a mess. Roddy and I had an argument about him taking Aunt Nettie's savings – then he had the heart attack.'

'He took your aunt's savings? What for? And you were there when he collapsed?'

'Yes, which is lucky as I could call an ambulance. Or you could say I caused the attack. So, not so lucky.'

Dali raised an eyebrow.

'I completely lost it with him.'

'I'm not surprised. I can't believe he would do that!'

'You'd better believe it. Wait until you hear the whole story.'

Dali rested his chin on his hands. 'Go on.'

'Roddy's overstretched himself. I've seen it loads of times when I worked in London – trying to get a quick return, taking out short loans. Building being held up for whatever reason and it's suddenly a crisis to make the payments.'

'Did he tell you this?'

'Erm, no. When I did the bookkeeping, it was remote because I was looking after Dorothea, so I needed all the passwords – and they've never been updated. He must have uploaded all the files for the chains of title and I trawled through everything. Everything.' Bella snorted. 'He needs to get security in there.' She clicked away on her laptop. 'I'm going to send you documents because I think I have the *right* to fix this mess, too. What's your email address?'

Dali rattled it off.

'By the way, did Dorothea contact you before she died?' Bella asked. 'You were on her to-do list.'

'She was in touch before she became unwell. She phoned and said she had business she wanted to discuss with me. But...' Dali leaned back in his large leather chair. 'I said I would come and see her, but she didn't want me to come to the house and in the end it came out that she wanted to rewrite her will. Shepherd – you know he looked after the family for donkey's years – died before Christmas.

'Actually, I didn't know. Jeez, I'm not party to anything.'

'Anyway. Dorothea said she didn't want to deal with Shepherd's brother, "the old dodderer" as she called him. She wanted to re-write her will and wanted me to do it. But, I don't know, it made me feel uneasy, as if someone was going to miss out and if it was you or Roddy, I didn't want anything to do with it. I said I would send recommendations. Being Dorothea, she told me I hadn't a clue how to run a business and put the phone down.' Dali laughed. 'She was some woman, your mother.'

'Try living with her.'

'What was in her will?'

'I haven't seen it.'

'You haven't seen it?'

Bella shook her head. 'No. I should have asked Roddy, but it's as if I'd lost my fight somewhere, so used to not being party to what was going on. But I've woken up now!'

Dali concentrated on his laptop. 'I've got the files. Let me have a look.'

'Look at my father's will first.'

Bella looked around the study while Dali read. Pictures of his life with Keren and the children dominated the walls, putting the framed qualifications in the shade. Her attention was drawn away when she heard Dali give a soft whistle.

'You weren't aware of this?'

'The fact McCaa Properties was left between Roddy and me? No, I was not.'

'It says here that Dorothea was to act on your behalf until you were twenty-one, when you would take over.' Dali clicked away on his laptop. 'You transferred your shares to Dorothea when you were twenty-one?'

'No, I did not. The company and shares were never discussed with me *ever*. It was always Dorothea and Roddy. Any time I went home, Roddy would come over and they would go into her study to discuss business, never in front of me. As much as she would boast to her friends about my 'high-powered' job in London, and my career successes, I was never invited to contribute to what they were doing. I learnt to keep my nose out of it.' Bella was all business, her jiggling leg the only sign of an undercurrent of anger.

'What are you going to do? Dorothea forged your signature. Roddy must have gone along with it. You could take him to court for this.'

'I was so angry when I saw it. And hurt.' Bella shook her head in disgust. 'The picture of him sitting in jail for years is very appealing. But as much as that thought is attractive...' She got up and moved around, pulling her thoughts together. 'What I want is to get the company out of this mess and for Aunt Nettie's savings to be returned to her account. I want to fix this deal so Roddy will always remember it was me who saved his skin and I hope it makes Dorothea spin in her grave. I want everything I'm entitled to and to make it so Roddy can't lift a finger in the future without consulting me. I want a negotiator's fee for pulling it all together so I can go and live in London and not worry about money. There. That's what I want. Can I do this legally?'

'Only if Roddy does a share transfer and you become a director of the company. He can hardly refuse; you have enough over him. I mean, it would be his word against yours, Dorothea is dead, but—'

'The signature on the share transfer is nothing like mine. It's Dorothea's writing; she didn't even try to disguise it.'

'I'm sorry Bella, I had no idea this had happened. I'd always believed your father left McCaa's to Roddy and Dorothea. I'm shocked at Roddy, though, being party to it.'

'He got more and more out of his depth as things spiralled. In his defence, I imagine Dorothea was behind it all in the beginning, cutting me out, but it doesn't excuse the continuation of it. All these years of lies.' Bella returned to her seat. 'I can fix this mess – it's the kind of work I did very successfully over the years: assess the takeover of companies, refinance, make the deal workable. It saved the companies and the shareholders. They get a smaller return but don't lose their investment. I need you, Dali, to be the intermediary. He'll take it coming from you. I don't want to discuss anything with Roddy. Don't want to speak to him or make him worse or hear his arguments and excuses. Could you act for me?'

'I'll go and see him tomorrow morning.'

'And I want to see a copy of Dorothea's will. Thanks, Dali. Thanks for seeing me at such short notice.'

'It's no problem. I'm glad you came to me. I'm so shocked at what's happened.' He got up and came towards her. 'Bella, I'm sorry about Keren. What she did all these years ago is unforgivable.'

Bella looked at Dali, saw the weight on his shoulders as he thought about his wife and her lies.

'She came to see me, to apologise and I've forgiven her. Things will never be as they were before. They can't be. But we came to a ... I'm not sure what ... a truce. I hope you two manage to work it out.' She pointed to all the photographs. 'You've had such a life together – don't let what Keren did ruin your lives, too. I suppose what she did, she did for love, however misguided it was. She's always been in love with you.'

'I know. I never noticed at the time, when you were with Jem. I'm sorry.' Dali laid a hand on Bella's arm. 'Jem's gone to New York.'

'Has he?' Even though she knew it was foolish, her heart swooped at the mention of his name.

'It's a short trip – to get "his people" to sort stuff for Fergus moving there.' Dali had drawn quotation marks in the air.

'Oh.'

'It's another world. Did you two get the chance to talk?'

'We've made our peace with it, I think. I can't dwell on what might have been. Thirty years have gone by and we're both moving away. Me to London, Jem to New York with his dad. A fresh start. You and Keren can start again, too?'

Dali put his arms around her and gave her a hug. 'You're a good friend, Annabella McCaa.'

She kissed his cheek. 'Thanks so much, Dali.'

Bella stepped into a cool summer evening and walked to Broughty Ferry along the Tay. A haar was coming in off the water, making the air bitterly cold. She slipped her hood up to keep warm, cutting off from the beach into Long Lane. Bath and bed were calling. Tomorrow she would start the fight to save McCaa Properties.

CHAPTER 48

Bella sat behind Roddy's desk, imagining the alternative life she might have had if her father's wishes had been followed. Would she have wanted to work in the property business with Dorothea and Roddy? Probably not. But it would have been nice to be invited. At least she understood Dorothea's desire to keep her out of things; she couldn't have tolerated her daughter finding out the truth. She heard footsteps in the corridor and Dali's head came round the door.

'Can I come in?' he asked.

'Of course. Have you seen him already? Did he sign the shares over?'

'He almost didn't have to.' Dali sat down opposite.

Bella was puzzled. 'What do you mean?'

'Initially, Dorothea left her shares to you.'

'She left them to me?'

'In the old will, yes. She left them to Roddy in the new will.'

Bella shook her head in disbelief. 'So, with the house remortgaged, she decided to cut me out of the shares, too? When was this?'

'End of February.'

Bella crumpled. 'Annabella' – underlined twice. What a fool she'd been to feel grateful that her mother was going to share information about the house, be honest with her, then to be betrayed completely by her in the end. Dorothea couldn't even honour her husband's will.

'What did Roddy say?'

'Not much at first. When I told him I'd seen everything and knew what he and Dorothea had done, he was embarrassed and contrite. He said he'd intended to transfer the shares to you once the company was out of the woods.'

'I'll bet.' Bella was disgusted.

'I think he was on the verge of a breakdown – stress and worry damaged his judgement. Or he just wanted to keep control, to keep you in the dark about what had happened in the past.'

'I have no sympathy. He didn't tell me anything. What kind of brother behaves in such a way?'

Dali shrugged his shoulders. 'I don't know. He's not the Roddy I grew up with. Here are the transfer papers.' He placed the document on the desk.

'He's fine with me negotiating a new financial package?'

'He blustered a bit, but in the end, I think he's relieved not to have to deal with anything.' They arranged to talk later and Dali left.

Bella stared out the window, thinking about her mother's actions. At the end, when there was a chance to right the wrong, she'd chosen to leave Bella out in the cold. Ten years of care. Ten years and no recognition from her mother. No respect, no love. Only the knowledge that Dorothea was a worse version of herself than she had ever imagined. She sat at her father's old desk. She would show them how it's done.

The next finance payment was due at the end of the month and Bella would have to adhere to the same deadline. Roddy's records were meticulous – curious for a company built on dishonesty – and she was grateful for that. Orion Investments was the broker for the deal – a good place to start – and she spent the morning going through Company House files, getting background on Orion and the finance company. Orion had used another broker as an intermediary and Bella pushed her chair away from the desk when she saw the name of the company director. Sam Evans – her ex-husband.

'Jeez Louise. Is all my past haunting me? What the hell is going on?'

It had been ten years since she'd spoken to Sam and he'd barely entered her mind at all in the intervening period. Funny how, over the years, she'd Googled Jem occasionally and hoovered up any news there had been of him in the press but had never had any desire to find out what Sam was doing. Bella's brain cranked up as to what his involvement might mean but she realised it made absolute sense for Roddy to go to Sam for advice. She had introduced them and he was probably the only contact

Roddy had who worked to such a scale of investment and with the right expertise. Alpha City Finance he was calling himself these days. Bella snorted. Alpha! What a twat.

Bella got online and could see he'd done well for himself, thank you very much. She clicked through pages of deals mentioned in the trades, until there was Mr Evans, her ex-husband, sitting on a luxurious sofa in front of a huge window overlooking the Thames – a profile in the Financial Times reporting Alpha City had been set up to broker corporate property deals. She blinked at the date – two months after their divorce was finalised and he was staying in a palatial waterfront penthouse? So that's what he had spent his share of their joint assets on while she created redundancy payments to make sure the staff didn't lose anything by the company's closure.

***

'Am I a *mug*?' she bawled down the phone at Shirley.

'No, you're not. You did the right thing.'

'Some of the admin staff had been with us from the beginning, I couldn't see them lose out. I should have seen it coming —

'You were excellent at your job and will be again. And Sam – he was a charmer, a player - and we both know he could be somewhat economical with the truth at times. You worked well together as a team for a long time. I'm still in shock about Dorothea and Roddy conspiring to keep you out.'

Bella laughed wryly. 'It would have made sense to her; the daughter who was never good enough. And Roddy? Cut from the same cloth.'

'So were you; he has no excuse. You should take Roddy to court, you're far too forgiving.'

'I'm not. It's... I don't want to give her any more head space. Roddy, I'll have to deal with in the future but in the meantime, I've got to make this re-financing work – for Aunt Nettie, for myself – to prove I can do it, and so I can rub Roddy's face in it. See, not so forgiving after all. Sam's involvement will stand in our favour... I need to trawl through their correspondence and find out how it became such a terrible deal.'

The friends spent the next hour hashing out the kind of finance package best suited to the circumstances, and how McCaa Properties could be saved from defaulting on their loan and losing everything.

Next stop was Aunt Nettie. She was so relieved Bella was going to take over after Roddy's attack that she cracked open the sherry and poured them both a small one. Bella swallowed a prayer as it went down. She had to make it work. If not ... she dreaded to think what her aunt's future would hold.

'You'll be able to work it all out. Poor Roddy.'

Bella had refrained from telling her aunt about the will and shares shenanigans. Her aunt didn't need to find out how awful her nephew and her sister-in-law had been. The priority was returning those savings to her aunt.

'And I'm better. No wobbles today so far. The carers are great, they come twice a day. You can go to London without any worries about me. I'll miss you, though.'

Bella hugged her aunt. 'I'll miss you. There's a lot to do before I even get there. I'll crack on in the morning; tonight, I'm going to relax a bit.'

Iain had been in touch asking if he should bring round pizza and she'd answered with a resounding 'Yes!' By the time she was home he'd called in the troops and Amina and Celeste arrived, too. A newly confident Celeste regaled them with tales of her sales experiences and Amina enthusiastically updated them with the new clothing designs. Iain continued his hero status by popping out for Ben & Jerry's to wash down the pizza and Bella brought everyone up to date with the accident, Roddy's heart attack and how she was going to save McCaa Properties.

'But won't you miss doing this?' Amina twirled her Bella backpack creation in the air and indicated the chair Celeste was sitting on. 'You've a real talent with your hands. Remember you sold all these chairs...'

Which brought Bella to Jem and his pity buy. She wondered if he was at Fergus's yet, and if Cassie was with him.

'Earth to Bella! You were completely lost there – what were you thinking about?

'London. And how I'm getting my life back. You can all come and stay once I'm settled.'

***

Being settled in London seemed far away as Bella waded through documents, plans and reports the next morning at the office. Her mobile pinged: Lorna:

Top right-hand drawer. I should never have taken it without asking you first. Forgive me?

Bella opened the drawer to find her mother's jewellery box. It sent a shudder down her spine to see it, as if Dorothea were watching her. She slid the drawer closed and locked it.

'Watch and weep, Dorothea – watch and weep.' Bella read and typed up notes. This deal could not fall through. Her aunt depended on her.

CHAPTER 49

Bella stood in the copy shop watching her hard work spill out of the machine. Everything had been emailed, but glossy brochures would be impressive to hand out at the meeting. Shirley had pored over them last night, making sure all t's were crossed and i's dotted. Confident with the presentations in her possession, she hopped in a taxi to the West End.

Lorna opened the front door.

'How is he?'

'He's doing well considering he had the stent put in yesterday, but it's supposed to be a speedy recovery, so let's hope so. I'll leave you to it; he's in the lounge.'

Bella walked down the hallway, feeling out of place in the house she used to call home. Roddy was propped up on the settee, covered in a rug, an array of tablets and drinks beside him on a table.

'How are you?'

He had colour in his cheeks but still looked tired. 'Better.' He gasped a breath. 'A bit out of puff, but better.' He sipped some water. 'I'll soon be at work. You don't need to be doing anything.'

'Roddy, I need to be doing everything. McCaa's ... it'll all be lost if we don't renegotiate the finance.'

'I was sorting it out.' Roddy's bluster sounded weak.

'No, you weren't. The current deal is a mess, you were plugging holes. And are we going to ignore how you and Dorothea cut me out of everything?'

'We didn't, not in the way it sounds.'

'You have to stop lying; it's pointless! I have proof.'

He covered his face with his hands and said nothing. Bella waited. 'Roddy.'

He looked at her for the first time. 'We had to jump in when Father died; neither Dorothea nor I knew anything about the business. We had to get on with it.' Her brother threw the rug off and swung his legs round to sit.

'Roddy! Half the company was mine and I never signed over any shares. How could you do it?'

The silence stretched out while Bella sat patiently waiting.

'I didn't see a will. I'd newly graduated and was working in family law. Dorothea said Father had left it to me and her and she needed my help. I didn't see the will for years and when I did, I was running the company, enjoying it. Then I got scared about the truth coming out, what might happen. You were off at university and it was easier. I knew it was wrong but I couldn't challenge Dorothea.'

A situation Bella could understand.

'I'm sorry.' As he apologised she was shocked to see tears appearing. 'I persuaded myself I was doing you a favour, saving you from being trapped, too. I've thought about it so much over the years. I wanted to make it right but... I can't blame it all on Mother. I couldn't stand up to her and I liked it; I liked being successful, but the price was always doing everything the way Dorothea wanted.' Roddy took a deep breath. 'She always said she would leave you the shares in her will. It was a shock when she left them to me. Perhaps she did it to keep it all hidden. And I was worried you'd find out about Father's will and what we'd done. I am sorry, Annabella.'

'These shares were mine. From Father. Things could've been so different.'

'I'm sorry.'

'And Aunt Nettie?'

'The development deal was a mistake; we tried to do too much too quickly. When Dorothea died, I panicked. And then I got desperate.' Roddy leaned his head against the cushions, as if confessing had taken it all out of him. 'It's probably too late.'

'No, it's not. I've been working on another deal and I'm off to London tomorrow to get all the parties on side.' Bella placed a copy of the proposal on the table. 'I will make this work. At the least Aunt Nettie will have her investment returned. At the most, McCaa's will be on their feet and I'll own half the company.'

Roddy wiped his face and examined the sodden handkerchief. 'What's wrong with me? I can't stop crying.'

'Think yourself lucky you don't have the hot flushes to go with it.'

CHAPTER 50

Bella joined the stampede of commuters boarding the Docklands Light Railway. A crack of dawn flight from Dundee to City Airport had landed on time and she would arrive early at Canary Wharf – time for her to go over what she was going to say once more.

Bella gripped the handle tightly, thrilled to be lost in a commute, one of the millions on their way to work, holding on for grim death as the train swung from side to side, pelting along the track. Dressed in a smart blue suit, courtesy of Save The Children, she inhabited a memory of her old self – a successful businesswoman on her way to an important meeting. Three hundred pounds had been transferred from Sharma's to her account to fund the trip. If all went to plan it wouldn't be long before she'd be in London for good, starting her new life from Alvin's Belsize Park studio. The negotiator fee should be enough for a small flat and to cover her expenses while she got settled and found work – but she'd have to earn it first. Then she'd deal with McCaa's remotely and let Roddy do the day to day running when he was better, but he wouldn't be able to make any decisions without her say-so.

She found it hard to forgive her brother but understood how difficult it must have been to confront the determination of their mother. As the train sped through a tunnel, Bella recognised how complicit she had been in how her life had turned out over the last ten years. She could have been stronger, defied her mother, forced support from Roddy, and justified the need for a personal life, respite and holidays. But at the end of the day, she too had been incapable of clashing with her mother, cowed by a lifetime of acquiescence and pity – pity for how small and meagre her mother's life had become.

Bella kept a tight hold of her old briefcase, dusted off for the trip. Her small, wheeled suitcase had two blouses inside, identical to the one she wore. She would not be caught out by the consequences of overheating at such important meetings. If she had to put on a replacement dry top, no one would guess. She had a stock of Pro Plus and a roll-on perfume that promised to keep menopausal women cool and scented – if she believed the advert. She was as prepared as she could be. The meeting with Orion Investments was at 2 pm and there was a pre-meeting with Shirley and Chris at noon. Carried by the throng along the well-trodden route to exit, she tumbled out with the crowd and dodged pedestrians as she caught her breath and her bearings.

'Hey! Watch it!' she called, as a be-suited commuter kicked her case out of the way. She'd committed the cardinal sin of stopping in the middle of the pavement and could hear tuts and mutters as people edged around her. Darting towards a deli truck she ordered an espresso and threw it down, instantly regretting it as blood thumped wildly through her veins. But the short stop had centred her and it wasn't long before she was on the twenty-second floor of a magnificent office building, being shown into a glass-fronted meeting room and directed towards an astounding array of refreshments by a young man called Damien.

'Help yourself to drinks, and would ya like breakfast? We have a French boulangerie and charcuterie in the building – what would ya like?' The trendy executive was determined to please.

'A drink will be fine, thanks.'

'Are ya sure? We have access to more traditional breakfast choices – a square sausage roll might tempt you? Or are ya vegan? Macrobiotic?'

'I'll help myself to orange juice. Thank *ya*.'

'We don't have *orange*.' Damien sniffed. 'But there is mangosteen? Caviche with avocado? Yubari Melon?'

'Yubari Melon.' Bella had never heard of it but was compelled to make a choice.

'Bolt from the blue, or what? You look good Ms Annabella McCaa.' Her ex-husband had entered the meeting room and kissed each cheek exuberantly. 'What...?' He scrutinised her. 'What's the scar on your head?' Trust Sam to notice.

'Car accident. Long story.' The assistant presented two glasses of the juice with panache.

'Excellent choice – this stuff's the real deal. Thanks, Damy baby, we'll be fine.' Damy baby discreetly left the room.

'This looks impressive.'

'It is. It is. I'm certainly on my feet again.' Sam ran his hand over a thinning pate. When they'd been together, he'd been very proud of his thatch of thick, blonde hair. Bella took cheap pleasure at the loss.

'I heard you were on your feet a long time ago with the uber extravagance on the Thames?'

'Oh, I got a brilliant deal. You know what this biz is like.' He gave her his trademark boyish grin; she imagined it still worked for him at times.

'Anyway, it's lovely to see you and what a coincidence I'm connected with Orion and Orion with McCaa's – and you've taken over? How is our Roderick?'

Bella's mouth was dry and she swallowed a mouthful of the Yubari Melon. 'He'll be fine. Thank you.' She placed her laptop on the table. 'But it's not a coincidence you're connected to Orion, is it?'

'What do you mean? I put Orion and McCaa together to create the partnership for the development. I've been friends with the directors for years.'

'But you're also a shareholder in ES Investments, who are part of the financing package getting a return from the interest and one of the companies who will gain if we default. When I looked at the deal you advised McCaa Properties to sign, it's verging on malpractice. You would have understood these terms had no delay room built in and yet you advised Roddy to stop using Sharma's as legal representation but go with your lawyers. Not illegal but, coupled with the payment returns and your advice, very smelly.'

'Woah! Not true, Annabella! And Roddy's a big boy – he made up his own mind. No one twisted anyone's arm to sign.'

'You took advantage of him. Shirley and Chris Jones have seen what you've done and I understand you're currently brokering another deal with them? Trecante?'

Sam lost his smile. 'Trecante is nothing to do with McCaa. I can assure you I've done nothing wrong—'

'It's a bit like leaving me to make all the restitution, because you knew I would, even if we didn't legally have to. And, I've never said this to you before, but if you had done due diligence on our US partners in that deal, you know we wouldn't have lost everything, because we wouldn't have gone through with it. That was on you. You lied.' Bella's voice was getting louder as she got into her stride.

'I didn't lie... they came well recommended.'

'You were supposed to check!'

'OK! I took some bad advice, I know.'

'And now you've given bad advice. Why? If news of this comes out, people will look at your other deals and any pending ones you've got and they'll be all over it – it's not a good business strategy. Chris Jones is seriously thinking of cutting you out of Trecante, whether you brokered it or not. Believe me when I tell you I will make it my life's goal to show everyone what you've done and how you purposefully advised a financial package that was virtually unworkable.'

'It was your damned interfering mother!' It was Sam's turn to lose his cool. 'She wouldn't let me do my job. Went on and on, without a clue what she was talking about. I couldn't believe she was living with you, not asking your advice, and treating me as if I had hay coming out my ears. She was the one who wanted a quick return, wasn't interested in delay precautions and wanted to dump Sharma's. In the end, I got sick of her. Yes, it was a precarious deal if things went off-piste, but what Dorothea wanted she got, as you well know, and it did give me satisfaction when she and Roddy signed on the dotted line, knowing there might be a shaky road ahead. I didn't realise it was going to be quite so shaky. Roddy never argued and Dorothea never listened.'

Bella picked up the remains of her Yubari Melon and threw the glass at Sam, missing him entirely but it bounced on the glass wall and found its mark on return, glancing off his shoulder.

'Ow!'

Yubari Melon dripped down the glass as adjacent office workers gawped.

'You could have brought another broker in – Toby Shuttleworth, for instance – you're still working together. Saved them from themselves. It's what the old you would have done – bring another opinion in if the clients were set on a course of action you thought might be tricky.'

Damien's head came in the door. 'Is everything under control here? Any more drinks?'

'*Get out!*' Bella roared. Damien ducked his head and shuffled away.

'Dorothea's dead. McCaa's is going down the tubes, my aunt's going to lose her retirement savings and I have nothing left. You are going to sit there while I go over the new deal structure and you're going to make sure it passes with flying colours at this afternoon's meeting.' Bella slid the shiny proposal across the table. 'I don't care if you had to deal with Dorothea as an extenuating circumstance, what you did was wrong. People have lost jobs, Roddy's heart attack, my aunt, and *nothing* left for me. And I put up with Dorothea constantly for *ten years*. You owe me Sam.'

Bella kept a steady eye on her ex-husband. He leaned back in his chair and regarded the ceiling.

'I never meant things to turn out how they did between you and me.' He looked at Bella. 'We could have retired if it had worked. I knew I was taking a chance and I should have told you. But I couldn't.' He gave a huge sigh. 'I felt such a failure and I'd let you down. I'm a rat. But you have to be a rat sometimes to be a success in this business.'

'No, you don't, Sam. And you're not a rat, or you didn't used to be. If our time together, your life with me, meant anything to you, support me here. Please. It's payback time. I'm aware it wouldn't fly in court but I could make things nasty for you. Not many would want to take advice from you again.'

He passed his hands over his pate and she wondered whether the constant rubbing was wearing the hair away.

'You'll feel better after, I promise you. This is a good deal; Orion comes out with an improved return. It takes longer, giving us working capital, and eases our payment schedule to be manageable once the development is complete.' Bella poured herself another glass of Yubari Melon.

'That's £32 a glass.'

She watered a nearby plant with it. 'Sam?'

'Okay. I read your email presentation and yes, of course it can work. I wouldn't expect anything else from you. I did think about calling when this was going on, but Dorothea was emphatic you wanted nothing to do with the business. Your proposal is good – the sticking bit is that partners wait longer for a return. And McCaa's have got a three-month repayment grace – might be hard for the others to take.'

'You can do it. Your persuasiveness is one of your many talents. We need money to pay my aunt; Roddy persuaded her to give her life savings for the development. You remember lovely Aunt Nettie?'

'I do, I do. You didn't say Dorothea had died in your email, just mentioned Roddy's heart attack. I'm sorry.'

'It was only in March but it feels a lifetime ago.'

Sam got up to look out the massive glass wall showing a panorama of Canary Wharf. 'I missed you so much, after you'd gone. If it hadn't been for all the mess... But we had good fun, didn't we?'

Bella took in the view alongside him. 'We did. Until it got serious and it just wasn't fun anymore.'

She held out her hand and they shook on it. 'This has to work, Sam, there's too much resting on it.'

CHAPTER 51

Before she left the building, Bella used the opulent rest rooms and re-did her makeup. It was impossible to stop it sliding off in the heat of the day. She'd forgotten about the sticky London summers and bad air conditioning, even in the poshest offices. As she applied more mascara, Bella thought how it would have pleased Dorothea to have dealt with Sam, keeping Bella ignorant of their contact, thinking she was being so clever and much more capable than her daughter. She wished Dorothea could see what a disaster it had turned out to be and how it was her never-quite-good-enough daughter who would turn it all around.

Arriving at Shirley's offices, Bella had to repeat the toilette process, this time changing her blouse. The tube had been packed, smelly and noisy and she'd melted while crushed up against a door. At one point, she'd had to angle herself away from a suspicious protuberance – a side of London she had not missed.

At 2 pm the boardroom filled up with all those party to the McCaa development, including Sam and his partner, Toby Shuttleworth, Chris and Shirley, and various bankers and lawyers, one of whom was Dali's representative. Bella's tension levels had ratcheted up as the meeting loomed, but when she stood up to give the presentation her nerves miraculously disappeared. No brain fog, hot flushes, sore breasts or tears. Channelling a version of herself from the distant past, she was clear, concise, and answered all questions. After a thirty-minute grilling, the bankers tussled over percentage points and return dates and then Toby stood up and talked eloquently about the depth and professionalism of the presentation, how Annabella McCaa's reputation preceded her – how she'd had a long and distinguished career with his colleague, Sam Evans, and Orion Investments had all confidence to agree the deal as offered with the caveat they would look at it again in six months. All being well, the deal would carry through until the development was complete and sold.

Bella couldn't believe it. They'd done it. She'd done it. As everyone shook hands and congratulated each other she looked across the room and mouthed 'Thank you' to Sam. He shrugged his shoulders and flashed his grin. Toby gave a thumbs up.

Champagne and glasses magically appeared, and they toasted the reformed partnership, and how clever they all were for making it work. The talk settled into tales of recent deals, percentage points, and who screwed who to get the best settlement. As trays of canapés were brought in, and as more champagne was poured and guzzled, Chris sidled up to her.

'Impressive. Very impressive. You didn't refer to your notes once. Remarkable. I want you as part of my team. Not compliance but working with Shirley brokering and refinancing. You could start on Monday if you want? We're so busy and there's no time like the present. What do you say?'

'Yes! Absolutely yes. Thanks, Chris. I can't wait.' He shook her hand and wandered off, while Bella sat down, taking a long drink from her champagne glass.

In the background, the babble went up as the drinks went down. Shirley took the next chair and pulled Bella to her, giving her a loud smacker on the cheek.

'For being a star and getting a job – all in one. I'm so happy for you,' Shirley laughed.

'I'm so happy for me!' Bella laughed too and tapped her glass against Shirley's.

'Congratulations to us!' They swallowed the champagne and thumped the glasses on the table, smiling inanely. Bella ran her hands through her hair and exhaled heavily.

'Are you OK?' Shirley scanned her friend's face.

'It's been a long day – a long few months.' Bella refilled their glasses. 'I'm going to pop out, take a breather.'

'Off you go. You deserve it.'

Shirley downed her champagne and Bella escaped onto the terrace; the frenetic, noisy bustle of London laid out before her. She called Aunt Nettie and gave her the news.

'It's all going to work out.'

'I never doubted you, sweetheart.'

'Chris offered me a job, starting Monday, working with Shirley as we used to before.'

'Congratulations Annabella! You've got everything you wanted, everything you deserve.'

'I feel so lucky.'

'Lucky? You've worked hard for it, young lady. But you sound a bit low.'

'Tired. It's been a long day and I'm going to head out to the airport soon. I'll see you tomorrow.'

Bella texted Roddy the news and he responded immediately:

Well done. I mean it. Thank you.

Her phone pinged again.

I hear congratulations are in order?

It was from Dali; of course he knew already. Bella breathed in the muggy London air and smiled. Jeez Louise. She'd done it. She had her life back.

CHAPTER 52

Time passed in a whirl: saying goodbyes, re-packing possessions for a removal Amina and Celeste would facilitate, finalising paperwork for the restructured finance package; and trying to keep her mind away from Jem, four thousand miles away. The insurance company had been in touch to confirm the Mini was a write-off, but the compensation would take months to come through. At least it was something – but she'd miss her dependable little run-around, now she could afford to keep it.

She climbed the stairs to her aunt's flat, laden with so much shopping her aunt wondered what she'd do with it all.

'There is online shopping!' she laughed.

'But you can't always get your favourite things and this'll keep you stocked up for a while.' The savings had been returned to her aunt's bank account and Bella had set up a monthly direct debit for Michelle. Not only had her aunt been persuaded to get rid of the cheque book, they'd downloaded the banking app and once the process of instant transfers had been demonstrated, her aunt was won over.

Incredibly, her indomitable relative was 100% back to her old self. The only tell-tale sign from the accident was a stylish haircut to hide where the surgery wound had been shaved, and a pink rinse. Bella would have her own small mark, but only the eagle-eyed, like Sam, would notice it behind her fringe. Seeing their battle scars made Bella imagine they were warrior queens – they'd fought the good fight against Roddy and Dorothea - and won.

'You spoil me. I'll miss you so much.' They hugged for a long time.

Bella met Dali at his office. 'I don't want any part of it. I'll keep my name on the documents until the six-month trial period goes by, but then all will revert to Roddy.'

'But it means losing what your father intended you to have, not to mention the financial security. The development will be lucrative when it's completed; you'll be set for life. You can't want to miss such a deal?'

'I do. I have everything I want from my father. He loved me. He was thinking of me and thought me good enough to be part of his business, whatever Dorothea's opinion. But the rest – it's all tainted. Tainted with Dorothea and her duplicity. Tainted with Roddy and his weakness. I spent a lifetime trying to please my mother, and now – no more.'

'You're sure?' Bella nodded as Dali slid the papers over for signing and she scribbled her inheritance away. 'If for any reason things go pear-shaped these get destroyed, right?'

'No, he can fall under the bus on his own.' Bella laughed. 'I don't want a share of the house, either. I'll take the negotiation fee and no more.'

'Bella! Think of the future. You can't throw everything away.'

'I can. It's my future, and it'll be whatever I make of it. No one else. I've got a job doing exactly what I did before, and the fee from the deal is plenty enough to buy a place. I don't wany anything to do with them and the past. I've got everything I want.'

Dali replaced the signed form in a file, shaking his head. 'OK. It's up to you I guess.' Bella chuckled seeing how it went against the grain for him.

'When are you off?'

'Tomorrow – the 6.38 am from Broughty Ferry Station. I'm going by train so I can have a final view from the curving bridge, and watch Dundee and ten years of my life recede into the distance.' Bella pulled her coat on and picked up her backpack. 'You and Keren are back together? She sent me a good luck card and told me.'

'There's so much history between us; the children – and grandchild – so we're going to give it a try.'

'I hope it works out. For both of you. I'll be in touch.'

'Good luck.'

Out on the street, Bella felt a huge weight gone from her shoulders. She'd made the right decision – she was in control of her life at last, beholden to no one.

***

At home she worked on the deal documents and emailed them off for signature, along with their pristine loan agreement. Everything was in place for her fresh start. When Bella finished packing, she stepped into a hot bath, used all her tools to defuzz her body, and soaked while a conditioning treatment revitalised her hair. Lying there she thought of Jem – more than a physical distance separated them. She imagined him out in New York with the elegant Cassie, or preparing for Fergus's arrival, together with his son. Tears tracked down her face as she allowed herself to grieve – for what might have been in the past and what could have been in the future. She had been madly in love thirty years ago but today they were more than an ocean apart and she was no longer the schoolgirl, teenager and young woman he'd been in love with.

Hair dried and everything prepared for the next day, she couldn't settle and, getting dressed again, headed to the beach, hoping the waves would soothe away the lurking anxiety. She sat on a bench in the fading light and tried to tune into the water gently ebbing and flowing. She would miss being able to do this at the end of a stressful day; she'd come to love Broughty Ferry, the beach and most of all the cottage.

'Belle.' She turned to see Jem standing beside her.

'Jem! What are you doing here?' She was completely thrown by his sudden appearance.

'There was no one at the cottage so I guessed I might find you at the beach.'

'When did you come home?'

'This afternoon. It should've been sooner but stuff came up at work and I had to get a much later flight. Do you mind?' He pointed to the seat and Bella shimmied along. 'Dali says you're leaving tomorrow?'

'I got the job I wanted, managed to sort things out with McCaa Properties – a lot has happened, but it's all worked out.'

'I'm glad... I'm happy for you; it's what you wanted.' Jem took her hand in his. 'Listen, I... I'm sorry about meeting you with Cassie like that.'

'It doesn't matter. I mean...' It was hard to meet his eyes, but she did.

'Cassie decided to surprise me. We'd only had a couple of dates; it wasn't even a relationship yet.'

'It's OK, it's nothing to do with me.'

'I didn't want to hurt you. It's over anyway – I mean... it never began.'

'You don't need to explain. We're going our separate ways. You in New York with Fergus, me in London. We've both got what we wanted.'

Jem released her hand and laid his arm along the bench behind her; she could feel the warmth emanating from his body and had to resist nestling closer. 'I suppose we have.'

They watched the waves ebb and flow. Reluctantly Bella stood up; it was time to say goodbye. 'I've got an early train.'

'The 6.38 from Broughty Ferry!' They smiled at each other 'Dad and I are leaving early too; I've booked a 6.45

taxi to Edinburgh airport.' Jem stood up beside her. 'Can I walk you home?' They walked towards Long Lane, the sound of the water receding as they turned onto the cobbles and at the cottage Bella fished keys out of her pocket.

Jem said, 'I hope it goes well in London. No doubt I'll hear from Dali.' Bella couldn't think of anything to say, not wanting him to leave, but aware she had to let him go.

He leaned down to kiss her cheek, then softly grazed his lips across her mouth and Bella melted. Time stood still and she could feel desire charging through her body. They looked at each other and, in a second, were kissing passionately. Taking the keys from her hand, Jem unlocked the door and followed her inside, where, urgently removing each other's clothes, they stumbled towards the bedroom.

Hours later, Bella lay with Jem's body curved around her, encased in his arms, grateful they'd had this time together before going their separate ways.

'Do you think you'll be happy doing what you did before? In London?'

Bella turned to look at him. 'What do you mean?'

'Nothing ... just I wondered if you might have thought of something else ... somewhere else.'

'This is what I want. I've worked so hard for it. Waited so long for it.' She turned away from him.

'I was only thinking ... the world's your oyster.'

'I don't want to start at the beginning again.' She wasn't sure what Jem was suggesting but it frightened her. She was so close to leading her own life, to being in a world she understood, answerable only to herself. In control of her own destiny. She didn't want to be hurt again. Bella closed her eyes tightly, embarrassed that tears were squeezing out.

'I'm not who I was all those years ago, Jem.'

'You'll always be Belle to me.' He made love to her again, with an exquisite slowness, and she savoured every part of him for as long as she could.

It was a silent farewell, too much and yet nothing left to say. Jem cupped her face, kissed her lips and the door clicked shut behind him, his footsteps receding softly down the lane.

CHAPTER 53

Bella sat in the half-light, feeling numb. When she roused herself, she flitted between the small tasks she still had to do and changing her mind about what to wear, emptying her case out, throwing things in, forgetting what she was looking for.

'Get a grip!' she shouted and managed to ground herself enough to get organised. She followed her morning ritual methodically; washed, dressed and put makeup on. She stopped when she picked up the hairbrush and saw in the mirror that the bedhead style she'd been so unsuccessful in achieving before Keren's party was there naturally, and she left it; loathe to brush away the evidence of her night of passion with Jem.

At 5.30 am she was twiddling her thumbs, so she pulled on her trusty backpack, zipped up her parka and dragged the cases to the door. The final chair she'd renovated was sitting there, beside the sewing machine. They would be sent to London with the other boxes and bags she'd prepared. After all Roddy's efforts, the sale of the cottage had fallen through; no planning permission could be found for the spiral staircase and the upper conversion.

It was the one thing she decided to keep, and Dali had organised Roddy signing the deeds over. She could rent it out, perhaps to Celeste. It was the first property her father had purchased and she wanted that connection to him.

After a final look round Bella locked the door and trudged the cases over the Long Lane cobbles and speed ramps, noisy in the deserted morning. She heaved them along the High Street, stopping for a short rest along the way. What had she packed? They were such a weight as she individually bumped them down the steps to the platform.

The morning was peaceful – the occasional distant seagull squawk and traffic noise didn't disturb her as she sat on the bench. Breathing deeply, conscious of her chest rising and falling, her hair ruffled gently by the wind, she savoured this unexpected peaceful meditation. So much had happened since Dorothea died; this tranquil interlude felt like the first moment she'd had to just... be. There was no one to care for, no problem to solve, no job to find, no money to save – she'd done it. In and out, inhaling and exhaling, finding a steady rhythm, focusing on her breath, trying to keep her thoughts away from where they threatened to go.

The peace was broken by the ping of her mobile. An animated GIF of popping corks came in from Shirley.

Thanks for the docs. We've got dinner tonight with Chris and Toby Shuttleworth – your first consultation! Safe journey, babes, I'll email the proposal and meet you at the station.

Bella re-read the message. Instead of filling her with excitement, her heart was heavy. Instinctively she knew her desires had changed; this job was no longer for her. Her fingers hovered over the keyboard but at that moment, the phone died, she'd forgotten to charge it the night before.

She got up and paced the platform, surprised at her immediate gut reaction to Shirl's text. She didn't want to work in finance, making deals and having meetings with the Sams and Chrises of the world.

A seagull eyeballed her from the other side of the tracks and she stared back. Jem was right. It had all been to please Dorothea, to win her approval, and yes, there had been an unspoken notion she would join the family business after graduation. Instead, her mother had been as keen as Keren she go to London – now she understood why. It was nothing to do with her capabilities, it was about hiding Dorothea's culpability.

When she told her mother about the breakup with Jem, Dorothea was delighted, had come to London and they'd spent rare mother-and-daughter time; a glimpse of a relationship they might have had. Any secret desires Bella may have entertained of letting Jem explain himself were forgotten under her mother's rare gaze of acceptance. They discussed her prospects – not in her career but who she might meet at the bank who was already rich and successful, sacrificing any chance of reconciliation with Jem on the altar of mother love.

No more. Bella's future stretched out before her. She could be and do anything she wanted in London. The hefty negotiation fee meant she could live comfortably while deciding on a new career. A creative business. She was only fifty-two years old and had no ties. Renaissance could be a reality!

She heard the train chugging towards the station and Bella got up, moving her cases to the edge of the platform, the only passenger ready to board. She was completely responsible for her own life and her own happiness, free to do whatever she wanted. Her choice. The train stopped and she reached for the carriage door handle, catching sight of herself in the window reflection as she did so. Her choice. Her decision.

She let go of the handle and stepped away.

The guard blew the whistle and the train chugged off as Bella stood, watching it disappear.

She didn't want London, either – what she wanted was to find out if she and Jem could try again. Otherwise, there would always be a 'what if' to go with the 'what might have been'. Jem knew her better than she knew herself.

The clock read 6.39 am – she had six minutes. She plunged the dead phone into her pocket and yanked the first suitcase up the steps before returning to haul the second one up. Seizing both handles, she thundered off down the road, dragging them behind her as she turned into the High Street, charging towards the sea front. The cases bounced and bumped along the pavement, the weight wrenching her wrists as the soles of her Docs thwacked on the concrete. Suddenly her body exploded with heat; slick moisture broke out down her neck and across her forehead, dripping down her nose, but she gamely struggled on, puffing and panting, her chest burning inside and out.

Her cheeks hot with effort and hormones, Bella ran on and on, before being brought to a dead stop when she could no longer see through the veil of sweat in her eyes. She unzipped the parka and yanked it off, using it to wipe her eyes and face, raking the hood across the back of her neck. She tugged the sleeves into a knot as she wrapped the coat around her waist. Picking up the cases she set off again at full pelt – Celeste would be proud.

She cantered along the promenade and Fergus's house was coming into view when a taxi pulled away from the kerb outside. Bella gave an extra spurt, as if she might catch up, then realisation sank in. She was too late. The cases were dropped from her hot hands and she watched the car turn the corner. Wheezing and gasping with the effort, she leant on the railings and looked out over the water. Too late. By seconds. Bloody-hot-flush seconds. She pulled her parka on and zipped up against the chill.

'Bella!' Turning, she saw Jem coming down the garden path.

'Jem!'

'You didn't get on the train?'

'No. I decided I didn't want my old life back after all. I want a new one.'

He picked her up and swung her round, his joy making her laugh.

'You didn't take the taxi?'

'No. Turns out Dad wants to be here. He wants to be with his friends and his garden and his house. Who am I to say where he should be? I'm staying with him.'

Bella stood on her tiptoes and kissed him. 'Do you think we can try again? Give ourselves a second chance?' Bella looked into Jem's blue eyes and was crushed against his body as he wrapped her in his arms and held her as if he would never let her go.

EPILOGUE

'Are we actually going to do this?' Bella was standing on the beach with Amina and Celeste. It was ridiculously early and they were quivering in their swimsuits.

'We have to.' Celeste was running on the spot to keep warm.

'Oh, my Gawd.' Amina was piling her luscious locks on top of her head and pinning them in place.

They looked out at the dark choppy water.

'On the count of three?' Bella suggested.

Amina and Celeste nodded nervously. 'One, two ... three!' They clasped hands and ran towards the water and as soon as their feet touched the waves they screamed like children.

'Jeez Louise, it's freezing!'

They waded in. 'This is torture!'

Bella held her arms aloft. 'We have to go for it.' And she launched herself into the water, dipping her body under the waves, electrified by the shock of the cold. She jumped up and down – anything to keep her heart from failing. 'It's better once you're in, come on.' Amina and Celeste howled and squealed then plunged until the three of them were splashing about, acclimatising their bodies to the bitter temperature.

'It's madness!' yelled Celeste. 'I can't believe I'm doing it.'

Bella floated, looking up at the morning sky, her skin almost inured to the cold – or she was numb. The waves buffeted her from side to side, then she struck out across the current, exalting in the energy firing through her body, invigorated and happy.

The friends swam closer and chatted together, as Bella had seen these other women do all these weeks ago. As one they headed for the shore and were soon towelling themselves down, rubbing briskly to find warmth and quickly pulling on their clothes – this was Scotland, after all.

'You could do a great line in towelling robes, Bella,' Amina said. 'Save the blushes of all the early-morning swimmers.'

'Great idea – recycled, of course!' Bella rubbed her hair and shivered into a thick jumper and leggings, feeling so utterly alive.

'Anyone for coffee?' Bella turned to see Jem striding towards them across the sand holding a tray of steaming hot drinks.

'Lifesaver.'

Jem handed them out and he and Bella stood close together as she sipped the hot liquid gratefully. She slipped her hand in his.

'How was it?' he asked.

Bella looked at Jem and smiled. 'Liberating!'

AFTERWORD

I hope you enjoyed The Liberation of Bella McCaa and if so, I would be extremely grateful if you could write a review on Amazon. This makes such a difference to a debut author and helps others find the book too. Thank you for taking the chance on a new writer.

Look out for my next book, a romantic comedy set in New York - *Just One Weekend*. Coming soon!

Join my mailing list over at www.catherineaitken.com.

Printed in Great Britain
by Amazon